GORÉE:

POINT OF DEPARTURE

ACKNOWLEDGEMENTS

I would like to express my gratitude to all members of the Barry, Diop, Faye and Gueye families, the "Four London Families" of yesteryear, for inspiration and indelible memories.

I am indebted to George Lamming, for the gift of his support; to Ayi Kwei Armah, Abdoulaye Barry, Margaret Busby, Margaret Cezair Thompson, Cheryl Gregory Faye, Diodj Faye, Ahmed Cheikh Gueye, Vivian Ama Gueye and Merle Swan Williams, for their suggestions and insights; to Jeremy Poynting, for his meticulous editor's pen; and to my family, at all points of the compass, for their unwavering love.

Last but not least, I would like to thank Michael, my most rigorous and loving critic, for believing in me and helping me to believe in myself.

GORÉE:

POINT OF DEPARTURE

ANGELA BARRY

PEEPAL TREE

First published in Great Britain in 2010
Peepal Tree Press Ltd
17 King's Avenue
Leeds LS6 1QS
England

ISBN13: 9781845231255

Supported by
ARTS COUNCIL
ENGLAND

For Africa's children

In everything the unseen moves
The ocean is full of songs
The sky is not an enemy
Destiny is our friend

From "An African Elegy" by Ben Okri

CROSSING OVER

1

MAGDALENE: ISLANDS

A journey across the sea. Yet another one...

It had been Saliou's idea and he'd suggested it only minutes into their chance encounter at Kennedy Airport. So freakish were the circumstances of that meeting that Magdalene did not need to be convinced: it was fate. She'd been bumped off a flight home after attending a festival of Women's Film in New York. He'd left his UN AIDS seminar early and was trying to get back home to deal with a crisis at the hospital. St. Lucia for her; Senegal for him. They found themselves at the counter of *Au Bon Pain*, trying to get a decent cup of coffee and a croissant.

They hadn't seen each other for well over ten years. When Magdalene realized who was standing next to her, gladness at seeing that beautiful face was followed by anger at the pain that face had caused – like a geyser of good feelings ready to gush high into the air only to find its path stopped by a granite boulder. He had been the first to speak.

"Marie Madeleine! *C'est vraiment toi?*"

Again there were two emotions at hearing the name by which he had rechristened her so long ago. She remembered how he'd caressed her with the sweeter sound of "Madeleine" – and how she'd resented being refashioned with the occasional addition of "Marie" – into the one who'd washed the feet of the Saviour with her tears. So many years gone by and still she could not see his face or hear his voice without conflicting emotions.

"Well of course it's me!" She took his hand and gave him a wide and dazzling smile. Saliou Wade did not try to escape its tyranny. Satisfied, Magdalene went on. "You see I get fat! No wonder you didn't recognize me."

Magdalene had long acknowledged, with regret, the fifteen

extra pounds that had crept onto her since she'd last seen this man. He was as lean as on the day they'd met almost thirty years ago. Lean and perfect in a classic French suit.

"In Ouolof, we say that at a certain age, a woman's body bestows on her the gift of authority. No longer a *jeune fille* or even a *jeune femme* but an adult, on the way to becoming an elder. Solid. Significant. Wise. That's how you look now." He paused, dropping his black eyes. "And it suits you."

Magdalene struggled for a moment. It was this kind of talk that had made her marry him in the first place, when life became his voice speaking of worlds much older than the one she knew. So plausible, with such powers of seduction. She recalled the enchantment of those early years with Saliou's patient voice explaining the intricacies of an ancient culture. He felt he could explain it. She felt she could understand. Both had been wrong. Magdalene felt herself heading towards a door which she preferred to keep shut. She veered away.

"Ever the gallant," she said lightly and went towards an empty table. By the time they were both seated with their coffees and rolls and bags and coats ranged about them, the waters muddied by their shock encounter started to settle.

"I called Khadi but only got an answering machine." Saliou fidgeted with a plastic spoon. "I'd hoped to at least talk to her…"

"She's in Boston for the next two weeks on some big case. You know these ambitious young lawyers! I only saw her once – on the day I arrived." Magdalene could feel the muscles in her face tightening as she rushed along. "Our daughter is a very busy lady!"

A false brightness bounced off every word. Magdalene did not go on. They stared at their styrofoam cups.

"I need to see her. I want her to come to Africa to see me," Saliou said. "The last time I saw her, she was fourteen years old and now, she's a… she's a…" His hand flipped over in a small gesture of despair.

"And whose fault is that? Once you went back and got married again, Khadi just didn't want to know."

"And what was I supposed to do? Wait until you decided what you wanted out of life? Unlike you, I knew what I wanted and how to get it!"

"Knew? Does this mean you don't know any more? What? Is there trouble in paradise?"

They were not shouting but there was an intensity in their voices that caught the attention of people near them – that and the fact that Magdalene was speaking in English and Saliou in French, the way they always communicated.

"Same Madeleine. Still looking for an argument. Still confused. Still *enfantile*."

This was absurd. It was as though they were still married, as though this were a marital spat about an open toothpaste tube or an unpaid bill. Was this need to square up to each other still a reflex?

"Infantile! Didn't you just say I was full of authority?"

"Your body! Your body! *Dieu merci*, you no longer look like a… a…" Saliou picked up a straw and waved it in front of her. But then, as if he'd had a thought like hers, his voice switched into its sparring mode, sharp, but no longer serious. "But look at you! What do you call what you're wearing? And your hair! Quite ridiculous!"

While searching for an appropriate riposte, Magdalene caught sight of herself in the mirror running the length of the wall. She *was* "outlandishly" dressed in a careless assortment of so-called ethnic styles, topped by a thatch of short, greying locks.

She thought of the women of Senegal, the poor, in their voluminous *boubous* and the rich, in their strict Parisian *couture*. Whatever the context, whatever the style, their elegance was innate. She threw her head back and laughed until tears rolled down her cheeks. At first, Saliou held back, discomfited by the attention of the people around them. But he could not hold out for long, letting go a big laugh that vibrated through his body.

So it was settled. They'd had their moment of heat, an acknowledgement of a love, old and not fully extinguished. They'd had their moment of impasse, where their two worlds clashed fruitlessly against each other. Now they could talk.

For the two and a half hours before Saliou had to go and take his plane, the only subject of conversation was Khadi. Saliou listened in silence as Magdalene poured out her worries about their daughter who, in the eyes of the world, was such a resounding success. In all the years growing up in London, she had not put a foot wrong. No sex, no drinking, no drugs. Exceptional performance at school, ending in an Upper Second at Bristol. What parent could want more? Even when she'd made the unexpected decision to leave England and continue her studies in the US, it had been done with the minimum of fuss.

"That's just the problem," Magdalene said, while Saliou watched fine lines of anxiety pull down the corners of her mouth. "I can hear no noise from that girl. It's as though the volume has been turned down. From her heart. That's our Khadi. All the sound and movement coming from her – and they call it success! – it's not coming from anything real. Her true feelings are locked away somewhere. And what grieves me most is that I didn't see it coming. One day I woke up and there it was. That child with the beautiful open heart, well, she was gone. Gone from me. The way she went from you years ago."

Saliou lowered his head. "If she's withdrawn from you, what about me? If ever I ask to see her or even phone, she's always busy. Never angry, never *impolie* but somehow she always manages to avoid me. Those years when I wasn't in touch with you at all – yes, I regret them now. I just assumed that everything was all right. And I had a new life…"

By the time they said goodbye, they were united in their resolve. Khadi must be persuaded to spend some time with her father in the land of her birth. They exchanged email addresses and went their separate ways.

That had been over a year ago, and since then delicate negotiations had taken place. It had been a hard sell and Khadi's initial resistance had been intractable. A combination of pleading and relentless patience had finally broken her down. But, as a true corporate lawyer in the making, she'd insisted on conditions – no more than twenty-one days; at a time convenient to her; and, above all, and for reasons she did not divulge, that her mother should be with her.

After this, things happened fast; the preparations were in place and the fine-tuning complete. Tomorrow she would be taking the noon flight from St. Lucia to New York, would spend a day with Khadi and the next day the two of them would fly out to Dakar. To restore a daughter to her father. To restore a daughter to herself.

★ ★ ★

Magdalene looked down at the profusion of wild flowers and grasses that had accumulated in her lap and sighed. All this restoring of people to each other... It had sounded so simple.

"Tomorrow and tomorrow and tomorrow..." Magdalene sighed again and pulled up another handful of grass.

Tomorrow's journey had a clear purpose – to help her daughter. But the nearer you got, what had seemed clear became hazy. Maybe Khadi didn't want to be helped. She was a twenty-seven year old woman, independent, with a promising career. But Magdalene could not be seduced by the marvellous façade. Something had gone wrong in her daughter's life. Perhaps this trip would help to mend it. But what about her own life? What about that?

The steady breeze off the sea kept the heat of the late afternoon in check and, for a moment, Magdalene closed her eyes. With the sun shining scarlet through her eyelids and the wind brushing past her face, she could hear Antoine speaking to her, in that rough-diamond, journalist way of his, telling her, when the long years of wrangling were over and her divorce from Saliou was final, that she needed to finish bringing up her teenage daughter in the Caribbean. With all I have to do here in London? she'd said, almost laughing in his face.

"Everyone has to make peace with the place where they're born. Even you," he'd said tersely. They'd never spoken of it again.

Antoine. The one who had introduced Magdalene to Saliou long years ago. Godfather to Khadi. Great friend to both Saliou and herself and then, when everything had fallen apart, her friend alone. Antoine, who, big talker though he was, when he had something important to say, said it only once. It was his voice that came to her as she sat on the rough hillside and listened to the waves breaking on the shore.

Since her arrival in St. Lucia almost two years ago, she'd made several trips to this place on the island's Atlantic coast. Half an acre of scrub land between Dennery and Grand Anse with its face to the wind, a mile's walk from the nearest road, covered with bush and twisted trees, and offering a broad vista of undisturbed ocean: this had been the surprise bequest in her father's will. Neither she

13

nor her three sisters, all well established in different parts of Britain, had known of its existence. And all, including Magdalene, had been puzzled by the uncharacteristic favouritism shown by the man who had spent his life in quiet acceptance of his wife's fierce determination to move the family forward. Magdalene never came to this spot without mixed feelings. It always seemed like a pilgrimage into a secret place in her father's mind – and as such, a burden. Sometimes it looked like a place of wild beauty; sometimes, a scene of desolation. This stretch of rugged hills and chaotic vegetation bordering on an untamed ocean was so unlike the malls and placid bays of the Caribbean side of the island. It dared you to try and carve out a niche in its solid rock. Today, Magdalene felt more unable than ever to meet its challenge. Her father's land required total commitment, nothing less.

For years, she had not given Antoine's counsel a moment's thought. It was only after Khadi had decided to go to law school in the States and Magdalene found herself alone in London for the first time that she'd started to think seriously about this return. She'd dithered. But the day came when Khadi called to say she'd been offered "a job to die for" in New York. In less than three months, Magdalene had put her small Victorian terrace up for sale, packed her cameras and equipment, made the rounds of all the support and awareness groups to which she belonged, visited her parents' graves under a cold English sky, and finally boarded the plane for St. Lucia, arriving many hours later at Hewanorra in a rainstorm.

Despite securing a teaching job and an apartment soon after her arrival, things were never right. All Antoine's talk about the virtue of going home was just that – talk. But it had taken Magdalene a long time to admit this. She attacked everything with a crusader's zeal. She'd alarmed the College administration by inviting her students to her home for film shows and bouillon. She'd combed the markets for objects that corresponded to her penchant for the eccentric. She'd accepted every invitation to fêtes or first communions or poetry readings in her effort to find a handful of people with whom she could feel at ease. In return, she'd received several marriage proposals. She'd scoured the fishing villages for the remains of her family who had not taken a boat or plane to "foreign". She'd bathed in the sun-warmed sea and been stirred by the stark symmetry of the Pitons. She'd felt something, but it never felt right. Having left England, the place she'd always associated with heroic struggle, surpassed only by her labours in Africa, here she found herself engaged in a different kind of fight, one whose magnitude she was unprepared for. Her body was grateful for the move: her skin lost its yellowish pallor and her joints no longer complained at yet another cold, damp morning. But it felt like yet another exile.

A glance at her watch told Magdalene that it was time to go. Rising to her feet, she took one last look at the ocean. It looked tranquil from the far horizon to within a few miles of the shore where it became agitated and uncertain. A plume of spray sprang like a huge fan around the apex of the hilly point that jutted into the water. They're everywhere, she thought, brushing the front of her trousers and turning to go… these hills, these mountains, sometimes in the shape of triangles like the Pitons, sometimes rounded into breasts, like at Les Mamelles.

As she walked, her mood became as agitated as the sea she had just left behind. Antoine. Her father. Home. Exile. St. Lucia. London. Senegal. Saliou. Khadi. Thoughts about them tumbled about with an intensity that was real but aimless. When she reached the car, she fiddled with the key, anxious to be back on the road, back to her to-do list, which included handing over her car to someone at the college. Just as she was about to get in, she became aware of another presence. It was a woman of indeterminate age making her way home, her clothing clean but threadbare, her dark face bright with sweat, her neck and spine perfectly aligned for the task of bearing the weight of the large basket balanced on her head.

"*Bo'jou*," the woman said, head straight and footstep regular.

Magdalene opened her mouth to speak, hesitated and then answered, "Good afternoon."

All the way back to town, Magdalene fretted. She'd shied away from speaking her mother language in the simplest of situations. And the woman with the basket. So solid, so sure, so dignified. Had the hard years she'd lived abroad brought her any of those things? In a few days, she'd be crossing the ocean to a continent full of such women.

The next few hours were spent on the other side of the island, rushing around and ticking things off her list. It was time for a break. The Regency Hotel was too full of tourists – but it was at least a space where she didn't have to think about anything or anybody.

She signalled to the waiter again. He finally made his way through the Friday night Buccaneer's Barbecue throng to where she was sitting, at the edge of the hotel's beachfront patio.

"Madam?"

"A Piton, please, and make sure it's very cold." She gave him a bright smile but noted that he was unmoved. She persevered. "England's the only place for warm beer. Doesn't work here." A second smile met a similar fate. She was losing her touch. The good news was that she didn't give a goddamn... She watched him manoeuvre through the sunburnt tourists heaping their plates with charred meats and listless salads and sipping from icy glasses adorned with wedges of pineapple and paper umbrellas. He was smiling and chatting as he went. She sighed. All she wanted was a cold beer and a view of the sun setting over the water. And a rest from island irritations...

"Madam." The waiter was back, again po-faced.

One look told her that the beer was barely cool.

She placed her hand around the glass as though checking the temperature of a feverish patient, then pointed at one of the giant frosty Pina Coladas at the next table. "You see that! We can both see from here how cold it is..."

"Pina Colada can cold easy. Beer, not so easy."

The day had been long and taxing and Magdalene was tired but his manner took her by surprise. Letting it go was not an option.

"But it's your job to get me my order, isn't it?" She started tapping the table with her finger. Why did this kind of conversation follow her wherever she went? Some things never change...

"I get you another." He leaned across her, towards the glass. "But it go be just like this one." There was the sound of teeth being sucked.

Magdalene grabbed the glass and wrestled it out of his hand, slopping beer onto the table and herself. She took a five-dollar note from her purse and pressed it into his hand.

"Consider yourself paid and tipped. Just make sure you don't come anywhere near me or this table for the rest of the night. Gaston Hippolyte is a good friend of mine." The waiter was still taking in the threat of the general manager when Magdalene jettisoned her North London accent and added, "*Ti bway, ou ka – fe pey'oui ek manman'ou hont!*"

"I… I didn't think you was from here. I think you was… from foreign," he stammered.

Magdalene was ready to launch a tirade on colonialism, locals, foreigners, tourism, mental slavery etc. All of the weaponry of her activist years in England brought to bear on this poor soul – young, slack, undereducated, untrained. But she couldn't bring herself to do it. The collapse of his hauteur was so pathetic. Still, she had to say something. She gestured towards the barbecue eaters, their skins covering the palette from burnt rose to brick. "They're foreign," she said. "You treat them just fine. Why's that?"

He stood rooted, his extended hand still clenching the soggy money.

"Why?"

"Because they real foreign. Real. Not like you. Or not like I thought you was. But you not real Lucian neither." He cleared his throat. "Madam."

He gave a slight bow and she released him. Island irritation? No. This was more like a body blow, leaving her winded and disorientated. He did as she'd told him to and left her alone. She sat sipping what was left of her beer, now blood warm, and watching the swift descent of the sun into the Caribbean. Cigarette fumes drifted her way and she felt all the old cravings. But no, she'd quit years ago. There was no going back.

The waiter's words repeated in her mind like a scratched record: I didn' think you was from here. I did think you was from foreign. The story of her bloody life. Nothing but journeys. Nothing but being told you don't belong.

Then she thought of the journey ahead of her. It was not going to be easy. When she'd told some of her women friends that she was going with her daughter to see her former husband and his new wife and family and would be staying at the family home, they'd all said, "You mad?" She'd strike a pose and fix them with her cat's eyes. "Of course!" But they all knew that anyway. She would be meeting Saliou's wife for the first time and although her imagination had not been able to settle on any one picture of this person, she could conjure up the life that had evolved out of the new marriage. There would be small children, their own five, plus others; there would be relatives from near and far; there would be seeming confusion but underlying order; there would be warmth as well as dissention; there would be community. Of that Magdalene was sure. The African family was like a city, vast and embracing to all of like mind, but full of perils for those who were not. Looking out on the gathering darkness, she remembered when she'd been part of that city and the day she'd left it all behind...

A different waiter approached, somewhat gingerly, and asked if he could light the candle. When he'd done, she took a wallet from her bag, opened it to a photograph and held it up to the flickering light. A photograph taken over twenty years ago, just days before she'd fled from Africa. Three adults and a little girl stared back. Khadi, Saliou, Antoine and me. Someone – a stranger – had come up and asked if we wanted him to take a picture of all of us. Khadi is stretched out between us and she alone is smiling. Saliou has her arms, I've got her body and Antoine's holding her feet. She's having the time of her life but the rest of us... It's all there in our faces. Each one of us an island. There's the ferry in the background. We're just about to get on it and head back to the mainland. After that ferry ride, nothing would ever be the same.

Magdalene put the wallet away and stared into the candle flame. Thoughts of Antoine returned. Here she was, back where she was born. Back home. Just as he had told her to... Magdalene could almost see him standing there in front of her, that hard-living friend who had been like a brother to them both... You said it was what I needed. But, my God, after Saliou and his *Afrique*, and then those long years of struggle in London, has it all come down to this? The Buccaneer's Barbecue on a Friday night?

Fat tears of wax rolled down the candle. There were things she missed about London – the BBC, good cheap red wine, Sainsbury's, Marks and Spencer's underwear, anything to do with film equipment, reliable electricians, reliable plumbers, reliable internet service, Brixton market, good bookshops, the National Theatre, friends you didn't have to keep explaining yourself to… God the waiter was right. She was from foreign! Or might as well have been. It was what they'd said about her in Africa. When they called her *toubab*!

A burst of music shook Magdalene from her reverie. She looked around and saw that the space next to the bar had been cleared, a sound system switched on and two decorated poles placed at a distance from each other. A young man and a young woman, both perfect specimens with ruffled shirts and gleaming midriffs, gyrated across the floor to a heavy beat, with the young man flailing a spangled stick and the young woman positioning herself near to the revellers, ready to put them through their paces.

"Ladies and gentlemen, it's limbo time!"

Magdalene groaned but morbid fascination trumped better judgment. Another night she might have managed a wry smile before looking away. But tonight, watching was agony. What struck her was the deadness in the eyes of the two dancers, so at odds with their brilliant smiles and flamboyant costumes. It was quite a feat, the complete absence of life in those eyes as their bodies worked hard to whip the audience into the frenzy promised by the hotel brochure. The young woman – a girl, really – placed the stick a few feet off the ground and began to wine while her partner bent back and slid under it. When he was through, he tripped lightly towards the crowd, grabbed an armful of volunteers and urged them to pass beneath the stick. The girl then slipped under while the young man – a boy, really – jooked his pelvis this way and that to the delighted shrieks of the tourist women.

And so it went on, with the stick getting lower and lower, the dance floor becoming more and more crowded as sweaty revellers tossed their inhibitions to the breeze and tried to force unaccustomed spines to bend back towards the earth. There was some good-natured pushing and shoving, peals of laughter as the stick kept being knocked down. The girl and boy with the dead eyes carried on dancing until the stick was only inches off the ground. They alone were able to bend their bodies almost in two and execute a movement which was neither sitting nor standing nor lying and which looked like submission before a god.

They didn't even know where that dance came from, not to mention the misery it represented… Her thoughts flew to Africa again and she felt a familiar pain in her chest. What would Saliou's family have made of the Buccaneer's Barbecue? With one wave of the hand, it would be dismissed with the single word *toubab*. The white man and his powerful, noxious and inexplicable world. How many times had she heard that word when she'd been married to Saliou? How many times had it been levelled against her as an insulting explanation of her behaviour? Even at this distance of years, her flesh throbbed with the injury of that word. To be identified with the Friday night barbecue eaters, the rum-punch swillers, the would-be limbo dancers – that hurt.

She stared out into the dark. From nowhere the words of a poem she'd heard someone recite in her student days in Paris came into her head. "Afrique, mon amour…" the line went… and that's all she could remember. But it was enough. Sadness took hold as she thought of her failed marriage and the strange, unreciprocated attachment she had for that great continent. Longing and loss were heavy on her heart. Antoine had once written long ago, "In all the years I've known you, you've stayed speechless before the power of Africa." She shook her head. How come this drinking, cussing, womanizing man wrote with the pen of a poet?

She blew out the candle, rose from the table and pushed her way through the holiday-makers.

She walked quickly through the hotel lobby keenly anticipating the quiet night air. But as she stepped outside she felt as much as heard the pulse of an overwhelming wall of sound. Then she remembered that Friday wasn't just Barbecue and Limbo night at the Regency, but the night for the district's street party. She gritted her teeth, put her head down and ploughed through a mass of revellers bumping, grinding, breaking loose. This was not the show on the beachfront patio. These revellers took in the whole kaleidoscope of colour. There were plenty of tourists but they didn't wear a capital T on their foreheads. And the locals laughed and danced like they were at home. She felt alien from them all.

Finally, she reached *The Lime* and the wooden kiosk outside which you could usually find a couple of taxi drivers playing dominoes with the concentration of chess masters. Despite the Friday festivities, Magdalene was in luck. There was one taxi driver available and, signalling to someone in the bowels of the crowd, he set off walking at a brisk pace that had her almost running to keep up. Within a few minutes, they were beyond most of the noise and crush, where the car was parked. He held the car door open for her and Magdalene was relieved to note that although he was young, he had a quiet, composed air about him.

"Thank you," she said, settling in.

"Where to, madam?"

"The Morne, please. Go halfway up and turn off at Bagshaw's."

She sank back into her seat, a great fatigue descending on her.

"*Moin lasse*," she said sighing and letting some of the weariness go. She looked up and saw the taxi driver staring back at her in the mirror with puzzlement. The patois she had abandoned so many years ago, had surged out of her for the second time that night, the patois that Saliou had said was a bastard language – the patois she'd been trying to force herself to speak since her return, with so little success, the patois that she'd longed to use to greet the village woman as she passed. Antoine's words came back to her. "But remember, Magdalene, the Antilles have their own power."

She stole a glance at the mirror again. The driver had looked away and she saw only his dark profile. Surprised recognition. That's what his look had said. A fellow islander. This gave her a rush of pleasure. She rolled down her window, looked out into the dark and let it enfold her. By the time the taxi passed the garish lanterns of the famous rum shop, the Hardest Hard, and started to go up the mountain, the anguish of the past hours began to pass. She put aside the weight of her unresolved problems. She forgave herself for the tantrum with the waiter. It's not about me, she thought. It's about her. The child laughing in the photograph and the woman she has become.

When Magdalene reached home, sleep came quickly.

Early morning found her at the window of her apartment, looking out over the sea. A tender grey light lifted the blackness from the waves. All was tranquil, the silence disturbed only by the quiet swishing of the surf, the gurgling of water in hidden caves and the first fluttering of early swallows. Between the darkness and the light, the sea and the land, there was a whisper of benediction.

I will go back across the sea with her and hope that something good will happen. Yes. Something good *will* happen...

Turning away, she resumed putting clothes into her case and preparing herself for the journey.

2.

KHADI: SPEAKING IN TONGUES

"What was the first thing you felt when you saw her yesterday?"

"Irritation."

"Why?"

"It reminded me of when I was at school and she would show up to parents' evening not dressed like a 'proper' mother. Even then, I knew that it was not how she dressed that was the problem... She was just not like everyone else... And I wished she was."

"And after the irritation, what then?"

"We stood looking at each other for what must have been a second but seemed like forever. Although she looked the same as she had a year ago, there was something unfamiliar about her. Something... tentative. Then, she took a step towards me – I didn't seem to be able to move – then she took me into her arms and held me tight. That was more like it, more the mother I know. So... straightforward. I knew the exact moment when she would begin to cry, cry and laugh at the same time. I've never known anyone else to do that to such effect. Quite unnerving..."

"Is that how you felt when she hugged you? Unnerved?"

"Now, now, I'm not a monster! I felt happy when she held me. She is my mother, after all, and I love her."

"Yes."

"Sometimes she's just a bit like hard work, that's all."

"Mmmmm." Naomi Fine tapped a pencil on her desk absent-mindedly then looked at her watch. "I'm sorry, Khadi, but it's time. I'm really sorry we haven't time to finish this. Give me a call if you need to, before you go. But if not, come and tell me all about it when you get back."

"Of course! I'll have all kinds of adventures to report. Terrific exciting stuff..."

"Khadi! You're going to be OK. It's all going to work out. You'll see."

When Khadi returned from seeing Naomi, she found her mother just emerging from bed. The rumpled nightdress and the smooth skin of her temples suggested that she had enjoyed a replenishing sleep. Her tiger eyes glowed as they rested on her daughter.

"Oh yum!" she exclaimed as Khadi unpacked the goodies from a brown paper bag. *Brioche, croissant au beurre, petit pain au chocolat* – all her favourite things from her Paris days, and all made with loving care by the master baker at "Chez Gerard".

"The coffee will be ready in a few minutes." Khadi glanced up and saw her mother hovering. "And no, there's nothing you can do to help." Another pause. "Let me do this, Mum. Let me get you breakfast on your first morning in New York... Let me do it, like I'm a grownup."

Chastened, Magdalene looked about her, sat down carefully and started fingering the seat of the smart black chair.

"Surprised?" Khadi didn't look up as she half filled large white mugs with bubbling milk.

"At what?"

"That it's so comfortable."

Magdalene checked her daughter's face. Although apparently absorbed in coffee-making, there was a smile flitting across it.

"Well... if you must know... when I first saw it last night, I wondered whether there was a single thing in your apartment that was for human use. I mean, just look at this place!" Magdalene's hand swept across the chrome, the leather, the marble, the wood, all gleaming and pristine.

"So, what you're saying is that you don't like it?" Khadi kept moving about, searching for plates, spoons, filling the sugar bowl, checking the coffee-maker. Her back was to her mother, but the tone of voice and the line of the shoulders told Magdalene all she needed to know. Khadi was still smiling.

"Don't get me wrong." Magdalene was up on her feet now, spreading her arms wide. "It's all very impressive. Where's that from?" She pointed to the stark black-and-white wall-hanging that dominated the room.

"Peru."

"And those?" She indicated a trio of bronze figures caught in the ecstasy of dance.

"Nepal."

"And this?"

"Botswana."

"Lovely," Magdalene murmured, trailing her fingers over the pale soapstone in the shape of a woman's head. Then she looked around her again. "Wonderful… if you like living in an art gallery or a design shop specializing in chairs that don't look as though they're made for the human bum."

Khadi was in the middle of adding coffee to the hot milk. With a lowered head, she stirred the cups with a tiny steel whisk and crowned both mugs with a dollop of whipped cream. She placed them on the table, sat down and waited. Magdalene didn't budge from her position in the middle of the living room.

"Do you?"

"Do I what?" Khadi raised her eyes, amber and shaped like almonds, the only inheritance from her mother, made dramatic in a face as dark as midnight.

"Do you like living in an art gallery?"

"Well," and Khadi allowed herself a full stretch of her long arms and fingers. "Now that you mention it, I do. I love surrounding myself with these things. I love the big empty space in the middle of the living room, I love the way the wood floor shines and that there's not a lot of stuff on it. And I love the one or two things that I've chosen – with great care – to put on the walls and tables. I love the fact that I own it. I love it all."

Magdalene digested the multiple repetitions of the word "love" in silence.

"And before breakfast gets cold, I love the way I've become a pretentious snob!"

"Oh, that's a relief!"

"What, that I'm a pretentious snob?"

"No! That you know you are. The crime is not in the being but in the not knowing you are!"

Khadi's apartment shook as a sudden gust of laughter blew through it. Magdalene joined Khadi at the table and, between guffaws and bites of breakfast, she wondered how she'd come to have such a daughter.

"I blame myself," Magdalene said, downing a croissant. "This is a reaction to me. Me and my mess. The piles of books on the floor. The yellow reminder notes stuck all over the place. The fact that we had to move a couple of times…"

"Six times in eight years, to be precise. Luckily, all within Finchley so…"

"So you wouldn't have to change schools."

"But I swear I knew more about the bedsits of North London than most estate agents."

"We never lived in bedsits!" There was mock protest in Magdalene's voice.

"That's true. We never did. It just seemed that way. Because at least one room was unusable because of all of your books and later your camera equipment. And another room was unusable because it was the nerve centre of whatever campaign you were working on. And besides, there was always some kind of refugee sleeping on the living room floor."

"Refugees? Since when did we take in refugees? A couple of friends – Malik, Jocelyne, Zahra – one or two others. All of them down on their luck – out of work, leaving a relationship, just arriving in the country. All of them… well… friends in need."

"As I said," Khadi said, picking at a crumb on the table, "refugees all." She flashed a smile. "Our house, whichever one it was, was like some international agency. Refugees, every last one of them. And you were their high commissioner."

Magdalene put down her cup. Was Khadi being flippant or had the talk suddenly turned serious? Magdalene studied her daughter's face but found only mild amusement. Yet she could not believe that the "refugee" speech had been altogether light-hearted.

"So that's how you saw things, Khadi?"

"No, Mum. That's the way things were." Still with a benign smile on her face, Khadi got up and started to clear the table, aware of her mother's intent gaze.

"What?" Twin fires blazed in Khadi's eyes for a second and then were gone. "What?" she repeated with an exaggerated New York accent.

"Well, my girl," Magdalene shrugged, "all I can say is that there are people who would pay good money for the childhood you had. Varied, colourful… rich. Not in money but in…"

"Experience! Yes, I know!" Khadi was on the move again, her restless hands taking up, putting down, reordering the objects in their path. "There were some real characters, I have to admit." She shook her head as though to dislodge the memory. "Yes, Mum." Khadi's voice dropped low. "Those years were certainly *mouvementé*, as the French would say. Colourful and *mouvementé*…"

Khadi's hands continued to stray among the debris of the breakfast feast but the rest of her body was rigid. Her back was to Magdalene and she heard her mother take a few steps towards her then stop. Khadi turned around, loosening the muscles of her face, neck and shoulders so by the time she was facing Magdalene, her features had been rearranged to express the same air of mild amusement as before. There was a momentary collision of amber eyes.

"And for all that colour and all that movement, this…" Khadi did a little twirl in the middle of the kitchen floor. "This is my reward."

Magdalene said nothing. All of a sudden, she craved a long drag of a cigarette. But there was no drug that could ease the tightening of the muscles of her chest. Something was not making sense. Was it what Khadi was saying or not saying? Was it just the unreality of this *Vogue* apartment that was so unsettling?

"How are you going to handle Africa, Didi?" A small tremor passed at the sound of the pet name discarded years ago. "There's nothing but colour and movement there and a total absence of this." The apartment was referenced with a slight gesture from her hand. "Don't you remember anything?"

"I was fourteen years old when I last went to see Father. Of course, I remember."

"So… you're ready to deal with the dust and the everlasting tide of family members and the dodgy toilets and the lack of privacy and the heat and the friends stretching to the horizon and the mosquitoes…"

"Apart from the dust, heat and mosquitoes, sounds very much like North London, Mum… Yes! We had plenty of dodgy toilets!"

"Khadi! Be serious. The life we lived in London – which is basically most of your life – was mid point between your father's life in Africa and the life you're living now. Yes, Saliou is a doctor and a very successful one and I'm sure he has a nice house and we'll be very comfortable. Or at least I'll be. Your standards of comfort seem very different from mine these days. But no matter how well off he is, he still lives in a poor country and you won't be able to get away from that, not for a second. Are you ready to look poverty in the eye, Khadi? And, on top of that, he's part of a culture that puts community first and the individual second. Are you ready for that?"

Khadi remained impassive. "You saw to it that I looked poverty in the eye as far back as I can remember. All those Oxfam posters pinned on my bedroom walls! At, school, I was the most politically correct person anyone knew. But now... I'm twenty-seven, independent, financially stable... And I say, well, I say that political correctness is something I can afford to do without."

Magdalene stopped in her tracks. If Khadi had made the air blue with her curses, it would have been better. She could at least have retaliated.

"Why are you going to Africa?" she asked quietly.

"Because you asked me to."

"That doesn't seem sufficient reason."

"It's reason enough. And, besides, we're only going for two weeks. It's just a vacation."

"You and I both know it's more than that." Magdalene went over and took her daughter's hand. "I'm just worried that you haven't thought about this thing more. Tried to prepare yourself for what you might see. And feel."

Khadi pulled her hand away and went back towards the sink.

"That's where you're wrong, Mum. Ever since I decided to go, I've done nothing but prepare myself." She opened the dishwasher door and began to load it. In a voice slightly raised over the clink of crockery, she said, "For the past twelve months, I've been seeing a shrink, twice a week."

Magdalene's mouth opened, shut, opened again, shut and remained shut for a full ten minutes while Khadi worked to restore her apartment to its immaculate condition. Something very primitive inside Khadi celebrated the silencing of her mother as the victory of a lifetime, but she maintained an unruffled presence whose fluid movements nevertheless dominated the space they occupied, occasionally throwing her mother a look of compassion.

Words reached Magdalene's lips but could get no further. Her head was full of questions and accusations. *So you've become a real American! Is having a shrink a necessary qualification for the lease on an apartment like this? What do you talk about? Me, I suppose. It's always the mother's fault! What's troubling you? Why can't you talk to me about it? Why can't you talk to me?* But Magdalene watched and said nothing.

From the first moments of Khadi's life, Magdalene had loved to look at her. Her child was beautiful. Apart from the eyes, Khadi was all her father – the narrow frame, the long limbs, the matte-black skin, the shapely head. Magdalene, with her own somewhat ramshackle appeal, had taken pride in the child's classic beauty. Very early, she had seen that the child was not given to self-expression through words. For Khadi, words were doled out with prudence and precision. It was her body which was the window to her heart. When other mothers talked about the thumb-sucking, foot-stamping, shoulder-slouching signposts of infant-to-adolescent development, Magdalene would counter with an extensive list of gestures, tics and facial expressions invisible to eyes other than her own. She used to tell her friends about the three points of the triangle: sorrow – the pulling of the left ear with the left hand and the covering of the mouth with the right; anxiety – a short hard sound somewhere between a laugh and a cough; and joy, ah joy was elevating the body on tiptoes and then twirling with arms outstretched. Magdalene had felt that she could read her daughter as a conductor reads a musical score. But now...

Now, as a bright New York sun streamed in through the window, Magdalene was faced with a realisation more traumatic than the news of the shrink. Through all this morning's conversation, Magdalene had watched her daughter, matching her movements with her words, trying to plot the correlation between the two. She felt she had understood Khadi's mood, could anticipate her reactions. But there'd been no clue that Khadi was working up the courage to tell her mother that she was having psychiatric treatment. The body that Magdalene thought she knew so well was now speaking in tongues that were strange to her.

She spoke at last.

"And has it helped? The therapy?"

"I think so." Khadi still wore a beneficent smile. "I've been looking at some issues in my life. But… it's an ongoing process, you know." She looked at her mother's blank face and shook her head. "No, perhaps not." Her mother had probably never had a repressed thought or feeling in her life.

Again, silence hung heavy between them.

"By the way, Mum, I'm having a few friends over this evening to meet you."

"But we're taking the plane tomorrow night. You're going to wear yourself out."

"Not at all. This is New York. I'll order in some tapas, pick up some sushi and a few bottles of wine…" Khadi's voice trailed off as images of the evening ahead met with the thought that a day and a half from now, the two of them would set foot on African soil at Dakar Yoff airport. From Khadi's chest came a short, hard sound, somewhere between a laugh and a cough, and she made a quick turn and headed for the bedroom, feeling completely exposed for the first time since Magdalene's arrival. When she re-emerged, her armour was intact.

Khadi's composure continued throughout the day as she prepared for, then hosted the party, made arrangements for her friend Tim to take them to the airport, slept, took her mother shopping the next morning, finished her packing. Whether she was walking the streets, talking to her mother or her friends, or even sleeping, the will to be in control of her every word and gesture did not relinquish its grip.

The goodbyes at JFK were meant to be brief and businesslike but, despite Khadi's best efforts, Tim was determined to turn the departure into high drama.

"Khadi, darling," he said, like all her New York friends, elongating her name so it sounded like Katy, "this is going to be such a fabulous trip! Crossing that big ocean and reclaiming your past! I mean to say, books are written about such things... movies... And here you are, living it... Maggie..." He turned to Magdalene, his newest best friend. "If I didn't know you, I would say that your daughter deliberately kept this from me because she knew I would have found a way to go with you all. But, imagine, she just told me a few days ago..." With this, the flood ceased momentarily while Tim made an eloquent gesture with his hands.

"What I need you to do, Tim..." Khadi's crisp voice stepped into the void. "...is to pick up my mail and water the plants. No more than twice while I'm away. Just when the soil is starting to go dry."

"Do I look like a person who doesn't know how to water plants? Is that what you think of me?" His features lost their customary brightness and he stood there like a sullen schoolboy.

Magdalene stretched up and placed a kiss on his cheek.

"We'd better say goodbye now, Tim. Take no notice of Khadi. She really is grateful for your kindness. And so am I."

"Well, all I can say is thank heaven for you, Maggie," he said, folding her in a bear hug. Then he took Khadi by the shoulders, held her at arm's length and waited until her reluctant eyes were raised to his. "And as for you," he said in a low voice, no longer playing the *grande dame*, "you go over there and do what you've got to do. I'm not joking now. I know this won't be easy. For most of us here, Africa is just an idea, one that most of us want to hold on to, sure, but if we're honest, it's pretty remote. But for you," he sighed, "it's real. Father, brothers, sisters – the whole nine yards. If anyone can bring back more than statues and fabric, it's you." As they joined the queue, Tim's voice could be heard ringing out, "And if anyone over there makes you unhappy, tell them I'll make sure they boil in tar!"

Khadi shook her head as she joined the security line and prepared to take off her shoes. Magdalene rewarded him with a wave and a smile. Tim pressed a snowy handkerchief to his mouth, turned and merged into the milling crowd, flicking the white cloth over his shoulder like a flag.

"You need to be nicer to your friends, Didi."

"I'm nice to Tim. I'm very nice to him, in fact. I just don't encourage his more, shall we say, flamboyant side."

"Don't you know anything?" asked Magdalene as she picked up her bag from the conveyor belt. "That's not a 'flamboyant side'. That's who he is! And believe me…" her voice and eyes tried to keep her daughter's attention despite the general hubbub around them. "Believe me, underneath that there's a good heart."

Khadi's refusal to respond made Magdalene want to go running for a cigarette. But the craving was momentary and she was not ready to back down in the face of her daughter's stonewalling. "Tim cares about you, Didi, and you treat him like shit." Magdalene's face was hot and her eyes were glinting. "If he didn't prefer boys to girls, I'd say he'd be my ideal son-in-law!"

"Oh, Mum, really! You're just as bad as Tim. Always making a scene!"

They were interrupted by an announcement that their flight was delayed. Khadi went off to reconnoitre and before long, they were doing the rounds of the food court, bookshops and women's room until they found themselves back where they'd started.

"And he's worth a hundred of those characters I met last night…"

"And who, may I ask, are we talking about?"

"Tim, of course!"

"Oh, I thought we'd finished with that."

"Listen to me," said Magdalene, indulging in a generous stretch, "those guys at the party last night, you know the ones who looked right and said all the right things. Not a human bone in their bodies. No feeling in their eyes. No laughter in their bellies. Nothing…" Magdalene rolled a long scarf into a tube, put it under her head and curled up like a cat. "Not one of them has what it takes," she said, yawning, "to give me my grandchildren. Such a shame about Tim…"

Khadi watched as, in moments, her mother transformed from moral lecturer to sleeper. By the time she had grasped the thrust of the treatise, Magdalene was in a profound slumber. What could she do with a mother like that? Always be on guard! Just when you think you're safe, she'll sneak in and land a blow. You'd have thought she'd be happy with the way I've turned out. But Oh no! It's never enough whatever I do. She tells me to study hard at school. So what do I do? I become a fucking lawyer. And now what was I supposed to have done? Squatted down and pushed out a baby for a man with a big dick who'd make me cook and maybe knocked me about. Is that what you really wanted me to do, eh Mum? Eh? Eh?

Khadi sighed and wiped a hand across her forehead. She leaned over and took the magazine that was slipping out of her mother's hand. Despite what Naomi Fine said about giving voice to anger, Khadi always felt soiled by its dark tide. My mother loves me unconditionally, nothing more, nothing less. That's it. There's really no more to be said.

From her leather holdall, she took a sheaf of papers, postmortem notes on recent litigation where she'd assisted one of the partners. She'd made it her policy to review each case at its conclusion. As she tried to find a comfortable position, she marvelled at the ease with which her mother's fifty-something spine achieved repose within the unforgiving contours of these chairs. Well, that's my mother – nothing, if not flexible...

With a highlighting pen, Khadi set to work on her papers, blocking out all distractions, focusing on the text. It was a good deal later when she glanced up and saw a fellow passenger walk by. He was an older man, not known to her, but there was something familiar about him. Oh yes, he walks like my father, has the same erect bearing. Oh God, I'll be seeing him soon. What will he be like? Old like that man, white hair but still with the ramrod back? What will it be like when he sees Mum? Will they be strangers, polite acquaintances? I couldn't stand that. Will they be friends, like nothing has happened? I couldn't stand that either. Because too much has happened. To both of them. To all of us.

The postmortem notes began to blur as these questions tumbled around in her head, merging into a single one. *How did I let myself be persuaded?* Khadi put her papers down and leaned back. It was not sleep she wanted, just darkness. Unlike her mother, she and sleep were not on good terms: she existed on no more than four or five hours a night. She closed her eyes. Sleep did not come but memory did. In fact, a memory within a memory......

It was a year ago and she was in Naomi Fine's office, admiring the elegance of the room with its subtle colours and the small but

33

quality paintings on the wall. There was one she particularly liked and wanted to get up and examine it closely. But she couldn't. There was silence in the room. This was only her second session but she already knew that the silence would continue until she started to talk.

"Dreams. You want me to tell you about my dreams. Well, I don't really dream, Naomi. I told you that already." Her tone was almost petulant.

"Yes you do. We all do. It's part of being human." The doctor's encouraging expression went counter to the message of her voice: there would be no dodging the question of dreams. "There are people, though, who suppress them almost immediately."

Khadi slumped back into the plush chair and looked hard at the small painting on the wall and beyond that, the window, framing sunlight on trees at the threshold of autumn. She longed to be a brush stroke on the canvas or a leaf on one of those trees, unnoticed, unconscious, one of millions of its kind. Instead she was in an office with a woman wearing big glasses who kept asking her ridiculous questions. She wanted to get up and leave. Take the subway to 34th Street and up the elevator to her apartment. But she did not get up. She ran her tongue along her bottom lip and leaned forward.

"There's only one." She could not see Naomi Fine's eyes, just her glasses glinting. "Dream, that is. And it's not really that. It's what happened. It's true. It just comes back to me now and then. Always the same. Never ever different."

"When you say it's true, what do you mean?"

"I mean…" Khadi sounded exasperated. "It actually happened. When I was four years old, my mother had had enough of her marriage to my father, so she took me from my bed in the middle of the night and we caught a plane to France. That's what happened. And that's what I remember when I'm sleeping. So I suppose that counts as a dream."

"Good, Khadi! We're making progress. Now tell me about the dream."

"But I just told you! That's it! There's no more." Khadi started twisting the hem of her sweater and tapping one of her feet.

"No, Khadi." The doctor's voice was smooth. "You've told me

the facts. What you haven't told me is your experience of that memory which has become a recurring dream."

Khadi pursed her lips and said nothing, rocking backwards and forwards very slightly. Then she placed both hands over her mouth and leaned over as though she were about to throw up. Her body was taut, preparing itself for the violent expulsion to come. Behind her glasses, Naomi Fine sat vigilant as the moments ticked by, waiting to see if she should intervene.

She didn't have to. Khadi stepped back from the brink. She took her hands away from her mouth and faced the therapist.

"I'm just little. Four. I'm asleep under my mosquito net as usual and I wake up and find that I've wet the bed. I start to cry. Why didn't my mum come to sit me on the pot? Finally Mum comes. She's in a hurry and throws a blanket over my wet nightdress. She picks up a bag with her other hand and we go running into the pitch darkness. There's a car waiting outside our gate and as soon as we get in, the car moves off. Mum's breathing very fast, as though she's been running. She doesn't say anything to me but puts the blanket right over my head and holds me very tight. I'm scared but the thing that really bothers me is the smell which is all around me, in my clothes and seeping through the blanket. *Pi pi.* Mine. But it's so late and I'm so tired, I fall asleep again."

Khadi was trembling a little, clasping one hand around the other.

"Go on."

"When I wake up, I'm still in a car but this time, it's another one. I look down and see that I'm dressed in different clothes, clothes I don't recognize. They are heavy and tickle my skin. The sun is shining but the air is strange, cold, and when it goes up my nose, I want to sneeze. There's a man driving the car and at first I think it's Papa but when he turns around, I see it's Tonton Antoine. My mother is looking out of the window. She looks tired. She turns and smiles at me. I want to ask why Tonton is driving the car and not Papa, why the air is hard and hurts my nose, why the sun shines but isn't hot, why the road is so wide and the buildings so tall, why we are not in our own house with Yacine making my breakfast. I take a deep breath to ask all these questions when my mother pulls the blanket up around me."

She looked down at her lap and at her mangled sweater.

"The air is cold as I breathe it in and there's a strong smell of urine, the same from last night, dry now but it's left its trail in the fibres of the blanket. My nose and mouth are filled with it. I feel like throwing up!" Khadi clapped her hands onto her mouth for an instant and then, deliberately, placed them back where they were before. "I can't ask my mother any questions. All I can think of is being taken out of my bed in the middle of the night and finding myself the next morning in a place where the sun is cold."

Khadi fell silent. Naomi Fine looked pleased.

"Well, Khadi..."

"I'm not finished..." Khadi broke in. "I don't know why this has all happened but I know it has something to do with the fact that I wet the bed."……

Khadi opened her eyes. She looked at Magdalene sleeping next to her. The memories retreated, the more recent ones with Naomi Fine encasing the old ones, like the gilt frame around the small painting, like the window outlining the autumn trees. Despite an official voice announcing that their flight was ready to board, Khadi did not move. She took deep breaths and tried to loosen the knots of panic taking hold of her. Tried to find her still centre, not vulnerable to dreams or memories. She did not succeed. But she was able to find a more familiar place in her mind, a place that let her appear serene. Leaning over, she shook Magdalene lightly.

"Come on, Mum. It's time to go."

Magdalene stirred, rubbing her eyes. "What? So soon?" She started getting her things together and then stopped and gave her daughter a searching look. "And how are you doing?"

"Just fine. Really. I'm ready." Khadi's words were like silk, her body in complete control as they joined the queue. When they entered the cabin, the flight attendant greeted them and Khadi gave him a radiant smile.

But both mother and daughter knew it for what it was. A performance. A fraud.

3.

SALIOU: PÈRE DE FAMILLE

"*C'est elle, ma grande soeur, Papa?*" Maimouna asked, scanning every female face as they entered the crowded airport.

"*Non, Mai. C'est pas elle,*" her father replied, guiding her along by the shoulders.

"*C'est elle, alors? Celle-là? Ou celle-là?*"

"*Maimouna! De grâce! Je t'ai déjà dit. Ta soeur n'est pas encore arrivée!*"

Saliou looked down at the pinched little face and sighed. "Come," he said in Ouolof and in a much less stern tone, "let's go back outside for some fresh air. Maybe we'll see the plane come in." He picked up his briefcase and ushered his young daughter towards the door.

On their way outside, they bumped into Alioune Beye, an old friend whom Saliou hadn't seen for years. Alioune, now Monsieur le Juge Beye, was returning to Martinique after a month visiting his elderly mother. It was he who informed Maimouna and her father that the flight from New York was delayed for two hours. Saliou shook his head and made a small irritated noise.

"You'd have thought they'd announce it."

Alioune Beye chuckled. "Don't forget where we are, *mon cher.*" He surveyed the boisterous crowd taking possession of the airport's main concourse. The vast majority of these were not travelling but members of large family groupings, bidding farewell or welcome to sisters, nephews, fathers, great-nieces, cousins, cousins of friends... anyone who was stepping, or had already stepped beyond the shores of Senegal to that ubiquitous place referred to by the elders as "*alla-bi*" – the bush. "Boy, you might not believe it but this..." he made a sweeping gesture, "this is what I miss in Martinique, even after all this time."

"You mean you miss the noise, dust, too many people, bad air conditioning, worse plumbing, not to mention gross inefficiency and corruption." Saliou said this with a smile, his fingers playing with the spiky little braids at the top of Maimouna's head.

The two men had been friends since childhood and their student days together in Paris. They shared an easy camaraderie, quite at odds with the formal greetings presented to them by passers-by for whom they were "Monsieur le Docteur" and "Monsieur le Juge".

"Alioune, you can't seriously be telling me that after all this time in *les Caraibes*, you still feel…"

"Out of place? Well it's not quite that. The family's there, after all. Did I tell you that Tutti just made me a grandfather? Yes, yes, *Dieu merci*…" The two men and the child snaked through the crowd, looking for a quiet spot. "No, Martinique's been good to me. I've been successful; I've been able to provide for my family here and over there. I've got used to having France in my face all the time. But then, that never bothered me the way it bothered you."

"So what do you miss?"

"I can't tell you what I miss, Saliou." He paused. "All I know is that I want to die here."

Saliou's eyes were warm on his friend as his mind roamed over the choices they had made in their lives, the values they'd inherited, the principles they'd hammered out as young men, the compromises they'd made along the way. The years had swept by them like a great river. And now here they were, with white hair and talk of grandchildren. But there was a difference. The conclusion that Alioune had just reached, about belonging in and to Africa, was one that Saliou had arrived at years ago.

"Guess who we're meeting off the New York flight?"

Alioune raised his eyebrows in query.

"Khadi." Saliou paused. "And her mother."

Alioune's face broke into a smile. "Khadi? Eh! She must be…"

"Twenty-seven."

"Ah! And very beautiful, I'm sure. She was such a beautiful child. Give her a big hug for me. Although she probably won't remember me." There was a marked pause. "And Madeleine. I didn't know you were in touch. How is she?"

Saliou seemed to struggle to find an answer. "What to say? She's still…"

"*Extraordinaire*?"

"Something like that," he conceded with a low laugh.

"And our dear Ndeye?" Alioune asked, measuring his words, "Is she looking forward to the visit?"

Saliou visibly straightened and assumed the bearing of the paterfamilias, absent in the previous exchanges. "Oh yes, no-one in the family is looking forward to meeting Khadi and Madeleine more than Ndeye." He was made aware of the wriggling child at his side. "And of course, Mai…"

Alioune didn't say anything for a while, then looking Saliou in the eye, he murmured, "When I was young, I used to think that everything proceeded in a straight line. Begin at A, keep walking without looking to the left or right and you'll eventually arrive at Z. But the older I get, the more it seems like life goes in circles. Departures, journeys, returns and departures again…"

Saliou was silent.

Soon it was time for Alioune to leave. He kissed Maimouna, embraced his friend and was gone. Maimouna watched her father as he watched his friend disappear into the crowd.

"Are you sad, Papa?"

He turned. "No, *petite*, not at all. Let's go and find somewhere to wait for your sister's plane."

After a few minutes of aimless walking, Saliou thought better of it and was soon talking on his cell phone. "Come, Mai, we're going to Tanti Marie's house. She's going out but we can go and relax there while we're waiting."

Five minutes' later, they were exchanging greetings and good-byes with his French colleague, Marie, who told them to make themselves at home. If they wanted anything, just ask *la bonne*.

Although darkened by shuttered windows, the morning sun made the house distinctly hot. Saliou and Maimouna jumped at the opportunity when *la bonne* suggested that they take their glasses of cold *lait caillé* into the yard. This was the place to be. The concreted space was long and narrow but its lines were softened by ranks of potted palms and the wooden fencing was obscured by the brilliance of purple bougainvillea. In one corner, there were a couple of adolescent mango trees, not yet bearing fruit but putting a whole section of the garden in dappled shade. The far fence kept out the dunes which stood like muscular bodyguards keeping back the sea. Despite the suggestion of sand in the air, the sea was the overpowering presence here. You could not see it, but you could smell it, taste its salt breath, sense its movement. And on its shoulders came a fresh, quickening breeze.

Maimouna set about exploring. Her inspection was both meticulous and carefree. She started with the dwarf palms in their clay pots, trailing her fingers in the loose dirt, letting them linger on the rough topography of the trunk, giving a barest touch to the fine hanging filaments of green, just enough to make the leaves tremble. She took her time, giving each tree her full attention and then she would move on to some other marvel worthy of her absorption. In this manner, she progressed around the yard, inhaling rosemary and thyme hiding from the sun on a window sill, crying out in delight when she discovered a couple of crusty turtles slowly digging their way into a spot of deepest shadow, stroking the vivid flowers tumbling over the fences, taking care to avoid their sharp thorns. Every now and then, she would leave her station and head for the far fence, going on tiptoe to get a glimpse of the ocean. For a moment, she would stand motionless, her whole body craned forward in the direction of the twinkling blue line that appeared between the sand dunes.

In all of this industry, she seemed to have forgotten her father who watched from the shade. This child would be a scientist, maybe a doctor. She would do something special in the world. He imagined how different this scene would be if he'd been here with his other children, his four boys. How they'd be tearing around the place, scrambling up the trees, conquering the space in a different way, a way which would need his constant supervision. But not Mai… she would be doing exactly what she's doing now if she were completely alone. Saliou let out a long breath. These women. What am I going to do with them?

And on the breath of that thought came the image of his wife, Ndeye, as he'd left her at home an hour ago. To all eyes other than his, she appeared serene, her forehead high and smooth, her eyes untroubled as she cast her calming influence over the bubbling energy of the household. But he knew that she faced this meeting with trepidation. This was the first love, the first mother. This was the one who was a rule-breaker, a quality unknown to Ndeye. This was the one vilified by family legend but who evidently still had a place in her husband's heart. This was the one who, by the laws of tradition, would have to be welcomed with unconditional generosity into her household. This was the one whose legitimacy came in the guise of the accomplished but alien daughter who was also the sister of her children. Even for Ndeye, diplomatic and self-effacing to a fault, the next two weeks were going to be tough.

Saliou thought about his marriage and the last ten years and knew beyond all doubt that there existed between him and Ndeye a profound though mainly unspoken love. Was he asking too much of her? But Khadi was his daughter, too, as much part of him as this enchanting child dancing in the sunshine. He was aware of the potential for distress, but when the blood called out, all other voices were silenced.

Saliou looked up to see Maimouna standing in front of him.

"Papa, what have you got in that bag?"

Saliou's mind was blank for a moment and then he remembered the parcel he'd brought with him from home. "Oh…" he said, reluctant to talk about it. "It's…" he was about to say "nothing" but one look at Maimouna's unblinking eyes reminded him that it would be pointless to try to fob her off. "It's for your sister."

She waited, a study in patience.

"Would you like to see?"

She clambered onto his lap and watched as he took from his briefcase a photo album bound in embossed leather.

"Here's a picture of Khadi…"

"But I thought you said she was a grownup!"

"She is now. But then, she was just a baby, about the same age as our little Lamine is now."

"And that is your Tanti Magdalene, Khadi's mother. You'll be seeing her soon too."

"There you are, Papa!" she laughed. "You look…" she couldn't finish the sentence as she studied the slightly blurred image of her father with unfamiliar clothes and a fierce halo of hair. "Where's *Maman*? And where am I?"

"Too many questions, Mai!" There was an edge in his voice, but Maimouna did not hear it. She was too entranced with these pictures, her mind trying to encompass notions of past and present and of worlds outside herself. Saliou's commentary ended as suddenly as it had begun, but they continued slowly turning the pages. When they came to the end, Maimouna started afresh, treating the photos to the same rapt attention she had given the turtles and the palms and the sea. She did this several times but eventually, the warmth of the sun and her father's arms got the better of her and, with the album still open, she fell asleep.

Saliou was glad. The intensity with which this child consumed life was exhausting. Glancing down at her sleeping form, he saw the album open to a picture of him, Magdalene and Khadi, sitting on a beach, the only one with the three of them together. He returned the album to his briefcase, recalling that when he was assembling the pictures of Khadi's early life, he had wondered whether to include this one. How would Magdalene feel seeing it? Would it bring back bad memories? Or were the memories bad only for him? He had looked long and hard at the photo, scrutinizing the faces, trying to find waning affection in his face and incipient betrayal in Magdalene's. He didn't find either. Just a happy young family on a day out.

And yet it was the beginning of the end. The day when it all started to fall apart.

Though both briefcase and album were shut fast, Saliou struggled to close his mind to their silent taunts. Now was not the time to be drawn into any maudlin analysis of things past. As the instigator of Khadi's visit, much was riding on his ability to hold things together. He alone would be able to persuade the older members of his family, some of whom still harboured ill-will against Magdalene, of the moral purpose of the visit. Only he would be able to constrain the herd of young cousins and nephews panting to meet the glamorous *Americaine*; reassure Ndeye; ensure that Magdalene was kept away from any danger zones which might provoke one of her outbursts. He had to continue – whatever he might be feeling – to be the *père de famille* for Maimouna and her brothers and the myriad other persons for whom he was the rock, the provider of all life. Above all, he had to bring his first child, the lost child, Khadiatou, back into the circle of belonging. It was for these reasons that he could not afford to think about the "happy young family on a day out". No, that was out of the question. And yet…

The tightness in Saliou's belly did not respond to reason; his mind would not relinquish that image. With the warm weight of Maimouna on his lap, he had to sit there trapped in memory.

Antoine. He had taken the picture… Yes, Antoine. The tightness in his belly was replaced with a cold anger. It was not a new feeling; he felt this way whenever he thought about his former friend, the traitor who had colluded with Magdalene in stealing his daughter away. It was more than collusion… Without Antoine, Magdalene would never have left. She could have been persuaded to consider the enormity of what she was doing, to us and our daughter. But Antoine… not only had he facilitated her escape, he had talked her into it in the first place! Marie Madeleine would not have done it on her own! Saliou shut his eyes against the increasing glare of the sunny yard and willed away this slide into foolish, pointless recrimination.

Anyway, Antoine was dead. How long has it been? At least ten years. And all that time, he'd made him suffer the indignity of anger. That's the problem with the dead. They always had the last say. But what was truly *épouvantable* was the fact that he felt as angry with himself as he did with Antoine. He should have seen it coming! He couldn't believe he didn't.

He recalled the moment when his unlikely friendship with Antoine had been cemented during their disreputable student days in Paris. A long night of heated political argument was drawing to a close……

"Until Africa becomes unified, until it becomes the United States of Africa… then nothing of any consequence can happen for Africans, wherever they are in the world." Antoine gave an almighty yawn and made a move to get up from the floor. But his legs were unsteady from an excess of sitting and red wine.

"You amaze me," said Saliou, lending a hand. "You're the only *Antillais* I've ever met who really thinks of himself as an African."

43

"And you're the only wine drinker I know who really thinks of himself as a Muslim!" Antoine dusted off the back of his trousers. "No, that's not true. I've known others…"

"No, seriously though…"

"That's your problem, Saliou. Too damn serious." Antoine poured himself another glass, emptying the last of the bottle.

"No, really," Saliou insisted. "How is it that none of the Martinicans and Guadeloupéens around here talk about Africa the way you do?"

"Well, *mon cher ami*…" Antoine downed the wine. "Could it be to do with the fact that I spent some of my childhood there? Me and my won't-say-a-word mother and that bastard husband of hers, my father."

"Well, now you don't sound like an African! When you're dishonouring your parents. Besides, you didn't just go to Africa with your father. He was posted all over the place as an army doctor. Indochina! Didn't you say you went to a couple of countries there?"

"All right, Saliou." Antoine looked at him with bloodshot eyes. "I'm this screwed up because I grew up travelling around with the French Army. The only black family I ever knew was my own – until we went to Africa. Cameroun first, then Mali." Antoine clapped him on the back. "Whatever shit I found – and there was plenty – it still felt good to be there. A kind of home. Even when we left to carry on travelling, I kept that feeling with me."

Antoine struggled to wind a woollen scarf around his neck.

"This climate is hell. I'll never get used to it… Then… then…" he said, trying to conclude what he had started. "Then we went to the Caribbean for the first time since I left as a baby. And that was another kind of homecoming."

They opened the door and the sharp winter wind froze their faces.

"This will sober us up," said Antoine. "But if I fall on my ass, pick me up, will you? That's what friends are for."

"*Bien sûr!*" Saliou answered, feeling a little light-headed. "Anyway, you're not just my friend. You're my brother." Their laughter rang out as they skidded along the icy pavement…

It was Antoine who had introduced Saliou to Magdalene, whose vivacity had made him notice her among the group of *Antillais* to which she belonged in her first year in Paris. She was trying to learn French after a sterile upbringing in London where her parents had forbidden her to speak their native St. Lucian patois. "It'll keep you back," her mother had said. But somehow, she had found her way to Paris and was trying to immerse herself in a new cultural landscape when Antoine "discovered" her and saw it as his duty to widen the vistas of her life. The first point in her journey was his friend, Saliou, and Antoine knew, from their first meeting, that a new sun had risen on both their horizons.

It was Antoine who had acted as mediator when Saliou's older brother Omar was dispatched to read Saliou the riot act about bringing a foreigner into the family. So skilful were Antoine's negotiations that even the redoubtable Omar had returned home with a good report. When Saliou and Magdalene married and moved to Africa, they both mourned the loss, not of Antoine's friendship – that would be eternal! – but of daily contact with their beloved friend. The moment they set foot in Dakar, however, the pace of their life quickened. So many things to do, people to meet, adjustments to make! The next few years sped by with Antoine making a lightning visit to stand as godfather when Khadi was born and then not being seen again until... until...

Saliou's mind had been racing along and now it slowed down again, slowed to a crawl. It was back at the photograph on the beach, the family day out......

"Saliou!" Antoine groaned. "Put your arm around your wife, for God's sake... Now, say..."

"Cheese!" piped Magdalene, trying to hold Khadi still.

"Not cheese. Say sixty-nine! That's it. *Soixante-neuf!*"

"For goodness sake, Antoine. Remember the child!" Magdalene wagged her finger at him.

"What! She can't count up to sixty-nine yet?"

The photo taken, Saliou and Magdalene sat on the sand while Antoine took Khadi out into the water again. The sun was warm without being overpowering and there was a balmy breeze. They didn't say much to one another but neither was there silence as they exclaimed at the antics of the splashing child and the man towering over her.

"We'd better watch the time if we want to go into the Maison," Magdalene said.

"Are you sure we want to bother?" Saliou asked.

"Yes. I'd like to go. And Antoine's never been."

So they called Antoine and Khadi out of the water and made their way to the slave house.

As they went through the Maison des Esclàves, they'd heard the commentary, seen the chambers and the chains and the Tunnel of No Return that led out to the water.

For Saliou, it was the same as always. A trip to the museum. A bit of living history. But for Magdalene and Antoine, it was something more. When they stepped back into the sunshine, there had been a change.

"Come on! We might just be able to get a drink before the ferry comes." Saliou tried to jolly them along. "Magdalene! Give us one of your smiles. You don't want Antoine leaving tonight remembering you miserable. Come on!" ......

Something had happened between them that day, Saliou thought, as he readjusted Maimouna in his lap, or something had come to the surface. From then on, we were on the path that led us here. Yes, Antoine, I tell you this in your grave. What you stole from me can never be replaced!

Saliou looked at his watch. It was time to go. Thank God. Thoughts like this gave you ulcers and hypertension. He tapped Maimouna on the cheek. And yet, without Antoine's treachery, there'd be no Maimouna or the boys. No Ndeye.

"Is my big sister here?" she asked, instantly awake.

"No, we have to go now." Saliou stood her up and smoothed down her dress and repositioned her plaits. "You have to look right, you know." He gave her a reassuring smile and added, "You look fine."

They were just about to get into the car when they heard a man calling out.

"Charity! Charity! Will you give charity to one of God's chosen?" They turned to see a man standing on the other side of the car holding a tin cup. There was something both familiar and unfamiliar about him. He was of indeterminate age, was blind and in rags. But he was not one of the legion cripples who crawled along with wooden blocks beneath their ruined hands and knees. He was upright, his head was shaven and his rags were clean. He stood in silence, his unseeing cloudy eyes looking straight ahead.

Saliou rummaged in his pocket, drew out a few wilted notes and placed them in the cup. The man grasped the notes and held them out.

"Silver. I prefer silver." The man paused, sensing Saliou's surprise. "I know the sound and feel of silver. With the paper, I am easily robbed. I am easily fooled."

"As you wish, older brother," said Saliou, replacing the notes with a handful of coins which sang as they cascaded into the cup. "God's peace be with you."

"It is the duty of a Muslim to give alms," the unsmiling man replied, not moving as Saliou, his brow darkening, went to open the car door. And then, for no obvious reason, the man added, "The sea is at peace today."

"How can you tell?" Maimouna stood before him, staring at the man whose cloudy eyes were trained towards some distant horizon. She resisted the tug of her father's hand, standing her ground until her question was answered.

The man turned his head in the direction of the child's voice and crouched down to her. She felt her father pulling her away but she was not afraid.

"Although I have no eyes to see, I have been given ears to hear. To hear, you must walk in silence with a pure heart. Do you hear her, little one? Do you hear the sea?"

Maimouna cupped her hand around her ear and stayed very still. "Yes, I hear the sea. I hear it! Do you hear it, Papa?" Her face shone as she lifted it to her father.

The man continued, speaking only to the child. "The sea is a spirit, little one. And the spirit is a woman in a lovely blue gown. When she weeps, the gown weeps with her. When she laughs, the gown laughs with her. When she is offended, she thrashes her gown about her with a terrible anger. But today she is gentle," he said, straightening up. "Today, she is at peace." He turned and continued along his way calling, "Charity! Charity! Will you give to one of God's chosen?"

Saliou muttered under his breath, "Everybody in this town

thinks he's a damn poet!" But as a good Muslim, he knew it was "*ba-hul*" – not good – to abuse the poor and the wretched. It was his duty to perform daily acts of charity, but it annoyed him to be reminded of it by the recipient! And he had not liked the way he had spoken to Maimouna. He had such high hopes for this child. She had already made a name for herself at school. Her acute powers of observation, her ability to apply herself without adult supervision – these all pointed to a brilliant future. In science, he hoped. But she had another side, an opposite side, one that the man with the tin cup had recognized, a dreamy side, susceptible to the irrational and the fabulous. He would have to be very vigilant and keep her away from such influences. It was his duty.

"We're not late, are we, Papa?" she asked as they sped along the highway. "They haven't got here yet, have they?"

"No, Mai. We're in good time." Saliou was happy to note that she was once more engrossed in details of the imminent arrival, as she fingered her dress and hair. They entered the airport concourse just in time to hear – the public address system was now working – that the flight from New York had landed. One of his nephews, an Immigration Officer, was supposed to be on duty so Saliou felt confident that Khadi and her mother would be out soon. A large crowd gathered and before too long, the first travellers emerged.

Saliou began to lose faith in his nephew when the stream of travellers started to thin. He had images of Khadi and her mother being targeted as wealthy Americans and of Magdalene becoming involved in some unseemly skirmish. He looked around for some other official who might be able to hasten the process, saw one and steered Maimouna towards a couple of chairs by the wall.

"Stay here while I find out what's going on."

She did not release his hand. "But Papa, what must I do?"

"You must sit here and wait until I come back."

"No. What must I do while I'm waiting?"

"Oh!" he said, anxious to be off as he saw the official moving away. He opened his briefcase and pulled out some paper. "Here." He fumbled in his pocket and found a pencil. "Draw something." He took a few steps and called over his shoulder, "Something for Khadi."

Saliou was only vaguely known to the airport official, but he persuaded him to make enquiries about the fate of the two women. Ten anxious minutes passed before Magdalene came out, flustered but smiling, with stories of luggage lost but now found. She was followed by Khadi.

"Father," she said, "we're here. At last." She embraced him lightly and handed him the laden trolley.

"We have to get someone before we go out to the car," he said.

They walked together, full of animated chatter, until they came upon Maimouna, a small island of silence, her head down, her hand hard at work.

Feeling their presence, she looked up, her eyes dark and wide at the sight of these exotic-looking women.

Khadi sat down next to her. "And you must be Maimouna?"

Maimouna nodded and lowered her eyes.

"And what do we have here?"

Khadi touched the paper lying in the child's lap.

"May I see?"

Again, there was a nod as Khadi slipped the paper from Maimouna's grasp.

Printed in large letters were the words "BIENVENUE A MA SOEUR ET MA TANTE".

"Look, Mum! She's done us a welcome sign!" Scarcely had Khadi let Magdalene glance at it when she noticed that underneath the lettering, there was a picture of a woman with flowing hair and a beatific smile. From her waist there sprang an enormous skirt that spun about her and undulated all the way to the edges of the page.

"Who's this, Maimouna?"

She hesitated for only a moment.

"It's the sea. She's happy today."

Magdalene raised her eyebrows, a half smile on her face. She noticed that Saliou was shaking his head and looking away.

Khadi took the girl's hands in hers and said, "I think she's the loveliest lady I've ever seen."

Maimouna rewarded her with a beautiful, shy smile.

A FARTHER SHORE

4.

NDEYE: THE VOICE IN THE DARK

By the time Khadi and her mother set foot on the paving stones leading to the house, Ndeye was already at the door, with her sons and the rest of the large household ranged in an untidy phalanx about her. For a fragment of a second, all around her seemed to absorb her anxiety and project it onto the two foreign women moving towards them. Then Ndeye saw Maimouna, radiant, gripping her sister's hand like a trophy. She smiled and in so doing opened to Khadi and Magdalene the true *teranga*.

Ndeye Diop, wife of Saliou, mother of Amadou, Malik, Maimouna, Omar and Lamine, proffered her hand first to Magdalene and then to her daughter, greeted them in Ouolof, then in accented but correct English and ushered them in. Once inside, she went through the list of names and relationships – "This is Nafisatou, the third daughter of my eldest brother: she will be starting at the high school next month" – ignoring the eye-signs being given by her husband, though aware that this inventory would be soaring over the heads of the jet-lagged visitors. The courtesies of hospitality required the giving of certain information and in her house these courtesies would be observed! And this was no dutiful adherence to form; all was done with grace. Within a few moments, these complex introductions had softened into a smiling, nodding dumb-show amongst those who did not share a language with the visitors and tentative forays into English among those brave enough to try.

Saliou beamed. "You won't have to worry about English! Madeleine's French still works after all these years. And, as for Khadi…" Here he paused and placed a proud but hesitant hand on her shoulder. "Well! Her French is better than mine. And what's more, she even remembers some Ouolof from all that time ago!"

On cue, Khadi said in flawless Ouolof, "It is good to be here among my family once more." There was a spontaneous burst of applause which continued even after she went on to say that these were the only words of Ouolof she knew. Saliou was first to embrace her; then came all the others. Magdalene stood slightly aside, her eyes bright with tears.

Ndeye smiled again, a smile unseen in the commotion. Her misgivings melted away as she observed the effortless manner in which Saliou's first child, the child of another woman, a foreigner at that, had entered her home. She had struggled with the prospect of this meeting, a struggle made even more difficult by the need to conceal her anxiety. Ndeye was not the kind of woman to show jealousy or resentment. With her tranquil nature and orderly mind, she hardly ever felt hot and corrosive emotion. But she did not exist entirely in the realm of serenity. Although she appeared to float just above the turbulent surface of events, replacing conflict with peace as if by magic, yet she was deeply grounded in the complexity of her world. Family – her husband, their five children, the huge network of relations on her side, the equally vast collection on his, the rambling life of this villa in the capital, the fate of the village from which she and her husband had come – this was the essence of her life.

When Ndeye had learned that the lost child and "the woman Madeleine" would be coming, she had felt a painful tug in her belly. And although she now stood there, every inch the progressive, educated African woman, in flattering French-cut trousers and a silk blouse, with a hint of *marron à lèvres* on her lips, despite all the European meals she had been planning, despite the fact that for months she'd been taking refresher English lessons with her Gambian cousin who taught at the university, despite all this, Ndeye had suffered a gnawing fear that somehow these two could destabilize the equilibrium of the life she had created.

But now they were here and she felt nothing but relief.

There was nothing to fear in either of them. Ndeye did not even have to sneak a look at Magdalene to know that the man who had loved and married this woman no longer existed. The image that

Ndeye had carried around in her head, (partly supplied by Saliou's family and partly furnished by her own imagination) of a fierce Western woman who smoked, drank, cursed, lived alone, made films, travelled the world, had no real home – well, where was she? All Ndeye could see was a small, solid, somewhat dishevelled figure dwarfed by the tall lean Wades and Diops of the household, a woman who seemed to be hovering between laughter and tears; someone who, though seeming to hold onto her daughter's dress for comfort, had no hesitation in stepping into the circle to receive her share of the communal embrace. Ndeye acknowledged that the startling eyes and the ready smile combined to give this woman's face an unusual vitality, but she could see that the light coming from those eyes followed one path. At the end of that path was Khadi. She's a mother, just like me! Whatever she is, whatever Saliou was to her when they were young, now she lives for that girl alone. Ndeye felt a great weight fall from her. This woman might shout and stamp her foot but it would always be about her daughter; it would never be about the husband of her youth.

"Fatou! Go and bring the juice from the *frigo*," Ndeye said. "Malik, take your sister and your Tanti to their bedroom. Amadou, help Papa with the bags." Her tone was unhurried and in the space between the words, there seemed to be a slowing down of time in which Ndeye saw the group break up into work parties, each doing her bidding, their movements lengthening and stretching out before the task. In the midst of this, Ndeye studied her stepdaughter. What had the fuss been about? What had her husband been agonizing over for so long? There was nothing dangerous here, though she noted, with a little regret, that she was the image of her father in ways that none of her own children were. There were those strangely coloured eyes, perhaps, but apart from that, Khadi's beauty was of a very familiar kind – tall, slender, with high cheekbones, an aquiline nose and a brilliant white smile. Why, Saliou has a bundle of nieces and cousins who look more or less like that! And what's more, there was none of that arrogance that she'd expected from people from "over there", none of that disrespect. The mother, more than likely; but the girl, no! Everyone seems to have taken to her. Look at Mai! She hasn't let go of her for a second! Yes, we should be able to manage this for a couple of weeks…

Then from somewhere deep inside came what Ndeye called "the voice". Her dead grandmother would have called it her spirit, her heart's pulse, her soul's song, that intuitive throb which guided her to the truth of things. In her adult years, she had spoken of her exchanges with this voice with no-one, especially not her husband, who would have called it nonsense, not worthy of a modern Muslim such as herself. But Ndeye knew this voice was real. It came to her at the heightened hours of her life, in peaks of great happiness and pain, keeping silent during the flat terrain of the everyday. In these "conversations" she spoke of her joy or sorrow; "the voice" answered, but not in words, never in words. Just sounds whose meaning was clear. In recent months, it had been hissing like a wild creature, a civet-cat, perhaps, vigilant in the camouflaging grasses of the savannah. It had warned her to be watchful. But the voice that came to her now was like music as she presided over the cheerful confusion as her family went about their tasks. She gave an imperceptible nod as Maimouna, refusing to relinquish her sister's hand, led the newcomers away, the rest of the youthful welcoming party bobbing like little sea birds in their wake. Khadi and Magdalene – yes, in her mind, she no longer had to call them "the lost child" and "the woman Madeleine" – they were part of the family now, part of this song that flowed through her veins.

When everyone had left the room, Ndeye paused to rearrange a pile of cushions on the sofa, walked through the dining room, soon to lose its museum status and actually be used, stopped for a brief moment in the tiled kitchen where *la bonne,* Fatou, was pouring cold passion-fruit juice into glasses and finally flung open the back door open and stepped into the yard. With its outdoor kitchen, where another *bonne* had started working on the lunch, its majestic *fromager,* its sour-orange trees, its assorted benches and chairs, its WC, its clusters of bright desert flowers, its swept sandy floor – this was the heart of the house. Here you could feel you were nearer to the village. Ndeye breathed in the odours of the cooking, the sand, the fallen fruit and the late morning sunshine. After months of worry, the song of her heart's voice was sweet in her ears and she felt safe in her kingdom. *Yalla bahana.* God is good.

That evening Ndeye stood calmly between Magdalene and Khadi

at the entrance of the dining room while Saliou greeted Omar and Hodia at the main door. As the oldest surviving brother, Omar was head of the family, and though only the titular head, Saliou being the principal provider for all-comers, his status as older brother was always recognized. If for Omar ceremony was important, it was even more so for his wife, Hodia. She gloried in her role as wife of the oldest brother, and her overt devotion to her husband was lived out to the letter. But whereas Omar was content with ceremonial respect, Hodia used her position to exercise a peculiar form of malice.

Ndeye's serenity dissipated. The dinner had all the hallmarks of a disaster-in-waiting. It was Omar who, long ago, had spoken on Magdalene's behalf when no-one wanted to hear that Saliou intended to marry a foreigner, a *catholique*, an *Antillaise*… It was Omar who had vouched for her good character. Only on his authority had she come into the family. It was Hodia, queen of the *mauvaises langues*, who had broken the story about Magdalene drinking alcohol and having "relations" with a *toubab* who worked with her. So when the catastrophe happened and Magdalene had run off with the child in the middle of the night, it was Omar who had felt so soiled that, until this visit was in train, he'd refused to have Magdalene's name spoken in his hearing. As Omar and Hodia approached, Ndeye was sure of two things: that Omar had only agreed to come and eat with them because of the respect he felt for Saliou and all he had done for the family, and if she could live through tonight's dinner, the worst part of the whole visit would be behind her.

Khadi stepped forward, looking every inch a *fille du pays* in the light blue boubou her father had arranged to be made for her.

"Good evening, Khadiatou," Omar said. "How well you look. Saliou, I think we can agree she is the image of our mother."

Dumb with anxiety, Saliou could only nod.

"Peace be with you, Uncle, and with your household," Khadi said in good Ouolof. "It brings me joy to see you again after such a long time." She said this in French and kissed him on both cheeks. She turned, smiling, towards her aunt, who was standing like a statue in a stiff purple gown covered in embroidery. Both her arms were weighed down with gold.

"Tanti Hodia, you are just as I remember you," she said with the briefest flutter of her eyelids. "I hope the children are all well." Hodia leaned forward to allow Khadi to embrace her in a rustling of starch and jangling of bracelets. Then she stood straight like a statue and pulled her thin lips back in a kind of a smile.

"You have grown well, Khadiatou," she finally said. "You resemble my youngest daughter, Ancha…"

Saliou winced. Ancha was the plainest one in the entire family, no contest.

"Yes, you are a Wade, one hundred per cent…" She gave her special evil cough. "Except the *toubab* eyes from your mother…"

"Which most people say are my best feature! Hello Omar. Hello Hodia. This is great, isn't it? Feels like old times."

Magdalene, who'd been standing behind Khadi, came forward, moving fast, talking fast and putting her hand out towards Omar. Her outstretched arm was steady and strong. To Ndeye, it looked like a man's.

Magdalene stood with her arm extended and her cat's eyes burning. She did not seem aware of the silence. She did not seem angry or concerned. She was just waiting for Omar to reach across and take her hand.

It was Khadi who broke the silence.

"Father. You see what happens when old friends get together after a long time? The joy! It's almost too much. Tonton Omar and Tanti Hodia are overwhelmed to see my mother. It's touching, really touching." All the time, she was smiling, looking from one face to the other, talking quietly, touching first her mother's arm, then her father's. Hodia had started twisting her head around and moving her shoulders, getting ready to make a dramatic exit. Getting ready to scream accusations of insult to the world.

Then, from the folds of his kaftan, Omar's arm appeared, moving slow and unwilling, like a creature creeping through the undergrowth. It seemed to take forever. His arm looked frail, its skin dull and wrinkled. Magdalene's arm never moved. It just waited for his to cover the distance between them. As soon as their fingers touched, she covered them with her other hand and although Omar tried to turn away, she looked him straight in the eye and said, in Ouolof, "Peace be on your household."

"*Leboon!*" called old Auntie Story, her voice strong as it rang out in the gathering darkness the night after the historic meeting between Omar and his ancient enemy.

"*Leppon!*" trilled the assembly, shifting young bodies on the straw mats and wooden stools, on the laps of their teenaged cousins and aunts, in the arms of the maids. Auntie Story was the focus of the semicircle which had formed beneath the old silk-cotton tree dominating the yard. At the edge of the semicircle sat Ndeye, cradling her youngest, Lamine, whose head was already nodding.

"*Amoonafi!*" Auntie Story challenged.

"*Danaam!*" the children countered.

With a seasoned performer's timing, the old woman paused. Auntie Story was the name given to her in acknowledgement of her skills when she'd come from the Gambia many years before. Now she made her tired bones more comfortable and began.

"Once upon a time, there was a cunning hare who used to live not far from here and his name was…"

"Leuk-le-lièvre!" the women and children roared.

"I'm glad to see that, foolish as you are, you remembered. *Leboon!*"

"*Leppon!*"

"Well, one day, Leuk and his friend and rival, a hyena named…"

"Bouki!"

"At least I know you're not sleeping! As I was saying, Leuk and his friend Bouki…"

Ndeye did not have to look down to see that the toddler in her arms was at full attention, his eyes aglow, any rumour of sleep banished. All of the children sitting there in the dark were like Lamine, terrorized by the cantankerous Auntie Story, all the while knowing that, among storytellers, she was the best. Ndeye loved the stories, always changing, always the same; she loved the tussle between the storyteller and her audience; she loved the intertwining of the lives of the very young and the very old, like green lianas curling around the gnarled limbs of an ancient tree.

But she was not listening.

This time, the adventures of the tricky Leuk and his slow-witted sidekick failed to draw her in. It was not the fault of the storyteller. Oh no, Auntie was in rare old form. The alternating waves of shouts and silence bore witness to that.

A day and a half had passed since Khadi and her mother had arrived. It had been a hectic time with a steady tide of friends and family coming to greet them. There had been a few moments of potential trouble but each time it had been overcome. They had all been about the mother, of course. Khadi had not put a foot wrong.

She just seems to fit in, thought Ndeye, and again she found herself in that place in her mind where she could talk to the voice in the dark.

Khadi. The foreigner's daughter. She looks right... fits in... There's something about the way she moves... Like she never left here. And she's quiet. I like that. When she speaks, it means something. Maybe even more than one thing. When she said to Hodia, "You're just like I remember you..." it sounded so polite. But did she mean something else? I hope so! Ndeye chuckled as Auntie Story's hypnotic voice spun its magic.

"...and there, skulking through the tall grasses, with his long brown ears pulled back was..."

"Leuk-le-lièvre!"

Ndeye closed her eyes against the dark and the rhythms of Auntie Story's tale and focused on the words and images of the night before. When Magdalene had taken Omar's hands in hers, there had been a collective sigh. Omar had returned Magdalene's words with a long and searching look and then had wished her peace. Saliou had led the way in to dinner, relaxing with every step he took. Magdalene's stories were funny, with just enough *piment* not to offend the devout. Once or twice, Omar managed a ghost of a smile. Khadi had not said much but when she did talk, it was perfect, in what she did say and what she didn't, and how she said it. Hodia had sat in mute fury during the whole meal but nobody seemed to notice.

Yes, we have been blessed, Ndeye thought, holding the baby close. No matter what, the family is strong, with many branches bearing the weight of the fruit. She knew, too, that she was at the centre of it all, and the voice in the dark sang in her ears with the voice of the kora, the favourite harp of the angels in heaven. Its cascading music rained down, filling her with its sweetness, despite the crescendo of boisterous cries as Auntie's story hastened towards its climax.

"How are you doing?" someone behind her asked, placing a hand on her shoulder. Without turning, Ndeye knew who it was, the person who was forcing her to leave behind the celestial song. It took her a few moments to make that return.

"We missed you last night, Hassim."

"Sorry. An emergency at the hospital. But I understand it went without incident. Or, should I say, without too many incidents." He chuckled.

"You should have been there, Hassim. You're always missing out on family occasions." Even in the dark, Ndeye could see the shrugging of broad shoulders. It was a customary gesture from this cousin, raised like a brother in her father's house, who was closer to her than all of her brothers of the flesh. "And why is that? Why are you always... missing? At baptisms, weddings, funerals, *fêtes* – you just about make it, but only after all of the important parts are over. Why?" Although there was no edge in her voice, there was an unusual insistence.

"Ndeye, you of all people. You know the answer." And of course, she did. She just wished more of the family appreciated Hassim the way she did. But she also wished that Hassim would stop cultivating his position as outsider.

Right then a great roar of approval accompanied the conclusion of the tale of the cunning hare. But there was one more thing to be done. The old woman raised her hand and gave an impatient wave. Her audience piped down at once.

"*Leboon!*"

"*Lepoon!*"

"*Amoonafi!*"

"*Danaaaaaam!*"

Story time was over.

A satisfied hum underlay the general hubbub as people started stretching their legs and milling about. Someone switched on an outside light; a few children started rubbing their eyes. All seemed changed.

"So where are they?" Hassim asked, taking Lamine from Ndeye. "Who?"

"The woman Madeleine and the lost child, of course."

"Shhhhhhh," she said in a low voice. "Don't go telling everybody what I call them." Ndeye paused. "If you'd come last night you would have met them," Ndeye continued, pretending to grumble but in fact, watching with amusement as Lamine's head started to sink down into his chest. "I left them watching the news with Saliou and some of the other men... Don't you want to know what they're like?"

Again, he gave that maddening shrug.

"Oh, there they are," she continued, pointing towards the far side of the yard. "At least there's Khadi. With Maimouna." A bald electric bulb shone down on the two figures, one tall and slender, the other small and elfin, casting sharp shadows on the wall behind. They were bending over, with the little girl handing the woman something to hold.

"So, is that the lost child?" Hassim didn't appear to notice that Ndeye's eyes were fixed on the corner of the yard where her daughter and stepdaughter were intent on studying Maimouna's prize collection of smooth stones.

Where had Maimouna been all this time? Ndeye's mind was suddenly racing. She had a bad feeling in the pit of her stomach. Why hadn't Maimouna been at the storytelling? She loved the stories more than any child she knew. She had been able to recite them verbatim since she was just a little older than Lamine. She was the one who would prefer to miss ice-cream, cinema, coiffure rather than be late for Auntie Story's weekly show. The only time she had ever thrown a tantrum was when she nearly missed a storytelling session because a birthday party had gone on too long. She had said then that she would hold her breath and not stop until she was taken home.

Maimouna was Ndeye's crown – and her daily cross. She didn't mind that her husband wanted their daughter to be a scientist – she would make a good scientist, but what about the other things? When she'd tried to begin her daughter's basic training on how to run a house, how to cook, how to be a woman in the world... Maimouna's body would be there and she'd do what she was told, but her spirit would be somewhere else – and she did not know where. There were none of these problems with her four sons. They could be relied upon to do the normal things. It was only Maimouna who could bring these rushes of anger and fear. Maimouna was different, and Ndeye distrusted this and wanted to prevent her from spinning out of control. And now Maimouna seemed wedded to the lost child, in some kind of sacred communion.

Over the past day and a half, she could not recall a single time when Khadi had not had Maimouna pressed to her side, her face turned upwards, suffused with an expression of intense... what? Even though it was visible from the other side of the yard, Ndeye could not tell what it meant. She squeezed her eyes shut and found her head filled with the voice in the dark. But the kora music had gone. In its place was a sound of menace, a hyena, perhaps, not the dimwitted Bouki of fable, but the real thing, its low growl circling and circling in the night, closing in on the young chicks sleeping in the hen house. The sound of this voice grew louder and closer until Ndeye could hear the rasping, famished breathing of the beast next to her ear. She reached over and snatched back her baby from Hassim.

When she looked over again, Khadi and Maimouna were waving and coming in her direction. Hassim followed her gaze.

"Doesn't seem either lost or a child to me."

"What she appears to be and what she is may not be the same."

But Hassim did not hear. He was already on his feet. In her loose white clothing, Khadi bore down on them in the darkness. Like the moon at midnight, Ndeye thought sadly. Just at the moment when Khadi stopped and stood before him, her amber eyes coming out of the shadows, Hassim bent down, picked up Maimouna and started tossing her in the air like a feather. The night air rang with her squeals as Khadi stood alongside, her loveliness unacknowledged.

5

HASSIM: ON THE RUN

"Well, I'm off. Don't want to keep the minister waiting... Sorry I couldn't have done this myself, but Hassim knows more about what we do at the Centre than I do." Saliou clapped Hassim on the back and added, "And look after them properly. These are important people." With a peck on Khadi's cheek and a nod to Magdalene, Saliou was gone, closing the door behind him.

Hassim stood with his arms braced against the desk, staring at the shut door while the clock on the wall ticked loudly. Then his eyes lit on some papers which needed to be shuffled a few millimetres to the right, a task which occupied his hands for a few more moments. When the papers – part of the mountain of work that required his immediate attention – were perfectly aligned, he gazed uncertainly at the two women sitting in silence on the other side of his desk.

"Well. Ladies." He felt one of his fingers straining to pound out a wild rhythm on the desk but was able to arrest it before it began. "Little did I know when I got up this morning that I would have the pleasure of your company again so soon after the, uh, great pleasure of meeting you the other night at Ndeye's house." He paused to quell the twitching finger and produced a wan smile, which Magdalene reciprocated, half-turning to her daughter. But Khadi's head remained in a forward-facing position. She did not smile.

"But, as you know –" here he glanced at Khadi – "your father can be most persuasive." His hands strayed again to the pile of files marked "Urgent". So much work to do, so many interruptions...

"Dr. Charbel," Khadi said, rising. "I must apologize for my father, and this situation. Last night he invited my mother and me to come and see the work of the Centre and of course we were happy to do so. But now, with this sudden meeting with the

Minister, you are being inconvenienced. So we'll be on our way, if you would be so kind as to call us a taxi…"

Hassim recognized the father in Khadi's voice and in the set of her shoulders, as when he was sending a message to anyone he felt was trifling with him. The morning was a shambles; now was the time for damage limitation.

"I won't hear of it, Mademoiselle."

Khadi continued to stand, stony-faced, in an attitude of imminent departure.

Taking his hands off the desk, Hassim straightened up and noted that Saliou's pain-in-the-ass daughter was the same height as him. "It is no trouble at all. If you will give me a moment, I'll see that my secretary rearranges my schedule for the next hour." When Hassim returned to his office and led them out, he was struck by the uncanny similarity of the two women's eyes. And yet so different: the mother's so warm, the daughter's so wary…

"And, Mademoiselle, there is no question of inconvenience. It is always an honour to be of service to your father." Khadi's antennae went up and she gave both his expression and his tone a thorough going-over. But she found not the slightest trace of irony, and in the split second that her puzzlement was visible, she was aware – and annoyed – that Hassim had seen it.

The next forty-five minutes were spent going through the Dakar Municipal Hospital, where Saliou was chief of staff. With Hassim adopting a detached, fact-filled monotone and the two women asking perfunctory questions, they started with the National Centre for Health Education. "The Centre", as everyone called it, boasted a spanking new waiting room, two gleaming examination rooms and an office with visibly prominent computers. Posters showed images of different kinds of insects, water gushing from a standpipe, a pregnant woman being weighed, another woman nursing her baby. One, grim with skull and crossbones, had the legend, "AIDS is a killer. Don't be a statistic".

"What kind of message is that?" asked Khadi, stopping in front of the poster. When Hassim didn't answer, she continued, "I mean, it just teaches people to be afraid of something without telling them how they can avoid it."

Hassim tried not to glance down at his watch but where he'd

succeeded with the errant finger, he failed with his eyes. Khadi did not miss this sign.

"Where does it tell them about condoms? Where does it tell men to be sexually responsible? Where does it tell women to refuse sex with a man without a condom?"

Why did this woman want to tangle with him so much? He was relieved, though, that she had removed the burden of politeness from him. "Unlike in America, here we cannot take everything and write it on the wall. Cultural constraints exist and must be respected." Hassim and Khadi had drawn close, almost head to head, their words moving through the air with the quiet hiss of threshing blades. "This is a Muslim country."

"And for all that decorum, you allow thousands of your countrymen to die?"

"We have the lowest death rate from AIDS in all of sub-Saharan Africa, less than one percent – which, by the way, is lower than the death rate among African-Americans." What right had this Black-American-princess to pass judgement on things she knew nothing about? She might have been born in Dakar, but it was better to deal with whites than people like her! At least you knew where you stood! Still, out of respect for Saliou, he kept himself in check.

"And, for the record, our main problem is not AIDS. The killer is poverty, pure and simple. Malaria, cholera, tuberculosis, unsupervised childbirth and yes, HIV – they're like thieves at the gate. It's poverty that lets them in." Hassim had not finished. "But these are not glamorous diseases and are of no interest to your American pharmaceutical companies."

Khadi's mouth opened and closed in infuriated silence. "I'm sick of being called American. My father…" She looked angrily at her mother who was looking on in amazement. "He lets everyone go on calling me *l'Americaine*. I'm sick of it! I'm British, Dr. Charbel! I just choose to live in America. And, by the way, it's not all bad!" By the time she reached the end of this speech, and turned away from them, it seemed she believed it less even than her listeners. Magdalene stepped forward and took Khadi's arm.

"Come. The doctor wants to show us the rest of the hospital."

"Of course." Khadi turned, patted Magdalene's hand, looked

straight at Hassim and said in a voice that shook a little, "Sorry. I've lost a few friends to HIV so it's a very sore point with me. I apologize for my little... outburst."

"Shall we continue?" Hassim felt no pleasure over his victory in this skirmish. He would do his duty and then get back to work.

Leaving the poster room, the computer and examination rooms and several other less pristine rooms, which Hassim assured them were also part of the Centre, they moved into the main body of the hospital where the tour took place in virtual silence. Hassim was conscious, though, of the effect this Third World facility was having on them, especially the lost child, as Ndeye called her. The hospital was in two sections: the parts funded by overseas aid, like the Centre and the two newly equipped rooms for Critical Care; and the rest of the hospital with its peeling paint, mats on the floor for relatives and air of struggle. But this is not a bad place, he reminded himself. It's not too overcrowded, it's relatively clean, the majority of patients leave, if not cured, better than when they come in.

But Hassim had seen the gleaming steel and glass palaces in America and remembered the intoxicating power of being in a place where science at its most advanced was placed in the service of human health. He had met surgeons who manipulated cutting-edge machinery designed by award-winning physicists and engineers; had consulted with biochemical researchers whose work had given rise to drugs that could halt the progress of cancer or schizophrenia; had attended conferences on the spectacular regenerative potential of the humble stem cell. It was heady stuff and there'd been a time when he leapt at any opportunity to cross the ocean and keep abreast of new developments. Then, he'd woken up and remembered where he was, his reality. That's when he stopped going and made way for others, often those more interested in personal advancement than science... But he didn't regret it. Hassim made his way through the hospital, *his* hospital. He passed the lines of the coughing, the sprained and the feverish as they waited to be seen; he asked a tired nurse to work another shift, gave words of encouragement to a diabetic amputee and adjusted the saline drip of a child with a bloated belly. As he did this, it was as though part of him had forgotten the two women that his boss, his brother-in-law, his friend, had deposited with him. He was in his world and he moved within it like a bird through the blue sky.

But he also refused to look at the faces of the two women. He wanted no part of their angst.

"Well, that's it," he said, steering them back towards his office, lightness restored to his voice. Before he sat down, he switched on the overhead fan, leaned around the door and called, "Mademoiselle Coly, would you bring us two bottles of *limonade*?"

He sat down behind his desk and once more there was silence, and he cursed whatever ancestral gene had deprived him of the capacity for small talk.

"Hassim. That's all right, isn't it? Dr. Charbel sounds so formal." After the rigours of the tour, Magdalene had come alive. She was doing several things at once, as was her wont, fishing around in her bag, wiping her nose with a tissue, slipping her shoes off. But most of all, leaning towards Hassim and fixing him with her eyes.

"Hassim. How do you manage? I mean, this place hasn't really changed since I lived here twenty odd years ago. And it was bad then. OK, there've been a few improvements. Big ones. The critical care rooms. The CAT scan. The Centre itself. All pretty impressive. But what about the rest? Still the same old rusty beds. And not enough of them. Not nearly enough! If the hospital were double in size, it might just be big enough. And really, Hassim, there are parts of the building that are crumbling!" She paused for breath. "And then there's the personnel. Not enough of them. Not enough of anything..."

Khadi wondered about trying to divert this torrent of words, but knew it was useless to intervene.

"I heard the nurses complaining about running out of something – I couldn't catch what... The queues at the pharmacy... It hasn't changed!" She turned to Khadi. "I'm sure that's why your father didn't want to show me around. He knew I wouldn't be able to keep my mouth shut."

"Madame..."

"No, please. Call me Magdalene. Or Madeleine, like everyone else here does."

"Magdalene. I can see that you talk directly about an issue – don't go tiptoeing around it. Seems to be a family trait..."

"Shit-talk. That's what we call it back home. And no, I'm not into that."

"Neither am I." Hassim put his elbows on the desk and then rested his chin on his clasped hands. He felt relaxed as he took on Magdalene's questions, big, yes but not destructive like the daughter's. "The answer is both simple and complex. Just like the country. Yes, in twenty years, we should have been able to provide better care for our citizens with the resources that we have. Yes, there has been mismanagement at all levels. Yes, there has been too much self-interest. Yes, it is our fault."

"You'll never get anywhere in politics, Hassim. Too honest. I would love to hear some of our leaders talk like that! Caribbean, African, whatever…"

Hassim continued. "And yes, the cards are stacked against developing countries like ours. Yes, the aid we receive has strings attached. And yes, the big power-brokers, like the United States…" he threw a look at Khadi, "they don't want to see us self-sufficient. But yes, it is our fault." He stopped, made a temple of his hands, touched his forehead with his fingertips and then concluded, "Though there are large areas over which we have no control. My concern is to improve the things we can. And there are many. For example, take the Centre itself. It's all about education…"

Apart from the whirring of the fan and the sound of Hassim's voice, the room was quiet. Magdalene, open and attentive, leaned forward, occasionally making little approving clicks at the back of her throat. Khadi looked on as Hassim was transformed from ticked-off subaltern and perfunctory tour-guide to this engaged patriot, speaking of how to make his country better.

There was a knock at the door.

"Doctor Hathim?"

"Come in!"

In came Mademoiselle Coly, with a tray bearing two bottles of Fanta and two glasses. She was a haughty young beauty, in the latest fashion, balancing on stiletto heels and tinkling with silver bangles. Conversation stopped and eyes converged on the scarlet-tipped, jewelled hands that placed the modest refreshment before them, as though making an offering at an altar. When she leaned over to place the tray on the side table, a dark curtain of

"Darling" braids swung forward, causing a brief halt to operations while she tucked the hair behind her ear. Next came the pouring out, a task performed with elaborate care. Every now and then her fawnlike eyes darted in the direction of Hassim but the effort to maintain the chimera of confident glamour was so great that she had no time to make eye contact with Magdalene or Khadi, whose appearance would normally have been the object of meticulous appraisal. Hassim squirmed in his seat. During the pouring of the second bottle, Mademoiselle Coly couldn't resist studying Khadi's Fifth Avenue shoes, perfectly positioned so that she could see without appearing to stare. She only just prevented the fizzy orange overflow that her audience was anticipating. When the second bottle had been poured, Mademoiselle Coly gave a decorous tug on her short skirt and faced Hassim.

"Will you be needing anything elth?"

"No. Thank you."

Mademoiselle Coly swept arrogant eyes across the two women, flashed a smile at Hassim and swung out the door.

"Wow!" Magdalene couldn't help herself. "What's that girl doing here? Did you see those legs? And those cheekbones? She should be on the cover of *Vogue*!" Magdalene was all fired up, laughter bubbling beneath each word. "She's got exactly the right combination of vulnerability and… and pouting insolence…"

"Mum, please! You're talking about Dr. Charbel's secretary!"

"Actually, my real secretary is on maternity leave." Hassim said. "They sent Mademoiselle Coly from the Secretarial School last week." He sighed but couldn't repress a smile. "I've been trying to teach her filing. Pouring Fanta, she seems to have mastered."

"That's for sure. She must have read in a magazine: how to break up a meeting and get noticed by serving *limonade*. And what a man-eater! No matter about the lithp! So, *mon ther* Hathim, you'd better be careful. She may well have you in her thights!"

Hassim looked open-mouthed from Magdalene to Khadi, who was shaking her head. How could these women be so familiar with him?

"But, Madame…"

"Magdalene."

"Magdalene. You can't be serious! Mademoiselle Coly is just

a child. While I, as you can see," he pointed to a few straggling grey hairs in his moustache and the small goatee covering his chin. "I will soon join the ranks of the elders." Suddenly expansive, he gave Magdalene a rare smile. Then, without knowing why, he added, "There's a Lebanese proverb that says, 'Let boys and girls play together. Let men and women be together'." For the briefest moment, his eyes sought out Khadi's, but she was looking down at her hands, lying still in her lap. Hassim looked at Magdalene and sighed. "The truth is that there are a lot of young women in this city who are obsessed with their appearance. My new secretary is by no means the worst."

"I can feel a story here." Magdalene hunted around in her bag and took out a neat little video camera. "Do you mind awfully?"

"Surely you can't want to film me!" Hassim looked discomfited. "I don't want you to damage your camera. But, if you like, I could take you back to talk to some of the nurses or the field workers at the Centre…"

"No, not you, silly. Your secretary! I think there's a story there. I think she'll talk to me. In fact, I'm sure she will. Mademoiselle Coly and her girlfriends. And what they think about life! I love it!" Magdalene was halfway out the door when she stopped.

"Hassim. I respect everything you're doing here. But I'm on holiday and can't take on the woes of the world. I really can't. But this! Let's see. Today's Wednesday and we're leaving for the Petite Côte on Friday. That gives me a couple of days to do a few interviews… Just as a start, of course… I can finish when we get back. A short feature on African city girls!" She pointed towards the outer office. "It's too delicious!" And in a whirl of greying locks and Indian scarves, Magdalene made her exit.

A moment later, she was poking her head around the door. "You will come with us to the Petite Côte this weekend, won't you, Hassim?" Then she was gone.

Khadi spoke first.

"First my father dumps us on you like orphans on a doorstep. Then I abuse you, and now my mother runs off to tell your teenage secretary she's going to be in the movies! Not forgetting to completely reorganize your weekend. You must think we're hard work…"

71

"You are. But a different kind of work. A change… People are always telling me I'm too serious." Hassim took a step away from Khadi. "Do you think it has occurred to your mother that they might think about nothing, these city girls? Nothing at all."

"No. That won't have crossed her mind." Khadi gave him a complicit smile. Hassim dropped his eyes and started examining his shoes: plain, brown and planted on the cold, hard surface of the office floor.

The white running shoes shone like dim lamps by the side of the bed when, at 4:45 precisely, the alarm clock went off. A few minutes after pulling back the mosquito net, Hassim was dressed, had laced up his shoes and was outside on the verandah stretching the long muscles of his back, his hamstrings and his arms. This was the time of day he loved, with its cool black air and silence. Turning to the east, he gave thanks for another morning.

He set off slowly past the row of small houses in the quiet lane. His shoes looked to him to have an eerie paleness and made, he was sure, a tremendous crunching din as they threw up dust along the sand and gravel road. As he jogged along, he continued his loosening-up exercises, tilting his head from one side to the other, clasping his hands behind his back and pulling them up, lifting his knees high in the air like the dressage of a thorough-bred. For anyone in the habit of watching him, there was nothing that signalled this morning's warm-up was in any way different, but for Hassim, as he left the lane and entered a larger but equally silent street, nothing was quite the same.

He concentrated harder than usual, making his body work as he had trained it to over many years. With each step and each new breath, he felt the numbness of sleep ebb away, and sensed the slow awakening of his muscles and sinews as the warm tide flowed through them. He felt his body respond with gratitude for being put first, before all other things. When he saw the traffic lights ahead, signalling the end of the first stage of his run – crossing the sweeping coastal road, *La Corniche* – he hoped he would soon reach a place in his mind where he would neither have to focus nor concentrate, where the act of running would free him to simply move through space and time. But it was not to be. Just as he approached the crossing, the lights turned red and despite the early hour, a couple of cars went by, and he had to run on the spot. He realised that today would not bring him one of those peaks when he felt as though he were floating beyond the turmoil of earth. Whatever other benefits might accrue, he would not be able to banish thought and feeling from his mind and heart.

He had taken up running when he was an adolescent, living in the rambling household of his uncle, old Malik Diop, Ndeye's father and brother of his own mother, Anna, who had died when he was eleven. His mother's death had left a hole that nothing could ever fill, and a troubling unease about his father, the mysterious Monsieur Charbel, his mother's missing Lebanese husband, about whom he knew so little, about whom no-one ever spoke, except to say how much Hassim resembled him. As he entered puberty in that compound, peopled with tall, handsome, black-skinned Diops, he had felt different. He was shorter than the others, skinny rather than lean, with characteristics that he no longer liked, although as a child he had been made much of because of these very things: his complexion the colour of a perfectly roasted peanut, his hair at the midpoint between a kink and a curl and his nose directly from the Levant. He despaired when he looked at himself in the mirror. He knew that although he was bright in school that never won anyone friends. So, on the suggestion of his uncle, he decided to try to develop his body so that he might do some wrestling, a sport loved by all. During his middle teens, he exercised and lifted weights and, although he didn't do much wrestling, he started to feel better about himself. And then, when he was in *terminale*, feeling crushed under the pressure to do well in the *bac*, he accepted a friend's invitation to go running one morning. That was it. Monday, Wednesday, Friday; week in, week out; year in, year out. Wherever he was, whatever was happening in his life, the thrice-weekly run was immutable.

And here it was, Thursday, and he was running.

The light changed and he crossed the road and was soon on the running track which bordered the road for several miles. Again, he brought his will to bear on the workings of his body, knowing that he was beginning a vital stage in his run. Now, on this long ribbon of pale paving, with the city on one side and the sea on the other, his body would have to find its rhythm, a place of balance where the strength built up over time would declare itself to the morning breeze and give his limbs the power to traverse the miles ahead. As his shoes struck the track with perfect regularity, he turned his attention to his breath, encouraging it to merge with his legs, as in a dance. Yes, the rhythm started to come; his body started to flow. This was the beginning of the feeling he craved, the reason behind the stern ministrations he made his body endure. Checking that there was no-one else on the track, he closed his eyes for a few seconds, his spirit open to the cleansing air, not seeing what was around him, yet aware of what he was passing: on the left, the outbuildings of the University; on the right, first the sands and then the breaking waves of the Atlantic. The sound of the water made him open his eyes and look to the right. A beam from the nearby lighthouse swept over the black ocean, cutting a moving white path right across it and Hassim thought of the woman, as he had seen her the other night at their first meeting, with her white clothes in the darkness, with the light spilling from her eyes, from her smile, the same smile she'd given him yesterday, in his office during those few minutes when they'd been alone. A groan escaped his lips.

He looked to the left and was glad to see the Medical School, dark but recognizable, coming into view. He had been happy there, finally feeling the acceptance that had seemed out of reach in the years following his mother's death. There were students from all over the country and all over the region and his sense of being different was offset by the more compelling imperatives of being young and radical. The all-night talk sessions, the campus *manifestations*, the reading of seminal texts – these had made him feel part of something solid, beyond the accident of birth, that rooted him to the community of his country in a way that the warm embrace of Malik Diop's household had failed to do.

Then there was the study of medicine itself. From those earliest times, Hassim brought to it a passion that was beyond the ordinary. Instead of going out to clubs or fêtes, he had preferred to pore over the thick textbooks on human anatomy, on the body's frame of hard but living bone, its rivers, its flesh, its networks and cortices, its entrails and its heart. Even now, almost twenty years since he'd been wide-eyed novitiate, he never ceased to marvel at the beauty of the body's separate parts and their ability to work as one. Way back then, as he'd struggled late into the night to prepare for the next day's classes, he knew, without articulating it, that the body was the model for the community. That men and women should be able to bring together their individual gifts to make something greater, something beneficial to all of them. Even in the greenness of his youth, he had known that his political consciousness and his life as a doctor were two shoots from the same stalk. Having made this discovery so early in life, there had not been time for much else. Certainly not emotional attachments. A sharp wounding love when he was studying in France, the kind of love that he swore he would never subject himself to again. A long engagement years ago that led to nothing. A few short, sad encounters since then. More recently, nothing at all.

He continued with these thoughts, though resentful that they were crowding in on what should be the purely physical act of running. Even so, without apparent effort, his stride and his breath, married now, pushed him down the running track, still a vague glimmer in the dark, still empty, still silent apart from his footfall and the murmur of the sea. As he ran along, he knew he was passing the *Institut Fondamentale de l'Afrique Noire* and the statue of Cheikh Anta Diop after whom the University was named, and felt a rush of pleasure. It happened every time. Yes, Cheikh Anta and those visionaries who had set up the Institute had wanted to show Africa to itself, to teach Africa to itself. They were heroes who had touched the lives of many. That's what he wanted for himself. No heroics. No glory, but to be the best he could be, to be of service to those who needed it most. But he felt that people suspected him, thought that he was pathologically serious (read boring) or it was all an act, hiding some ulterior motive... The lost child thought that...

The light was changing. A shroud of deep grey coloured the air, making the buildings that had loomed impressively in the dark look dismal. He was leaving the University behind and with the bend of the coast, he saw a residential district emerge from the gloom. His legs stretching into an easy lope, he observed that the houses still looked asleep with no sign of stirring, though he knew that in the bowels of each house a woman would already be up and working. She might be resenting the snores of the rest of the family; she might be enjoying the solitude. More likely, she would simply be doing what she had been brought up to do. There was a heroism in that which had nothing to do with fancy degrees and political cant... Hassim's face darkened into a scowl. The lost child! He gave his head a violent shake and an arc of sweat flew from his scalp and his brow. He summoned his will once more.

He was reaching the midpoint where the district of Claudel gave way to the fish market and the abattoir. He had always given a metaphorical importance to this part of the run, which he called the Golden Triangle – the glory and the horror of the city. First there was this affluent neighbourhood, the place where Saliou had his Clinique Aurore, a private maternity clinic – the one source of friction between the two friends. Though it had none of the elegance of Fann or Pointe E, it was the place for an acquisitive bourgeoisie on the move. Whenever he ran past the comfortable, shuttered villas, he thought of what lay behind them – the huddled, rat-infested, garbage-strewn, music-filled lanes of the Medina, where many of the country's greatest talents, its most notorious swindlers, and the majority of his patients came from.

Then the fish market. Although the track did not pass the market, in his mind's eye he could see the part of the beach given over to it. The sun would be rising soon, so some of the pirogues would already be confronting the waves and others getting ready to go. Fishermen would be spreading out nets to be mended. Market women would already be negotiating for the pick of catches not yet made. He always regretted that the track ended before reaching the market. It was one of his favourite places, reminding him of his happy early life on the Petite Côte when his mother would take him down to the shore to select the freshest fish.

Finally, there was the abattoir, the point where the track ended, where he had to turn to get back to his place of departure. It was set back from the road but its blazing lights could clearly be seen. As always, the abattoir could not be shaken off with a mere change of direction. When he'd been a medical inspector some time ago, he'd had to make occasional visits there. Whenever that happened, he had not been able to eat meat for a week. He was used to the sight of blood and living flesh. It was the images of slaughter that haunted him – the beasts struggling and suffering, their piercing screams rising and falling into final choking gasps, the steaming intestines, the pools of blood, the ranks of hanging meat. And the impassive, spattered faces of the executioners.

Thoughts of the Golden Triangle jostled in his mind on his journey home, always turning on where he fitted into this equation and how he could best be an agent for change. When his legs began to send out signals of fatigue, he refused to acknowledge them and forced them to maintain their pace. He wanted to keep his head full – of questions of work and duty and country. He did not want empty spaces vulnerable to intrusions from frivolous distractions. This was what this run was for. To ground him in his own reality, one which, at the age of forty, he should know, to remind him who he was and why he had been put on the earth.

He continued to push hard. The University was on his right but this time when he passed it he felt none of the usual warm pride. He dared not look at the water on his left. It had a bright silver hue and seemed to be in a state of quiet anticipation. But he did not want to look at it and be reminded of the white road on the black water. The thoughts he wished to have were starting to loosen and collapse. With every step, they waned. He ran on, at war with his body and his mind. He could see the end of the track up ahead. Several hundred meters from the crossing and the traffic lights, he made the sudden decision to come off the track and end the miles of running with a sprint across the sand. He would test his body to its limit.

The moment his foot landed on the sand, he could feel its cloying grasp. He battled on, though this shifting element robbed him of his strength. But the enemy was not just at his feet. At his back, he felt the rays of the rising sun, moving across the face of the water. He felt the dawn as a great burden as she moved across the water towards him. Not heeding the pain he was inflicting on himself, not heeding the red light as he dashed between the cars, not heeding the greetings of people passing by, Hassim raced on, away from the light on the water that was reaching out to claim him. He ran like a fury until he reached the verandah of his house, still quiet, still lonely. He held on to the railing as his chest heaved and his heart pounded and his sweat poured down. For many minutes, he stayed this way, unable to think, unable to breathe. At last, he sat down on the step, wiped his moustache and mouth with the back of his hand and put his head in his hands. Then, he lifted his head, made a temple with his fingertips, touched his forehead with them and breathed a single word.

Khadi.

6

KHADI: BEYOND THE CITY

"Hassim?" She sounded genuinely surprised. "What would make Ndeye think that there is some problem between him and me?"

"Well first because he didn't come up for the weekend..."

"From what I hear, Hassim never comes to these things. In New York, people would say he's a person who needs his space. But here, he's antisocial. All because he has something better to do than... Anyway... as I said, none of this has anything to do with me."

This came out more robustly than Khadi had intended and, stealing a sideways glance, she saw that Saliou was processing the sharpness of her tone, all the while giving blasts on the car horn to a group of cows strolling across the highway. Contradiction upon contradiction, thought Khadi. Untethered cattle wandered alongside this magnificent highway while goats lived fat and happy off the arid, dead-looking scrub that the highway cut through. Another was sitting next to her father. Here he was, only inches away, frowning because she'd said something he didn't like. As though he had the right. No. Don't go down that path.

"No, Father, there's absolutely no problem between him and me. It was kind of him to show us around the other day and if he didn't come up to the Petite Côte, you can be sure it wasn't because of me. Besides, didn't he invite me and Mum to go upcountry with him on Wednesday? And didn't we say yes? Hmmm?" Saliou visibly relaxed on hearing the conciliatory note in her voice.

"Yes, you will enjoy that. There's nothing like going into the heart of the country to see how we really live. And Hassim... well, he lives for his job."

Khadi shrugged her shoulders.

Saliou glanced into the mirror at the sleeping forms of his three young sons collapsed in an untidy heap on the back seat.

"They put up a good fight but in the end…"

"…*même les guerriers les plus forts sont vaincus,*" Khadi said, catching her father's eye in the mirror. "You used to say that to me when you carried me up to bed. You thought I was already asleep. And I was, almost. But I always remember hearing the bit about the warriors being vanquished."

"What else do you remember?"

"I remember being sad that sleep had defeated me yet again." They both smiled and looked away. "But it made me happy that I was among the strongest warriors…"

"You still are."

Saliou grasped the wheel a trifle more securely and honked at the animals again.

The car sped towards the city and the setting sun. The road, almost insolently modern, traversed an ancient landscape. A broad flat plain whose vegetation had struggled for survival for millennia. Stark, stunted bushes, flat-topped, like tables. Sometimes they clustered, at a respectful distance, around a monumental baobab, grey, leafless, tormented, but still the dwelling place of the spirits. On the left stretched a continent of unimaginable proportions. Somewhere to the right lay the sea.

"You are far from New York." Saliou said after a long silence.

"And London. And Mum's St. Lucia. And every other place I know." Khadi fidgeted in the tight space in which she was sequestered with her father, who was now inviting her to speak about her life. She did not want to make comparisons between the societies that had formed her or justifications for the choices she'd made; she did not want to do that with anyone – let alone this person, who, as she was growing up without him, had taken on almost mythic qualities… No, he would not make her talk against her will. She would steer the conversation in another direction.

"It's a good thing the whole country doesn't look like this," she said, waving her hand at the passing vista. "Just like it's a good thing that… that… It's a good thing that you told me what to expect before we went to see Yaye Coumba. I would have been so lost without it. Even with it, I was pretty lost."

"You did fine. What a character, eh! No-one's quite sure how old she is, but she's well over a hundred. She can still make me tremble. Still sharp…"

"That's putting it mildly." Khadi pulled a shawl around her shoulders. The air conditioning made the car cold.

"Even Ndeye doesn't quite know how to act with Yaye. No, you did very well."

Khadi nodded. Why doesn't he say it, that there is only one person who knows what to do in the presence of an icon, and how to give it humanity. Only one. And they are all trying to keep her from me… She looked outside. There seemed to be a thin bright cloud hovering over the land, held in place by the rays of a retreating sun. Probably dust.

So much dust everywhere, especially at the Petite Côte. Very picturesque, yes, with its fishing boats and fishing nets and fishing people. And, very much home to Ndeye and Saliou. And Hassim? But so taxing. So much visiting to do; so many greetings; so many smiles; so many meals; so many gifts; so much walking around the villages meandering up the coast. And so much dust, despite the nearby ocean.

The old woman's house, at the very edge of the last village, had been the final stop of the weekend. When Saliou, Ndeye, Maimouna, Magdalene and Khadi had set off along the beach to see Yaye Coumba, Khadi already felt exhausted. Her arms hurt from carrying the presents she'd been given: all those brilliant bundles of cloth, woven baskets and silver jewellery. Her mouth and ears were weary from labouring to understand and speak the alien tongue which flowed around her like a river in flood. Her cheek muscles were quivering with the effort of all that enforced smiling. She knew this part of her trip was meant to be where she would feel the embrace of the authentic African world, far from the taint of the city, of the influence of the *toubab,* and all his deforming values. Her brain told her this but her body and her spirit had had quite enough of this return to the source. She did not want to have to squat over one more latrine. All she'd wanted was to make the quickest possible getaway back to the contaminated city, in her father's cool, comfortable car.

They'd found Yaye Coumba sitting under a shady tree, with a

gourd in her lap. Someone had just finished sweeping and a pall of dust hung in the late afternoon air. As soon as they'd entered the yard, the rumble of the surf became louder. It was the strangest thing. From a distance, the old woman, wearing cloth of brown and black, had looked like part of the tree, a buttress root, perhaps. As the group approached, however, the fragility of her body became more and more apparent. By the time they'd reached where she could see them, two things were clear. Yaye's physical self had only a tenuous hold on life, but the initial impression of power had been no illusion.

Yaye had surveyed them all from behind the milky film covering her eyes. Saliou had stepped forward.

"Yaye, it is…"

"The third grandson of my youngest sister, Aicha. Come, Saliou. I am old but I am not without my sight or my wits. You have learning. Can you not see this?" As she grasped his two extended hands, she trained her cloudy eyes on the three hesitant women and the child behind him.

"Who are these? Your wives?" The voice was firm with a hint of irony in it.

While the women dithered, Maimouna broke free from her mother's grip, bobbed respectfully before her aged ancestor before sinking to the ground and snuggling up against the folds of Yaye Coumba's dress. The old woman looked down at the child and placed her withered hand on Maimouna's head, where it stayed for the entire visit. During the next thirty minutes, Ndeye had stammered, Magdalene had mumbled, Khadi had whispered – while Saliou had behaved like a cossetted schoolboy, his grey hairs momentarily forgotten. Even at her great age, Yaye Coumba's penchant for handsome men remained intact. Only Maimouna seemed beyond the old woman's power to transform and intimidate. She'd sat at Yaye's feet – still, watchful and when, from time to time, she felt the craggy fingers stray across her cheek, smiling. When it was time to go and all the extravagant wishes for health and prosperity had been exchanged, only the embrace of Maimouna had brought a light to the dim eyes.

"Father…" Khadi looked out of the car window again. It would soon be dark. They had not yet reached the sprawling conurbation which eventually turned into the capital. Despite the fading light, she could still see unmoving forms lying at the side of the road – more of the carcasses she had been seeing all along the highway – cattle, goats and cars, all looking like deflated balloons. Then there were stretches of land where lakes of broken glass and garbage glittered like a distorting mirror. Occasionally, something blue lifted itself from the surface of the mirror and hovered in the air. One of the millions of plastic bags in their steadfast march across the countryside, cast away with indifference and left to scar the land for the next thousand years. This place is too much for me, she thought. It overwhelms me. I can't take the heat... the filth... She glanced at Saliou again. He seemed perfectly at ease. Khadi thought she even saw a small, satisfied smile playing about his lips. No. This has to stop. My soul is working overtime, trying to manage this, and there he sits, without a care in the world.

"Father. What have I done to Ndeye? Why doesn't she want Maimouna to spend time with me any more?"

"What?" Saliou's head made a sharp turn in her direction.

"Maimouna. Ndeye seems to want to keep her away from me."

"But Maimouna was with us at Yaye's house!"

"But that was different. Yaye Coumba asked for her to be brought. No! What I mean is that, given the opportunity, Ndeye will make sure Maimouna and I aren't in the same place. It's as clear as day."

Saliou did not answer. He put on his indicator, pressed his foot on the accelerator and overtook two cars, a ramshackle minibus and a truck lumbering along under a load of cement. By the time the manoeuvre was complete, he was ready to speak.

"Has there been some falling out between you and my wife?" His voice was soft but Khadi heard in it something just short of aggression.

"Not at all. Ndeye has been very kind to me." As she said the word "Ndeye", she heard it with her father's ears, heard the discourtesy of calling his wife by her first name when she should have been calling her Tanti. So many concessions had been made for her already, but Khadi was not ready to go into reverse.

"No, from the first day, I couldn't have asked for a warmer welcome from Ndeye." The words made a hollow clang as they fell from her mouth. "No," she repeated, "she was nice to me from the moment I set foot in the house. But something's happened. I don't know what. And it's to do with Maimouna." Khadi felt a constriction in her chest. She had to get to the end of this. Because she needed to make the case for Maimouna and because, for the first time, she saw her father wrong-footed. Something in that pleased her.

"I don't understand, Khadi. As you know, my work keeps me away from home a lot of the time. But, as far as I'm aware, Ndeye has been her usual self, looking after the household, making sure that everyone is happy." It was Khadi's turn to be stung. In her father's seemingly innocent words, she heard a husband's oblique declaration of love for his wife, his new wife, obliterating Magdalene, and her, his first child.

"Father, when I first arrived among all the people who came to... greet me..." (*who came at me*, she almost said) "the one person I felt an immediate connection with..." – Khadi could hear her voice faltering but she pressed on – "was Maimouna. The sister I always wanted but never had. Until now."

When she had begun to say this, Khadi had wanted to stir things up a bit, had wanted to wipe the smug look off Saliou's face, the look that said, "Yes, I'm righting all the wrongs of the past in this trip", but now she felt that she was the one who might be the loser here. She was in deep water, but she had to go on.

"The first few days, things were fine. Maimouna was my shadow. She was happy, I was happy. I felt that whatever else happened, this trip was worth it, to have found such a sister. Then Ndeye started making sure that Maimouna was kept busy, that wherever I was, she was not. Always the excuse that she didn't want her making a nuisance of herself. When Ndeye knew very well that nothing would make either of us happier than to spend the day together! You must have noticed it this weekend. Whichever car I was in, Maimouna was not. Whichever house I was in, Maimouna was not. Always! It's not fair! I want to be a sister to Maimouna and I'm not being allowed!"

Her father was thunderstruck. Where was the daughter with the impeccable manners? Who was this peevish stranger? There was such a childlike urgency in her words that Saliou pulled the car over onto the verge and switched off the motor. They sat in silence.

"I'm sorry you're so unhappy here." He paused, measuring each word. "We've all tried to make you feel at home, to feel part of things. The last thing anyone wants is for you to feel in some way deprived of what we have to offer here... Of course, it's not much and it's not what you're used to and I, more than anyone, should have been more... aware of that." Khadi's bottom lip quivered and she looked down at her hands. When Saliou spoke again, his tone was grave. "No one has been deliberately keeping Maimouna away from you. Of that I am sure. Ndeye has not lived abroad and knows family life only as we live it here. She may have thought that Maimouna's affection for you was becoming a burden. Or she may not have wanted Maimouna to be treated differently from the boys – who are, after all, your brothers too..."

"But Maimouna *is* different!" Khadi cried. "Everyone knows that! But maybe you don't realize how brilliant she is."

There was a glint in Saliou's eyes, which did not tally with the careful, even tone of his words. "Yes, we all know that she is... unusually intelligent. Perhaps gifted in ways that we're not aware of yet."

"Do you know how well she reads? Have you seen how well she draws?"

"I'm always bringing books home for her!" said Saliou.

"*Les Contes de la Fontaine!* Do you think they will stretch her?"

Saliou's brow darkened but he said nothing.

"Do you know that since I arrived she's started speaking some English with me? Good English. In less than a week! Have you had her tested? Her IQ has to be..."

"Khadiatou, *arrête!*"

Khadi stopped mid-sentence.

"You have known Maimouna for, what, a week? We have known her since before birth. We have seen how quickly she absorbs everything. We have seen how closely she observes. We were there when she read the newspaper for the first time. She was not yet four years old. We do not need your intelligence tests. We already know!"

Saliou waited until his breathing had returned to normal. "She is beyond her years in many things. But, even so, it's our duty to prepare her to live in this world as one among many, without the burden of being too special." As he spoke, Saliou realized that, for the very first time, he was articulating feelings about how to deal with his second daughter. It was the one subject that upon which he and Ndeye did not agree. "Perhaps this has been at the back of her mother's mind in the last few days."

"Father…" Khadi had recovered from the first rebuke she could remember being given by him. The timbre of her voice had softened but her determination to be heard had gone nowhere. "We all want what's best for her. There are schools in the U.S. which specialize in children like Maimouna…"

Saliou laughed. "I don't believe what I'm hearing."

Still, Khadi did not admit defeat. "I could find out…"

Saliou turned and looked Khadi full in the face. She dropped her eyes to where her hands lay, impotent, in her lap.

Sighing, she said, "Well, what about the time that Mum and I are here? You don't want her growing up feeling special, even though she is. Fine. But why can't you let her be special while I'm here? I'll be gone soon enough, in less than ten days. It'll be nothing for you. You have all of this…" Khadi gestured towards the sleeping boys. In her mind's eye, she saw Saliou and Ndeye sitting out in their back yard, talking to friends who had dropped by, their five children and others from the neighbourhood playing, each group seemingly oblivious of the other, discrete, almost unaware and yet the adults providing an arch under which the children could grow. "You have this all the time. But me…" Khadi swallowed hard. She had a sudden bleak vision of herself sitting alone at the table of one of their North London flats, doing her homework and listening out for the sound of her mother's key in the door. "For me, there have been precious few attachments. Mum… One or two others. Give me a chance to get close to Maimouna while I'm here, Papa. Give me a chance."

Saliou took her hand. His anger had evaporated. Why "Papa" all of a sudden, the title she had dropped when she was fourteen, when she'd last been here, in favour of the formality of "Father"? He shook his head, feeling out of his depth. He knew a cry from the heart when he heard one. But how could he comfort her?

"I'll talk to Ndeye and let her know that you are happy for Maimouna – and the boys, for that matter – to be with you whenever you like. That you don't need protecting from them. That you enjoy being with them!" Even as he said the word "them", he knew she was thinking "Just Maimouna." He knew it and it frightened him.

He started the engine and pulled out into the highway. From the corner of his eye, he was relieved to see that Khadi was no longer straining forward in her seat. Again there was silence as they drove through Dakar's outlying districts, the villages and townships that had been consumed by the insatiable city. Although night had fallen, there was plenty to look at out of a car window: street vendors hawking their wares by lamplight, groups of young boys and girls taking their evening promenade and on every sandy space, games of fiercely contested football.

"Precious few…" Khadi kept hearing these words ringing in her ears as the blurred lights and muted clamour of the city passed by. She closed her eyes, hoping that her father would be too preoccupied to notice her fluttering hands and the quickness of her breath. "Precious few…" The words – her own – still floated on the air, still made her feel naked. Her difficulty with relationships and the near flawless camouflage of her emotions – these had been at the heart of her sessions with Naomi Fine. Khadi could almost see the therapist's large glinting glasses, mirrors in which she was meant to consider her own reflection. How she had hated it when some truth had broken through, uninvited, irretrievable! And now, separated from Naomi's patient gaze by time and thousands of miles of ocean, here it was again, a disclosure from some raw source, presented, like a gift, to her father: "There have been precious few attachments in my life…" Her father? It felt as though she had placed something on a Facebook posting for the world to see. *Khadi's dubious relationships: remote father, hovering mother, safe, unappreciated, gay best friend. Lovers, a long list of them. But never love.*

The headlamps of Saliou's car swept along, illuminating cart and animal and human, shedding light equally on skyscraper and shack, leaving no chic villa, no crude hovel unexposed

Meanwhile, in the darkness of the car, Saliou rehearsed what he would say to Ndeye, who had left the Petite Côte a little earlier and would be at home waiting for them. He would have to put all this to her in a way that would not alarm her. It would not be easy. But there was one more thing he had to say to Khadi before they arrived home.

"Khadi," he ventured, "I'm glad you love Maimouna. I hope that some day, you might be able to feel that for all of us." He drew breath. "But don't forget that Maimouna, however special, is just a child. Seven years old. If there is an… emptiness inside, she alone will not fill it. Perhaps…" Saliou's voice became tentative, "you should try to reach out more, you know, for more… adult relationships…" He stopped, defeated.

"Don't worry about me." Khadi's voice was brittle. "I know how to handle adult relationships." No more revelations tonight, she thought. Not happening! Then she remembered Maimouna and her manner softened. "I just want the chance to stop being an only child and to be the kind of *grande soeur* that Maimouna – and the boys, of course – deserve."

For the rest of the drive home there was idle chatter. When they passed through the wrought-iron gates, the driveway and front door were floodlit and beneath this light, a tableau unfolded. Magdalene, at the side of Ndeye's car as it was being unloaded, waved as she saw their car approach. Ndeye, who was at the front door, heard it, turned and smiled. Saliou nodded, opened the back door of his car and started waking the children. Khadi got out and was slowly walking towards her mother when all of a sudden, Maimouna appeared, running in the direction of her brothers. When she saw Khadi, she rushed towards her instead and immediately started telling her of the adventures in her mother's car on their drive home.

As Khadi bent down to Maimouna, Saliou and Ndeye exchanged a look. Magdalene saw it and wondered what it meant.

A few days later, when Khadi opened the door to Hassim, it was clear that she had been waiting for some time. She was in a vivid fuchsia *boubou*, dangling earrings and a splendidly tied head wrap. But her manner had none of the charm that was supposed to accompany such apparel. Her mouth was sullen, her tone gruff.

"It's only me coming," she said, without preamble. "My mother's sick."

Hassim was opening his mouth to respond when a coughing, sneezing commotion broke out behind Khadi. Magdalene stepped forward, clutching fistfuls of tissues with which she dabbed her streaming eyes.

"Allergies," she croaked between sniffs. "The dust never used to affect me this badly. Must be the menopause." For someone in such bad shape, she was curiously upbeat. "You two kids have a good day." And with that, she pulled her dressing gown around her and vanished back into her room.

Hassim started to smile but Khadi stood rooted, blocking the door. "She did it on purpose."

"And how do you suppose she managed that? If she's found a way of generating such spectacular symptoms by a sheer act of will, then she's something of a medical miracle. She must be studied."

Khadi did not budge.

"Well?"

"Well what?"

"Well are you coming or not?" Hassim struggled to sound severe. Despite all his reservations about her, there was something about this woman's company that he found hard to resist. Her absurd childishness always gave him permission to dispense with conventional niceties.

"You don't have to come, you know. It's all the same to me."

"Oh but I do. If I don't, it will mean that I'm afraid to be with you. And I won't give them the satisfaction of thinking that!" There was the fact, too, that since Sunday night, Mai hadn't been under such heavy manners and she felt she had to show Ndeye and her father she appreciated that. Going away with Hassan would prove that she was capable of those "adult relationships" her father had been going on about the other night.

"No! Let's get going," she said in the tone of one taking a foul-tasting medicine. Lifting her chin, she flounced through the doorway in a way that reminded Hassim of his youthful secretary. As ready as he was to needle Khadi, he did not quite have the nerve to draw that comparison aloud.

Once in the vehicle – an s.u.v., a gift from the Canadian government, with the Centre's logo on the side and the back loaded with equipment – Khadi sat with her arms folded and her lips pursed. Hassim put the keys down and waited.

"Doesn't it annoy you, this ham-fisted attempt at matchmaking?"

"Not in the slightest. I think it's rather endearing."

"Which part? The part where other people get the right to interfere in my life? Or the part where they get to tell you that you can't find a woman on your own?"

"Oh, both of those. But…" he said, starting the engine, "what I like most is the part that makes you behave… well, like this." Pulling onto the road, Hassim burst out laughing. Khadi threw up her hands and wondered what kind of madman she had contracted to spend the day with.

Hassim's good humour did not last long as he fought his way through the choking fumes, swirling dust and bedlam of the morning rush-hour: newly polished Mercedes Benzes jostling with horse and carts carrying whip-wielding *borom sarrett*; overloaded *cars rapides* driven by maniac schoolboys, emblazoned with Koranic verses like "Alhumdoulilahi" and posters of Madonna in black leather; vendors walking through the stalled traffic to hawk their wares – plastic potties, face-cloths, pirated CDs, sliced oranges, aluminium pots, bottles of water, fresh-baked bread, brassieres, nappies – everything you might or might not need first thing in the morning on your way to work. Khadi closed her eyes and feigned sleep. In the corner of her mind, she chuckled at the stream of expletives coming from Hassim, delivered *sotto voce*, just in case she was not really asleep. When at last the city was behind them and the invective at an end, she opened her eyes, saw that the traffic-jam scowl was still on his face, and inquired loftily, "Well where are we going and what are we going to do when we get there?"

He was about to respond to the regal air – so irritating! – but thought better of it. It was really too tiring, this seesawing between the good Khadi and her evil twin. It was going to be a long day. Better to take it easy and try not to react to her every word and gesture. So he told her they were stopping at the hospital at Thiès where he would be conducting a workshop for the primary health care workers of the region. That would take a couple of hours. Then they'd be taking a member of this group back to his village so that Hassim could check on a couple of patients there. They'd be delivering medical supplies to both places.

He spoke matter-of-factly but Khadi noticed how the scowl had been supplanted by a calm and focused look. The world of his work was the only place he really wanted to be. Khadi thought about her own work: fevered planning sessions with big-city lawyers in Manhattan; solitary nights surrounded by thick books in her living room; the elation of the corporate kill and the bragging bonhomie among colleagues that followed. Nowhere was the repose she saw in Hassim as he contemplated the morning ahead.

"What?" he asked, noticing her furrowed brow.

"Nothing."

"Right. I hope it isn't going to be too boring for you." But he said it in the way of people who know that "it" is the most fascinating and important thing in the world.

As soon as they entered the hospital, Hassim was too busy to be uncomfortable. At first Khadi thought that the welcome he received was due to his rank, as the boss from the capital. But she soon saw that the esteem came from a long relationship during which the nurses, midwives and health educators had learnt that he could be relied on to fight for them in the corridors of power, just as they fought for the sick, the ignorant and the young in the far-flung and forgotten villages. Although Khadi was at first the object of undisguised curiosity, this soon vanished and Hassim took centre stage. He was well prepared, and though there was plenty of good-natured parry and thrust from his audience, he neither flaunted his dominance nor ceded control. New guidelines for education in birth control and sexually transmitted diseases were thoroughly discussed, rationales given, procedures explained, recommendations invited and noted.

Khadi was impressed. Though it took place in a run-down room in a provincial health facility, it could have been a university seminar of the highest quality. But she did not show what she felt during the workshop or after it when Hassim was surrounded by people handing in their monthly reports, or in the canteen, amidst the laughter and relaxation, or afterwards when supplies were being distributed or later still, when it was time to say goodbye. Once or twice an admiring smile almost surfaced, but was beaten down. During the whole morning in Thiès, she kept to the fringes.

"Khadi Wade, this is Ismaila Diouf. We're going to be taking Ismaila back to Sinade. He's been the nurse there for almost ten years. Knows everything." Hassim was in the middle of reading from the sheaf of reports in his hand. "Mademoiselle Wade is from America…" All of a sudden, he heard what he was saying and, without even looking at her, made the adjustment. "*Pardon.* Mademoiselle Wade was born here but lives abroad. She's the daughter of Dr. Saliou Wade."

"*Enchanté,* mademoiselle." Hassim heard the courtly quality in Ismaila's voice, so different from his own brusque manner. He felt ashamed. For her part, Khadi, too, was all decorum, extending her hand and producing the perfect greeting. Ismaila had not required Khadi's full pedigree to be enchanted. Her beauty and poise were enough. This is what she's used to, Hassim thought. Everything just given to her. Everyone sees what poor Ismaila sees. So few people see her other side. And yet it's that other side – that's where she really lives…

"Let's go," Hassim said, shaking his head as Ismaila rushed to open the door for her.

Sinade was no more than fifty kilometres away, but as soon as they left Thiès, the dusty road became scarred with frequent potholes. Then the sky turned suddenly dark and released a roaring rainstorm. The windshield wipers did little more than increase the sense of alarm rising inside the jeep as solid sheets of rain slapped against the windows. At last, the inevitable happened. In trying to avoid the deep gashes that the water was opening up in the road, one of the back wheels swung out over a ditch, just a little too far. There was a loud noise, they lurched to the side and came to rest at an angle, stuck fast.

Ismaila was the first to jump out while Hassim checked the back to secure the container of medical supplies they were taking to the village. There were costly syringes and bottles that could be broken. There was an insulated pack of live vaccine that had to remain chilled. They could not afford to be marooned there for long. When Hassim found that nothing had been broken, he went out to help Ismaila. The rain was so violent that Khadi could scarcely hear them as they tried to coax the wheel from the ditch. She sat and waited, hearing snatches of their truncated dialogue and their groans as they pushed. Then the noise of the rain became so intense that she couldn't even hear that. She felt alone and unable to stand it any more, she flung open the door and, seconds later, was drenched.

"What are you doing?" she heard Hassim shout. "Get back inside!"

"Surely there's something I can do!"

"Yes. Get back in the damn car. Now!"

"Don't you talk to me like that! Because I'm a woman…"

"Oh, for the love of God…"

"How will you be able to push it out of the ditch with me inside the car? Tell me that! And why can't I help you to push?"

"Mademoiselle, please go back inside. We have almost got it out," Ismaila pleaded. "You will get wet." This almost brought a laugh from Khadi. The wheel was still wedged tight and after only a few moments outside, her clothes were already stuck to her like a second skin. Ismaila's distress did not move her.

"Hassim, I will not go back inside and twiddle my thumbs."

"Just get in the car! I don't give a shit what you do once you're in there."

The heavens continued their assault as Ismaila gave his boss a supplicating look.

"There are three of us. Two will have to push. One will have to drive. Which job do you want?" Despite the rain, Khadi could see the men very clearly. Ismaila had the lean tensile strength of a man whose ancestors had tilled the soil for generations, but it was Hassim who had the muscle – shoulders, arms, legs – all in sharp relief beneath the saturated cloth.

"I'll drive."

"Fine." Hassim turned and said a few rapid words to Ismaila. Turning back to Khadi, he said, "We're going to have to rock it and get it out on three wheels. When I give the signal…"

"What signal?"

"I'll bang on the back… When you hear the signal, drive

forward." He handed her the keys and was about to return to Ismaila. Instead he opened the car door and found her behind the wheel, staring down.

"It's a stick shift."

Hassim's eyes widened. "And?"

"And... And... I don't know how to drive a manual..."

"Because, of course, in New York City, Madame is accustomed to..."

"This isn't the time to be scoring points! We've got to get out of here!"

"Well I certainly do. Before you drive me out of my friggin mind." He paused. "Well?"

"I'm a fast learner."

"You better be. Move over!" There was a sloshing sound as sodden garments moved across the front seat. "The gears are in the shape of an H: First, straight ahead; Second, straight back; Third, ahead halfway, to the right then forward again; Fourth, straight back. Neutral, in the middle of the H. Reverse – go as though you mean to go into Third but instead of going forward, continue going as far to the right as you can. Each time you change gear, you have to press down the clutch. The other pedal you know. Even automatics have an accelerator. When you want the car to go forward, take your foot off the clutch, then give it some gas. Got it? Now you try."

Khadi gripped the gear stick, breathed in, pressed on the clutch and slid the stick into gear – First, Second, Third, Fourth, Neutral and Reverse.

Hassim got out of the car. "When you hear the signal, put it into First and accelerate. Not too fast, not too slow. Just enough to get us out." And then he was gone, leaving Khadi to contemplate the letter H.

She did not have much time for reflection. The car was rocking. The gentle rolling back and forth gathered strength and became a more resolute pitching from left to right. She could feel beads of sweat forming on her brow. Then it came, the knock on the back of the car. Press clutch down, push stick forward, let clutch up, press gas down. A terrible shudder transformed the jeep into an animal struggling to get up, as if with a broken back

94

leg, smoke and mud spewing from the back. Khadi heard another knock and wondered what this signal could mean, but her foot was glued to the accelerator as all memory of the configuration of the letter H fled from her mind. Then, as if by magic, came one final heroic push at the back which coincided with Khadi's belated success in engaging first gear. The jeep leapt out of the ditch and flew forward, lurching in and out of muddy potholes in its path. It went into a skid, sending up a fine crescent of spray before finally coming to a halt.

When Hassim and Ismaila reached the jeep and peered inside, Khadi was slumped over the wheel. Then she looked up with a radiant smile and said, "I got it into neutral. You're right, Hassim, it really is an H!"

Thirty minutes later, vaccine still viable, hypodermics and vials all intact, occupants somewhat the worse for wear, the jeep entered the village. It had not rained in Sinade so the villagers were astonished to see their beloved nurse virtually unrecognizable under a layer of drying mud, as was the man accompanying him. The woman was equally dishevelled, her *boubou* drooping and spattered, her face streaked and her head tie listing dangerously to one side. But the villagers were generous people, grateful for the supplies and – once they knew who he was – for Hassim's presence among them. They confined their expressions of glee out of earshot of the trio, and offered practical help. Hassim was shepherded to Ismaila's lodgings and within a short while, both emerged, clean and in fresh clothes. Khadi's rescue took a little longer. Water had to be heated for her to bathe with; her *boubou* washed and put in the sun to dry; clothes had to be found... It all took time and when she finally came out into the sunshine, Ismaila and Hassim were hard at work in the clinic.

For once, she didn't insist on appearing busy. She sat in the shade of the overhanging thatch and watched the life of the village as it passed. She felt as though the rain, the fear and the excitement of the recent hours had cleansed her in an unexpected way. There'd been her bath: standing at the back of the house on smooth pebbles in a small enclosure surrounded by palm fronds, dipping from a bucket of warm water with aromatic leaves floating on top, scrubbing away the mud and anxiety with a cake of green Marseilles soap and a bunch of tied grasses. Then there were the clothes: a wrap made of simple woven indigo cloth, worn under a long loose tunic of patterned cotton. On her feet, a pair of plastic sandals, her own shoes being sodden. No earrings: she had lost one in all the confusion. Nothing on her head. Just the short tight coils of her hair. And, beneath the wrap and the tunic, nothing either, western under-garments being rare in these parts. In this peaceful, newborn state, she sat and waited for Hassim.

It was late afternoon when he came for her. For a moment he stared.

"You look different."

I feel different, she wanted to say but said instead, "When are we going back?"

"As soon as we've eaten. Come. It's ready."

They were the guests of the *chef du village*, with Ismaila basking in reflected glory. In addition to the two hypertension cases, he had shown Hassim scores of other people who had simply turned up when the word got out that he had come with a doctor. The visit had been useful and the people showed their gratitude by sharing a delicious *yassa,* making gifts of the borrowed clothes, boiling eggs for their journey and producing a basket of sweet miniature mangoes. When they left, Ismaila's eyes were not the only ones full of tears.

The return was uneventful. Hassim and Khadi didn't talk very much and when they did, conversation flowed, then stopped, then flowed again. He talked about feeling alone in old Malik Diop's house, but how he'd found work that he could do and how it had made all the difference. She talked about growing up feeling alone in London, but how she had found consolation, not in her work – that was just a job she happened to be good at – but in these newly-discovered siblings, especially her sister, Maimouna. It seemed much easier to speak to each other in the dark with the engine murmuring beneath their voices. But when they passed the place where the jeep had fallen into the ditch, all each could see was the other under the rain – Hassim with his strength rippling beneath that second skin and Khadi in a deep pink garment, silken with rain as it clung to her.

"Do you mind if we stop off at the office? I have to pick up some papers for tomorrow."

"OK. It's still early."

Their footsteps echoed as they walked through the silent corridors of the hospital. It was dark and, outside his door, Hassim fumbled with the keys. Inside, he switched on the light. The unforgiving glare of the fluorescent tube made them both wince. He set about looking for his papers. She sat down and fingered the clothes she was wearing. She wondered what Mademoiselle Coly would think if she saw her now.

"Here they are." He stood with the papers in his hands but made no move to go. Distracted, he put the papers down on the edge of the desk. "Khadi?"

She did not look up. She did not reply.

He came around to the front of the desk, to within inches of her. A sharp panic seized her. She looked down at her clasped hands and made a sound, somewhere between a laugh and a cough.

"Khadi? What's wrong?" His voice was tender. "Why won't you look at me?"

Her eyes darted about the room, looking for the way out, taking in the unadorned walls, the concrete floor, the tidy desk with one pile of papers precariously perched on the edge, the harsh light overhead, the slightly peeling door. I need to be out of here. I need to be out of here. Now!

Sensing her anxiety, he pulled back and started to walk around the office, talking, as though to himself.

"It's been so long since I... I promised myself that never again would I... And I knew it! From that first day." He made a temple of his fingers and tapped his forehead, not looking at her.

"I've tried not to feel this," he said, at last. He crossed the floor, crouched down before her and took one of her hands in his. "But I do feel it. I do." He bent over and kissed her slender fingers.

She thought of all the lovers she'd had, none of whom she had respected, whom she'd allowed to touch her body, but never her spirit. Now here was someone whose life was lived with honour, someone who was a stranger to shallowness, who would take no shit from her, and yet whose heart was moved by her. Someone who would drown her.

She stared at the plastic sandals and held her breath. He took both her hands and began to rise to his feet, coaxing her from her chair until they stood face to face. Still she would not look at him. In her ears there roared the sound of rushing water. She tried to plant the peasant sandals into the concrete floor, to summon resistance to this flood which would surely engulf her. She shut her eyes and fought to repel his touch on her wrists, his fingers light yet probing, as though taking a pulse. It was the gentleness that broke her. Her eyes flew open and collided with his, liquid and black. At the edge of those pools, she lost her balance and the drowning began.

The current was pulling her down, always down into ever deeper water. Her head, only just above the surface, she waged a desperate struggle. But her mind had become empty, would say nothing to her body, alive with the promise of imminent pleasure. She gasped for air but found her mouth stopped by his lips as the current drew them down. She was conscious of a dim line of light above, something beyond the dark swirling waters into which they were tumbling, something that might save her. Her hand reached up for it but only encountered his hair. She lingered a while, straying through the rugged fleece, forgetting... She remembered the light again but only her arms, in their upward yearning towards the light, obeyed the quiet warnings of her mind. But they too were thwarted as the loose patterned tunic was pulled along their length, over her head and then down it floated, like a luminous serpent, snaking its way down to the deep. Other garments followed, settling softly on the ocean floor. He murmured something and the sound was sweet, as sweet as his skin was salt. She knew all was lost as she felt the indigo cloth fall from her waist and make of the floor a rippling sea bed of the deepest blue.

They became one body, a lithe sea creature coiling and twisting, curling and heaving, like a wave on the water. As they rode down to the deep of the ocean, her mind was in hiding, her spirit rejoicing, enfolding her lover. They flowed down together, in rhythm like a dolphin, like dancing, her hands skimming over him, his arms like a cradle, their voices like music, their eyes seeing nothing because of the blindness, the blindness of sweat and the blindness of weeping. But still they strove onward as the weight of the ocean pressed down hard upon them. In the dark of surrender they were one.

Then she looked up and saw the light shining. His moaning dismayed her; he was heavy. She lashed out her arm as his weight pressed on her and it hit the desk leg, knocking off the papers, which scattered like foam on the water. "This is no day for drowning!" her mind repeated, and all she could see was the light on the ceiling, the glaring, hard light Hassan had switched on when they'd entered.

The waters receded.

The spell was broken.

They dressed quickly and in silence. Khadi helped Hassim to pick up the papers from the floor and put them back into the files. Hassim was flustered and unsure. Where was Khadi? The fragrance of her gift to him... the beauty of her song... Could they have vanished from the earth so swiftly? When he could take it no more, he said, "I thought... I hoped... that this was something good..."

Khadi had her back to him, retying the knot of her wrap. She could not let him see her frantic attempts to retrieve the scattered fragments of herself. She could not let him see her mouth's quiver, the tremor of her hands. She drew back from the brink. When she turned to face him, she seemed in charge of herself, pleasant, but detached.

"Why, Hassim! I'm surprised at you, being a doctor and all. This was a question of two bodies needing release. Nothing more. Eh? No need to look so glum. Because it was nice, very nice. And I know you're not going to read anything more into it than that!" This she delivered with a smile.

Hassim looked as though he had turned into stone. Khadi walked to the jeep with an easy step and even seemed to be humming during the short drive to Saliou's house. When they arrived, she wished him good night and watched as he sped off into the darkness. Only then did she start to tremble.

She walked through the house quickly, hoping she wouldn't run into anyone. She was in luck. Everyone was outside in the back yard. When she was a few feet from her bedroom, she heard light footsteps running towards her.

"Khadi! I saw you drive up. I was waiting for you to come home to tell me what you did in Thiès."

The child came skipping towards her, holding her drawing book in her hand.

"I'll tell you tomorrow."

Maimouna stopped in front of Khadi, a puzzled look on her face. "Why are you wearing those clothes?"

"Why? Why? Why can't you see that I'm tired? And, speaking of whys, why won't you leave me alone?"

She slammed the door behind her. Inside she shut her eyes. Weeping and shaking, she slid to the floor, images of two shattered faces burning in her brain.

7

MAGDALENE: DAKAR CITY GIRLS

"Mum…" Khadi said to the top of Magdalene's head. Her grey hair and long scarf were all that could be seen as she crouched to complete a travelling shot, ending with the moist parquet of litter on which they were standing. It was a place of darkness and light. Two markets, conjoined and contrasting. The one running along the length of the street was bright with fresh fruit and sunshine. A right turn down a side alley and there was the other one: labyrinthine, enclosed, dark and yet flooded with the brilliance of silver and gold. Magdalene's quest for the key to the mystery of Dakar city girls had led her to the jewellery market. Adornments for the ear, neck, wrist and finger glittered under glass, guarded by salesmen who carried on subtle negotiations with the women of the city as they calculated how many instalments it would take to purchase which piece in time for which wedding.

"Mum, I think I want to go back now. When you finish here."

"Already?" Magdalene kept her eye on the small video monitor as she rose from a squatting position and let the camera zoom in on a rope of heavy silver, being caressed by a woman who seemed resigned to not being able to buy it.

"Why's that? I thought you said you were going to help me today."

"And I thought you said this was going to be a tiny little film! Now it's starting to feel like a big Hollywood production. Spielberg or something…"

"Hardly," laughed Magdalene, finally turning to look at her daughter. "But, you know, love, you're looking a little off colour. Feeling OK?"

As they stood in the narrow, dark passageway, someone pushed past and Khadi had to press herself against a stall selling traditional incense – *chourail*. As she inhaled, its powerful fragrance made her head swim. She felt as though she were caught in a vice of precious filigree, forced to breathe its sickly sweetness. Magdalene, on the other hand, was perfectly at ease, turning to smile at the people clustering around her camera, ready to chat. But she looked again at Khadi and started to pack up.

"We just have one more stop. Another friend of Mademoiselle Coly who works at the Novotel. Hope she has more to say than the two we saw this morning... Pretty useless. Yep. Both pretty and useless." Her words came out in an unbroken stream as she zipped up the camera case. Turning to her daughter, she stopped and said, "Just one more, sweetheart. It won't take more than..."

"Mum. I'm going home. I really don't feel so good."

The plaintive tone told Magdalene it was pointless to insist that she stay and have lunch as planned. She hailed two taxis, and waved off Khadi who headed back to Saliou's house.

At the gleaming front desk of the Novotel, Magdalene asked for Mademoiselle Ba and sat in a plush chair to wait. A clone of Mademoiselle Coly approached Magdalene with the same metropolitan glamour sitting uneasily on the village beauty.

"I'm sorry, Madame," she said, sitting down breathlessly. "Someone called in sick and my supervisor has just told me I have to fill in." She glanced to her left at an imposing figure in animated conversation with tourists but whose eyes ceased to smile as soon as they lit on one of his underlings.

"So you're not going to be able to take me to any of the places we discussed last night?"

"*Desolée*, Madame." She was already on her feet, pulled in by her supervisor's glare. "But take this name and number," she said, pressing a piece of paper in Magdalene's hand. "She might be able to help."

And she was gone, painting on a smile as she resumed her post.

Magdalene was on the verge of tossing the paper and its childish handwriting away – it probably pointed to another waste of time – but some old reflex learned from the tough years in England prevented her from doing so. Just one more try that might lead somewhere. And after a few minutes on the phone, she felt she had been right not to give up on her afternoon.

Half an hour later, Magdalene was being shown to her seat in a hotel restaurant by Mademoiselle Anne-Marie Secka.

"Will you be having lunch?"

"Yes, I'm starving," Magdalene replied. "Will you join me?"

"No." The young woman's briskness was softened by a smile. "But I'll be free in forty-five minutes. After that, I'll have an hour and a half to take you to see some of the places that you're looking for. So…" Once again, the smile, gap-toothed and nowhere near the perfection of a Mademoiselle Coly or a Mademoiselle Ba but, unlike theirs, genuine. "I'll send someone to take your order."

Comparisons with the elegance of the hotel she'd just left were inevitable. That could be transplanted to Paris or New York – at least the lobby could. (Look a little more closely and the cracks would soon appear.) But, here there was no attempt to mimic the first-world. The décor of the restaurant was simple, but in rich colours, freshened by an abundance of plants and punctuated by the occasional mask or textile. Fans whirred lazily overhead and full-length jalousies were flung open affording a broad view of the hills and the sea. When the steaming plate of chicken in peanut sauce arrived, Magdalene remembered once again that she was in Africa.

That was the odd thing about this trip. For days, she could go about her business, watching Khadi, interacting with Saliou and his family, exclaiming at all the change or lack of it, having fun, being the self that she was in London, in St. Lucia, wherever – when all of a sudden, it would hit her. She was in Africa again, feeling its energy, its power but never once being overwhelmed by it. For this she was glad. And the food was so good… She wished Khadi had come.

When she had taken her last satisfied bite, she laid down her fork and looked outside. *I will lift up mine eyes unto the hills, from whence cometh my help… The* words of the psalmist provided a frame for what she was seeing – the two rounded hills known as Les Mamelles, after which the hotel was named. Beyond the hills, there lay an immense sea that rolled across until it reached a green island with another pair of hills that reminded lost sailors of the safety of their mothers' breasts. Only a week ago she was sitting on her father's land looking at those hills and here she was, looking at them again. Had she followed them here? Or had they followed her?

Magdalene saw from her watch that she still had fifteen minutes to kill before Anne-Marie was ready. She walked out onto the verandah and, enjoying the luxury of a good stretch, sat on a bench in the shade. *Ventre plein, nègre content.* That saying always used to raise a laugh among her friends in England. She never understood why. Here it was normal, to eat your fill and bask in the contentment that followed. Leaning back against the wall, she absorbed the afternoon sun and the cool sea breeze and closed her lids until only an indistinct brightness remained. She remembered having the same feeling as a child, sitting out in the dappled backyard with her sisters after a lunch of roasted breadfruit and fried fish. She had felt just like this – full, warm and happy.

Yes, happy. From the outset, she had never had any real anxiety about her own return, only her daughter's. Now she was here, she was surprised at how easy it had all been. After the first night, with Omar grandstanding and Hodia being Hodia, everything else had just fallen into place. She had thought she would have to be on her p's and q's with Ndeye, not wanting to alienate or alarm her in any way, but nothing of the sort seemed necessary. Ndeye was the perfect wife for Saliou, competent, charming, "modern enough" and in supreme but discreet dominion over all things domestic. And her children – all delightful, although when it came to star power, little Maimouna was the clear winner. And Saliou, himself. A changed man, Magdalene said aloud, and then looked around quickly to see if anyone had heard. But nothing moved except a lean cat, making its stealthy way to the open wooden doors.

Saliou. Magdalene half-closed her eyes again. He was different now. He had finally grown into the dignity that, as a young man, he had tried to force himself into, like an ill-fitting suit. He had earned those grey hairs with every life he saved, every student he taught, every mouth he fed. And he was imperturbable, or seemed so. It had always been his manner, but to people who knew him well, there used to be signs of inner disturbance. How well she remembered those one or two occasions when his soul seemed to be on the point of catching fire. But the explosion never came. He always managed to apply the brakes just in time. But now, all these years later, everything appeared covered in a self-control that went so deep it seemed to be his actual nature.

"Madame?"

It was Anne-Marie Secka.

"Shall we go now? I have already engaged a taxi. This is going to be interesting. I've never been involved in research before." She drew breath only long enough to enable Magdalene to fall in step beside her as they walked towards the entrance of the hotel. "I'm going to take you to see what we call the "three C's" – *couturière*, *coiffeuse* and *chaussures*. They are the three things those of us who want to present ourselves well in Dakar cannot do without. Let us start with my seamstress!"

In the drive back to the city, Magdalene and Anne-Marie chatted like old friends. But beneath the small talk, each was carefully assessing the other. The assistant manager of the small hotel on the outskirts of town was light years away from the other young women Magdalene had met in the past few days. At first glance, the blunt cast of her face and figure would be called plain in a country noted for the willowy lines and aquiline features of its citizens. One of her legs was much thinner than the other and twisted outwards ever so slightly. But she carried herself with confidence and in her hands all the demands of fashion, so slavishly followed by others, were tempered to meet her own unique requirements.

Anne-Marie Secka had ideas and these she expressed in ways that were often formal, sometimes cryptic, but evidence of a sharp mind was always reflected in the arresting alertness of her face.

"How much do you think that the average working city girl spends on clothes?"

"Oh, at least a third," Anne-Marie said without hesitation.

"That's an awful lot. Why so much?"

"Because... because..." For the first time she seemed to be groping for the right answer. "It's not the clothes themselves. It's what they can do for us. We always need to present ourselves well. So that we can be noticed."

"Noticed for what? By whom?"

She looked at Magdalene with unblinking eyes. "By the pow-

105

erful. The rich. By people who can help us to get where we want to go."

Magdalene did not smile. "These 'people' sound like men to me. Are you sure they will help you to get where you want to go? Or is it you who will help them to get what they want?"

"Madame, I see that you get right to the heart of things. We are alike." She looked out of the window at the curved white line of surf that hugged the coast road. "Unfortunately, there are many young girls who come here from their villages looking for a man to save them. And, yes, once in a while, you will hear about some girl who has been set up in a nice apartment with a maid to cook and clean for her. While the rest of us live in conditions which are... could be better." They shared a quick glance at this understatement. "And sometimes there's someone who becomes the third or fourth wife of a minister. But then some of us know better. We are looking for a job with possibilities. We are always looking for the next opportunity."

"How many of your friends are like that, Anne-Marie? Like you?"

She said nothing for several long moments. At last she said, "Look! We're here!"

Magdalene followed Anne-Marie into the seamstress's workshop, dark, despite the mounds of brilliant fabric and buzzing with sewing machines. They ran into a secretary friend of Anne-Marie's and all work stopped when she modelled a striking outfit.

"Isn't she beautiful?" Anne-Marie's normally firm voice was hushed with admiration.

When the fashion plate left, Magdalene had a polite but halfhearted conversation with the *patronne* of the shop and took some perfunctory footage of this lowly source of Dakar high fashion. It was the same at the hairdresser's and at the market stalls selling stiletto heels with pointed toes. But none of it was of interest any longer to Magdalene. Her curiosity had been piqued by Ann-Marie – so strong, yet full of contradictions. She wanted to hear more of her story.

"Why don't we stop for a coffee?" Magdalene asked when the swift tour was over and they found themselves in front of a café on the Avenue William Ponty.

Anne-Marie looked hesitant as she glanced at the striped awning and the round tables on the pavement.

"I... I don't drink coffee..." Idly watching the life of the avenue pass by fell outside what she had agreed to do this afternoon.

"Well, a soft drink then... And what about one of those patisseries? Don't they look delectable?" Magdalene lingered over the last word, her tongue almost tasting the sweet crumbly morsels. As she saw Anne-Marie's resistance weaken, Magdalene began to feel she would tell her something.

"No more than fifteen minutes, Madame. I need to be back at the office to sort out a few..."

When they sat down, Anne-Marie was ill at ease, tapping her French shoes on the pavement and pulling the hem of her skirt down to conceal the wasted leg. But eventually she relaxed and they talked for almost an hour. Although she took care not to give specifics, there emerged a picture of her life, starting with the solid values of her village in the South, the hopes of her school days cut short by lack of money, her decision to head for the capital, the hard slog to get to her present position. There was never a hint of self-pity, simply a commitment to forge ahead with the few assets that had been given to her.

"It sounds like your life is nothing but work," Magdalene said, slowly stirring her coffee.

"Well, what else is there?"

This sounded too much like Khadi.

"What do you mean 'What else'?" she asked, staring at Anne-Marie. "There are friends, family... Marriage. Children. You can have all of these!"

"Madame..." Despite Magdalene's urging, she never called her anything else. "I have friends. A few. And, as for the family, that is... *permanente*. They supported me and I will support them." She pulled back in her chair and looked into the distance. "And as for marriage... I'm not against it. But if it doesn't happen, I will survive. What matters to me is that I find some work to do that will make me feel..." She raised her hand, flexing her fingers as though they were holding an invisible ball. "...that I have done something with my life."

"But I don't understand you girls! When I was your age, all I

107

wanted was to be in love. To be married and happy." Magdalene found herself getting quite exasperated. "Okay! I found out later on that it was not what I thought it would be. And then I found out how important worthwhile work can be. But never..." Magdalene leaned close and looked into dark eyes which, for a brief moment, had become the almond-shaped amber eyes of her daughter. "Never did I regret looking for, seeking out that feeling. That big experience."

Seeing for an instant the image of Khadi waiting for Hassim in her bright pink gown, Magdalene said, "It is a terrible thing to see love coming and slam the door in his face."

Vendors shouted, exhaust-pipes misfired, political discussions raged, cell phones rang, beggars declaimed, marabouts intoned. But between Magdalene and Anne-Marie, there was silence.

"It is time to go, Madame," Anne-Marie said at last. Magdalene roused herself, paid the bill and flagged down a cab.

Within sight of Anne-Marie's hotel and the sloping hills behind it, Magdalene said, "Did you know that we have hills called Les Mamelles on the island where I was born? They look just like those. Right by the sea."

"Really?"

"I vaguely remember some story about why they called these hills that name. Do you know it?"

Anne-Marie shrugged but in the end added, "Everybody knows it. Since we were that high." She gestured with her hand. "Just a tale. What our grandmothers told us..."

"Well?"

"Madame?"

"Well, will you tell me?"

When Anne-Marie said nothing, Magdalene took the initiative. *"Il était une fois..."*

With a grudging gap-toothed smile, Anne-Marie began. "Once upon a time, there was a young girl called Khari." Magdalene looked up. "She was good and kind. She knew how to cook and wash and clean and tend to the crops and the animals. But..."

"There's always a but..." broke in Magdalene.

"But there was a problem." Anne-Marie paused. "Not only was Khari ugly but had been born with a hideous humpback."

Magdalene made a snorting sound while, with an unconscious hand, Anne-Marie pulled at the hem of her skirt.

"All of her life Khari had to live with this affliction and all of her life, the people of the village mocked her for it. No matter how clean her yard was, no matter how tasty her meals, no matter how unending her generosity, the result was still the same – the same taunts, the same snide remarks, the same cruelty. 'It looks like you have a baby tied to your back!' they used to shout. 'Show us the baby!'"

Anne-Marie Secka was at one with her tale, no longer aware of Magdalene sitting absorbed at her side.

"One day she could take it no longer. Nobody noticed when she gave away her goat and her chickens, when she ploughed over that patch of earth that had borne so many good things to eat, when she swept her yard and fixed the latch on her hut and went walking towards the cliff.

"She was not afraid as she looked at the ocean swirling around far below. She looked forward to being embraced by the kind mother she had never had. Looking far out to where the sea met the sky and throwing off the cloth that covered her, she leapt out into space."

Anne-Marie stopped.

"But the sea goddess was not feeling charitable that day. She did not feel like welcoming any new intruder into her domain. So as Khari fell, the goddess caused a wind to blow which flipped the girl over so that when she landed, she landed on her back. Seeing the girl there, naked and exposed, the goddess relented and covered her with the tide. But because of her deformity, her breasts remained above the waters."

She stopped again, waiting for her breathing to return to normal.

"And those breasts became the hills that we call Les Mamelles."

Magdalene could only shake her head, wipe her eyes and murmur, "Oh, Africa!"

Just as the car was drawing to a halt, Anne-Marie said in her professional voice, "I hope I have been of service to you, Madame. As for me, it has been most rewarding spending the afternoon with a maker of films, something I have never done before." She relaxed into a more natural tone and added, "I enjoyed talking to you very much. It is not every day... And you even got me to tell that story... I usually don't talk about such things. And, anyway, in this world, nobody wants to hear the story of an ugly girl." She ended in a whisper.

Magdalene took the young woman's hands in hers and held them fast. "You have many gifts, Anne-Marie. Never forget that." Without a word, Anne-Marie got out and walked away, her head high, her unequal legs taking her where she wanted to go.

On her way back to Saliou's house, Magdalene decided she would scrap the project of the Dakar city girls. She was ashamed that she had thought she could do a "tiny little film" on them. Anne-Marie Secka had shown her the dream and the nightmare of these "baubles" that decorated the streets of the capital. Time did not permit her to do them justice. So she would leave the whole thing alone.

But she was haunted by the story of Khari and Les Mamelles. Ugliness creating beauty... The random cruelty of life... The great, unpredictable mother of the sea... And then, as usual, her thoughts swung back to Khadi.

THE GREAT WAVE

8.

KHADI: SLIPPING INTO DARKNESS

To avoid being a witness to the risks the driver was taking as he tore through the lunchtime traffic, Khadi put her sunglasses on *and* closed her eyes. The dark soothed her and she was able to let go of the choking feeling she'd had in the jewellery market. She was glad to be away from Magdalene and at the same time sorry. For the past few days, ever since the debacle with Hassim and then with Maimouna, Khadi had been staying close to her, needing the security that she could provide. Even so, she had told her mother nothing about either incident.

Her mother was a mystery – always busy, seemingly relaxed and happy. For the life of her, Khadi couldn't understand why. How could she come to the home of her former husband and his new wife and their children, and behave as if everything was just fine? It didn't seem like an act. Her mother had many gifts but acting was not one of them. That was her own forte. As she got out of the taxi and walked towards her father's door, she wondered whether there'd be a day when she did not feel alone.

The house was unusually quiet, only the slightest murmur coming from the yard. Khadi went towards the sound and found one of the *bonnes* playing with little Lamine. Maimouna was tracing an intricate design in the sand with a pointed stick.

"Where is everyone?" asked Khadi.

"*Dem-na.*"

"Gone? Where is Madame Ndeye?"

"*Dem-na.*"

"And Monsieur?"

"*Dem-na.*"

Fatou's grunted monosyllabic responses – were they obsequious or arrogant? But Khadi had no time to bother with all that.

Her attention was on Maimouna who had dropped her stick and seemed about to creep off into a corner. She'd had the same mournful expression ever since the night Khadi had snapped at her. God! It was unbearable to see her this way. Wallowing in self-pity would have to wait. She would have to make reparation for at least one of that night's disasters.

"Mai," Khadi said softly. "Do you have anything special to do today?"

Maimouna shook her head without looking up.

"Would you like to go into town with me?" Maimouna picked up the stick again but didn't answer. "We could get some ice cream. And... and maybe go to the beach." The little braided head started to rise and the stick once more fell to the ground. "We could go to... to Gorée. We could get the ferry and go across to Gorée!"

"Oh yes, Khadi! Yes!" And the jumping began – into Khadi's arms, out again, around the yard, her toddling brother in pursuit.

While Maimouna was dressing, Khadi wrote a note to her father and Ndeye, saying that as she'd found Maimouna at home with nothing to do, she'd decided to take her to Gorée for the afternoon. They would be back in time for dinner. She would try to call them sometime during the afternoon.

Before she left, she handed the note to the taciturn maid and asked her to make sure she gave it to Madame the moment she returned. With a feeling of excitement, she ran to the gate, flagged down a taxi and hurried back towards the house. Waiting at the doorway was Maimouna, resplendent in a dress Magdalene had given her. It was white with small red flowers scattered over it; red clasps pulled her plaits into fierce bunches at the sides of her head. She was not shy about her elegance but spun round and round with her arms flung wide.

Khadi hugged her and laughed, then said, "What's this?" She took a book from the child's hand and saw that it was an atlas. This had been another of Magdalene's presents for the children.

"You don't want me to bring it?" Maimouna seemed worried.

"Of course you can bring it. But why an atlas?"

The child relaxed. "Because when we went to Gorée the last time... it was a long time ago, when I was young..."

"When you were young..." Khadi fought back a smile.

"Yes. Six."

"Go on."

"Well when Papa took us to Gorée last time, there were so many people on the ferry from other countries. And they were all talking different languages. And I couldn't understand what they were saying. And even when Papa told me they were from France or some other place, I couldn't really understand," Maimouna said in a breathless rush.

"But why the atlas?" Khadi insisted.

"Because..." Maimouna's voice was patient. "Because now it won't just be words I don't understand and people I don't know. With the atlas, when you tell me where they're from, I can look at the map and see the country and see where it's near. What part of the world it's in. And I can hear them talking, and even though I can't understand the words, I'll know that is the language of their country." She paused. "It will be something that I can start to know." She paused again. "Because when I see and hear, in the end, I can understand. I can know."

"OK. OK. We'll take the atlas." Khadi said, wondering about the vistas inside that small head. "But let's hurry now. The taxi's waiting. We don't want to miss the 12:30 ferry." They bundled into the car and were off.

Despite the season, the sky was blue, without a single rain cloud. They reached the *embarcadère* five minutes or so before departure time and found the waiting room full. There was an festive atmosphere as the throng pressed towards the door opening onto the dock. There were French, Italians, Germans, British, Americans, West Indians, Guineans, Malians. Senegalese. The Western tourists carried a multiplicity of photographic equipment and sunscreen; the Africans carried food, babies and merchandise to sell. Khadi's eye lit upon a quotation – framed in a place of honour – by the poet president, Leopold Sedar Senghor, about the *signares de Gorée,* those fabled mulatto beauties for whom the island was also known. As for Maimouna, by the time the *Coumba Castel* had pulled into dock and the scramble for seats had begun, she could barely contain herself.

They went onto the top deck where they soaked up the sun, the salt air, the sight of container ships unloading and the prospect of the open sea as they left the harbour. Khadi watched as Maimouna wrestled with her atlas, whose pages wanted to dance in the breeze. But she was determined and, holding it down with one elbow and forearm, leaving the other hand free, she could concentrate on listening. There was a middle-aged couple speaking French behind them, so she quickly found the France page. She didn't quite lean back to put her ear closer to their conversation, but she might as well have done so intent was she on placing them in a context she could understand. All she wanted was the mention of a place. She was soon rewarded. She looked up at Khadi.

"Yes. Bordeaux. They said Bordeaux."

"It's a big city," whispered Khadi. "It should be on the map."

Maimouna's finger went racing across the page until at last it came to rest. There it was, Bordeaux, a dot on the western edge of France. She traced a line down but the map ended and she could go no further. Khadi saw her disappointment, turned to a world map and showed her where France and Bordeaux were in relation to Senegal.

"Where's Gorée?" the child wanted to know.

"It's too small to be on the world map." Khadi explained.

And so it continued all the way to Gorée. From the many tongues, Khadi picked out Italian, English, and a kind of French with a Caribbean music to it. For her part, Maimouna identified Ouolof – that was so easy as to be ridiculous – and Serrer, the language of her relatives in the Petite Côte. This led Maimouna into tracing family journeyings on the map.

"Papa started right here, went up there to France to study and then came back here again. Maman has always been here. Tanti Madeleine was born way down there in the Caribbean and went up to England. One day she went to France and met Papa. And you, Khadi, you were born right here, just like me but you went up to England when you were a little girl. Then you crossed over and now you're in…"

"New York. Right there."

"It doesn't look that far," said Maimouna with a little sigh, her finger still firmly on the spot.

"Mai," Khadi began slowly. "How would you like to come and stay with me in New York?"

"Me? In *Amérique*?"

"Yes, you."

"I… I…" Although her words faltered, the child's eyes shone with a steady light. It's now or never, Khadi thought.

"You could go to school there. Live with me and go to school. They have some wonderful schools over there. Tell me, Mai, does your teacher ever tell you to stop asking so many questions? Do you always find your work easy? Do you always get everything right?"

"Not always!" Maimouna cried, unsure about this line of questioning. "But mostly." She hung her head, mortified.

"Well, the kind of school I'm talking about is for children just like you! Full of questions! Full of energy! Heads always buzzing with things!"

Realising that she was not being criticized, Maimouna looked up smiling and relieved.

"Yes, there *are* other children like you. And these schools give them lots to do. You can read any book you like. Do as much drawing as you like. Painting too! Do science. Learn how things work. How they grow. Play an instrument – violin, piano, anything…"

"It sounds… wonderful!" And the child's face became so transparent that Khadi thought she could almost see her mind trying to "hold" this new treasure. Then a cloud passed over it.

"But Papa, he has to work. He won't be able to come."

"Well, no. In fact, it would just be you and me." Khadi felt the ground slipping. "But you'd come home for your holidays."

"Maman wouldn't be there? Or Amadou? Or Malik? Or Omar? Or Lamine? Or Fatou? Or Auntie Story? Or Tonton Hassim? Or…"

"No," Khadi answered, beginning to realise that the scenario she was presenting was beyond the child's imagination.

"Nobody?"

"Well no. Just you, me and ten million other New Yorkers."

Maimouna's eyes drew away from her sister's, out towards the water. "We're here!" she exclaimed.

Khadi looked up and saw that, like the conversation, the crossing was at an end. The island of Gorée was upon them, floating like a dark gold slipper on the sea.

It seemed to have caught everyone by surprise and talk was suspended as the ferry moved along the coast. Only a few miles in any direction, the island could be caught in a single snapshot. And it was, time and time again, as conversation was replaced by the whirr of cameras clicking and panning.

"Tanti Madeleine should be here," Maimouna said.

Khadi could only nod.

As the ferry made its approach, the island seemed to glide by, caught in its own dream, haunted by its legion phantoms, ensnaring all those who would look on its brooding fortress, its lissome palms, its houses washed in yellow and red ochre, its placid beach. The captain positioned the boat to dock and, as he did, it seemed to be set upon by a flock of large birds, flying towards the boat, dark against the sky, then plunging into the sea only to return to repeat the whole manoeuvre. It was an illusion. The birds were children from the island who delighted in competing with each other in feats of daring – and relieving tourists of coins thrown into the water. They put on a breathtaking show that left everyone on board torn between admiration and alarm.

Khadi held Maimouna back as the crowd surged forward. It gave her time to collect herself. She'd forgotten what it meant to be here. Even if she'd been able to excise the fading memory of coming here as a tiny child with both her parents and the clearer memories of later trips as an adolescent setting herself up in anger against her father, even if she'd been able to delete all this, there was no way to prepare for the island's powerful aura. No, there was never a way to steel oneself against it.

And here she was with Maimouna. She always made Khadi feel more… the only word she could think of was "human"… but at the same time, she felt more vulnerable, with every action, every gesture seeming so much harder than anticipated. Just keeping up with her was exhausting. She was just a child but there was so much hunger in those eyes, so much passion in that mind… And so much love in that heart. Its purity made Khadi despair of the murkiness of her own.

There was no gangplank but deckhands helped passengers as they stepped across the gap between the dock and the gently rocking boat. Wanting an escape from her thoughts, Khadi observed how similar the male travellers looked, no matter where they were from: jeans, T-shirts, caps. The difference was in the women, between the dressed and the undressed, between the revealed and the hidden. The Western women with their naked arms and backs, their bare legs, their cropped windblown hair were all about confident exposure, as opposed to *les Africaines* with their boubous sweeping from shoulder to ankle, their heads tied or elaborately coiffed, sometimes with a shawl draped around the neck. There was a difference too in the way they moved. The Western women were brisk and birdlike, their sexual challenge edgy and overt. The movements of the African women seemed languid in garments whose apparent modesty was a veil for whispered seduction. Which kind of woman was she? She remembered the indigo cloth and where it had led her. She was both. She was neither – an enigma even to herself. She was in the right place: Gorée, place of enchantment, place of horror, where survival and annihilation were fused in the very rock.

Khadi took her sister's hand and they got off the ferry.

By the time they'd reached the end of the jetty, they'd agreed a plan for the afternoon. Lunch. In the absence of beach wear, wading in the shallows. A ramble around the island. A visit to the *Maison* in time for the four o'clock ferry. They chose the restaurant closest to the beach. Khadi played with her food while Maimouna polished off a heaped plate of *poulet frites*.

"You eat a lot for such a skinny little thing."

"Maman always says I don't eat enough," Maimouna said between mouthfuls. "She says that a woman has a big job to do so she has to start getting ready from the time she's a little girl. *You have to eat well to be a strong woman.*" She glanced around, just in case her mimicry of her mother had been overheard. Khadi pretended not to have heard and gave her instructions about how far out she could wade.

"I won't go far. I can't swim."

"That's another thing you could learn in America."

But Maimouna was now the one to pretend she had not heard. Instead, she turned on her heel and raced off to where the small waves broke on the sand. Khadi sat in the shade of the awning, finishing her bottle of water. Her thoughts strayed in the direction of Hassim. No! she had to concentrate on a relationship that was possible. But even this was not as straightforward as she'd thought. It was true what Ndeye was always saying: Maimouna was work. No sooner had she come to this conclusion than she saw Maimouna hurrying back with a man and woman in tow. They were the parents of her new playmates, and were now to be Khadi's companions while wading and building sand castles took place.

The couple was from Guadeloupe. It was their first time on the continent and they were earnest in their joy at being back in the arms of the Mother. Khadi had met many such born-again Africans in America. Inwardly she sighed as, for the next hour, they plied her with details of their search for roots, starting from the Babylon of their homeland, the travails of negotiating the French education system, the challenges of studying African culture and integrating it into their lives, ending in the victory of setting foot on African soil. And then, of course, the heartbreak of Gorée island. They had just reached that part of the narrative when the mother started waving to her two children to come back. Their ferry was arriving. They trooped back, grubby but smiling. As the family prepared to take its leave, the father declared, "It has been the high point of my life to bring my children here to Gorée. For us to see where we started. To see what was done to us." There was a pregnant pause with the mother nodding significantly.

The boy, bigger and older than Maimouna, turned to her and asked, "Didn't you say you were from here?"

"Yes."

"Well then your forefathers sold mine into slavery."

Maimouna's mouth fell open. She looked at her sister in appeal. Khadi wanted to wring the boy's neck but before she could, his mother took him by the shoulder. "Shaka! Really! What a thing to say! Sheba! Come along! We've got to go!" Gathering up their belongings, they made a hasty retreat to the jetty, leaving Khadi to face Maimouna's questioning eyes. She held her for a while and gently asked, "When you were here the last time, did you go to the *Maison*?"

"No. Papa went with Amadou and some grownups. I stayed on the beach with Maman and the others."

"Do you know what the *Maison des Esclàves* is?"

"Yes." Maimouna frowned with the effort of dredging up a few haphazard facts. "It's a house where slaves lived. Everybody knows about it. People come to see it... Slaves had to work very hard and then..."

"Do you know what a slave is?"

"It's a person who... doesn't have a house of his own. Who... has no money... No, that can't be... I don't know."

"A slave doesn't own anything, Maimouna. Not even himself. Not even his own body. The only thing he owns is his thoughts. And, in the end, he doesn't even own them."

The child could not respond.

"Do you know who these slaves were? The ones who were here?"

Maimouna shook her head.

"They were African people, just like you, like Papa, who were taken from their families and brought here to Gorée."

"But why?"

"Because other people, people from Europe, wanted them to go somewhere else to work for them. The African people didn't want to go but they were made to go."

"But why couldn't they just say they didn't want to go? When I really don't want to do something, I just say so."

"They were forced, Maimouna. With chains and whips and many other terrible things."

"And where were they forced to go?"

"To America. To the Caribbean."

"What! Like where Tanti Madeleine is from? Like where you're from?"

Maimouna seemed to be struggling with a long list of whys. One question was the clear winner.

"Is it true what that boy said? About his ancestors and mine?"

"I'm afraid so, Mai. But it's only part of the story. Listen, we still have over an hour to walk around before the *Maison* opens again. I'll tell you all I know about this place. So you can understand. So you can know."

Khadi took her sister by the hand and began their walk around Gorée. They visited the old church and the Museum of the Sea.

They saw old men sitting in the shade, playing dominoes, oblivious of their presence. Once a small boy, one of the stunt divers from earlier on, approached them and asked for money. They bought beaded necklaces, for themselves and for Ndeye and Magdalene. Despite the locals and visitors moving about, all seemed quiet, enshrouded in a net of dull gold. They climbed the hill overlooking the Atlantic and looked at the monument of a stricken ship broken apart, its two sections floating in different directions, but bound by the sea. All the while Khadi talked and told the child about this place and what had happened here.

Maimouna asked many questions, sometimes the same question in different guises. There were so many things which did not connect with the world she knew: cruelty on this monstrous scale; the notion of "white people" so unlike the jovial strangers she was used to seeing in her city; the idea of being a slave which, she was learning, was so different from being poor. And she'd always thought of "black people" as "Americans", like the ones she saw on TV – the Cosby Show people, Beyonce, Oprah Winfrey and the West Indians who played football for France – rich and famous people, or people like Tanti Madeleine and even Khadi herself with all their cameras and watches and expensive things. How was it that all of these people had had fathers and mothers stolen from Africa and turned into slaves? Was she responsible? It was a bitter blow.

Khadi saw the child's distress and tried her best to diffuse it.

"Maybe we shouldn't go to the *Maison,* Mai. We could go back to the beach. I'd come in the water with you this time." Khadi gave a false, bright smile.

"Oh no. We have to. I need to see."

When the doors of the Slave House opened at three o'clock, Khadi and Maimouna were first inside.

A house on two levels, of unexceptional size, painted the colour of rose petals mixed with blood. In the courtyard, a pair of stone steps curling in, as though in an embrace. At the centre of these encircling arms, a doorway, a light, a glimpse of the sea. Around the periphery of the courtyard, several rooms for the storage of different categories – fit men, childbearing women, pubescent girls (the sailors' choice), children, the sick, the recalcitrant. For the suicidal, there was always a swim in the water beyond the doorway, bristling with dorsal fins. Chains, potent despite their rust. A single twenty-five pound lead ball. Walls slick with the salt of ancient tears. Rough floors of sand and pounded excrement. No windows. No looking back for the human cargo of the ships that could almost be seen bobbing on the ocean. No looking back for the black gold of the Americas. The voice of the tour guide, floating above the thundering silence, laid it on the line, testifying, eulogizing the millions of dead at the bottom of the ocean and the millions who survived with the unhealed wounds of rupture. And always the magnet of the final doorway, inescapable, beckoning towards the light, towards the sea, towards the empty horizon.

Khadi rubbed her eyes when they stepped outside into the street. She didn't want Maimouna to see that she had been crying. The child said nothing as they walked along but held tight to her sister's hand. They returned to the same restaurant. Khadi ordered ice cream but Maimouna barely touched hers. During their short time in the *Maison*, the weather had changed. It was now grey and ugly and the waves breaking on the sand had muscle behind them. When they saw the *Coumba Castel* puffing towards the jetty, they were both grateful that it was time to go.

There was a crowd on the jetty by the time they reached: people just arriving, people wanting to leave.

"What's taking them so long?" Khadi asked after they'd been there more than five minutes.

"They're having trouble getting people off," someone ahead of her said. "Choppy," he added, pointing to the water.

Several more minutes passed before all of the arriving passengers were off and still more went by before Khadi and Maimouna were at a point where they could see what was going on. An angry tide was rolling in, making it impossible for the ferry to make a snug fit alongside the dock – and there was no gangplank. The boat rose and sank, drifted off and came slamming back, making all attempts to get on board hazardous. The leap of faith was no longer a cliché. From time to time, a hardy soul jumped across the gap and made it look easy, but for the most part, passengers had to wait for an opportune moment for wave and boat and dock to align and make the leap possible. The exhortations of the deckhands did not help.

"*Mais, Madame, sautez! Qu'est-ce qu'i ya?*"

"*Ne m'emmerdez pas! Espèce de couillon!*"

And so it went, the shouting, the cursing.

When Khadi and Maimouna were almost at the head of the queue, Maimouna turned to get a last look at Gorée.

"Why didn't they tell me about this before? I just thought this was a place to go for a boat ride, then the beach. My mother and father. Why didn't they tell me?"

"They didn't want to make you upset, like you are now." Khadi was only half concentrating on what she was saying. She was trying to see if there were any pattern in the apparently random widening and narrowing of the gap between the boat and the dock.

"But they should have told me! I should have known!"

"Why? You're seven years old."

"I didn't know and I should have. I should have." Maimouna's voice, high and sorrowful, went keening on the wind. But Khadi wasn't listening. She was preparing for the jump.

"Maimouna, forget about all that." Khadi used her lawyer's voice. "It's too dangerous to try to lift you across. We can't cross together. We have to go one by one, so let go of my hand now. Face the ferry. Look at it carefully. Listen for my voice and when I say 'Go!' jump as far as you can. See that man there? He's going to catch you. You'll be quite safe." She looked into Maimouna's eyes and saw that they were still pierced through with sights of the *Maison*.

"Maimouna!" She gave her a shake. "Pay attention! Listen for 'Go' and jump." The child seemed to hear, squared her shoulders and clenched her fists. Khadi happened to look at Maimouna's feet and saw that her shoe laces had come undone. She knelt down.

"Look at your laces!" she said crossly, handing the child the atlas she'd been carrying around all afternoon. "You were going to jump with your shoes falling off?" She secured the shoes with tight double knots and stood up, never taking her eyes off the treacherous rolling of the boat.

There were people all around, those already on the ferry and those behind them on the dock, but Khadi felt alone with the task of getting the child across to safety. The boat seemed to be edging towards the dock. Yes! It definitely was! In a few seconds, it would be as close as the rubber tyre buffers would allow. She opened her mouth and with the boat reaching a manageable distance from the jetty, shouted, "Go!"

Maimouna sprang from where she was standing, an arrow aimed at the deck of the ferry. What happened next took place in a fragment of a second but for Maimouna, time slowed down. Just after takeoff, she felt her fingers loosen and something fall from her hand into the water. It was the atlas. As she soared through space, the loss of that small weight destabilized her and, with the island scowling at her back, she found herself wavering in the air as the book plummeted into the sea. Then she caught herself and continued her flight across the gulf. But the damage was done. One foot landed flush on the deck but the other one could not find a purchase, slipped and sent her tumbling backwards, her head cracking against the jetty before disappearing beneath the churning water.

Khadi froze. A moment of silence. Then all hell broke loose. *"Xale-bi deffa dano! Xale-bi deffa dano! Woye! Woye!"*

Two deckhands leapt in. They too disappeared. Impossible to see anything except rubber tyres, the looming hull of the boat and an oblong of black water. The captain tried to ease the ferry back on minimum power, to put some distance between the rescue and the boat's propellers. Amid the screams of onlookers, the heads of the deckhands broke the surface, took breath and then went down again. There was the sound of running feet and then the air went dark with the flying bodies of the coin divers of the island, this time only the oldest and strongest of them, plunging into the ocean that they knew so well. The water foamed white as, again and again, their youthful limbs pulled down bubbling columns of air as they searched the deeps. They were not down long. When they surfaced, they had Maimouna with them. They supported her head and neck in a lifeguard's hold and, forming a relay chain, one by one they pulled her through the fretting waves and brought her around the jetty, across the cove and laid her on the sand.

Khadi had galvanized into action. Between catching sight of Maimouna's red and white dress and seeing her stretched out on the sands, she had found an Englishwoman who knew CPR, had commandeered a cell phone, phoned the Municipal Hospital, ordered an ambulance, left a message for Saliou, had spoken to the ferry's captain and organized two groups, one for a makeshift stretcher, one for a makeshift gangplank.

The CPR woman set to work on her straight away, compressing her chest, sucking out water from her mouth, breathing life into it. Sweat broke out on the woman's forehead but she kept working, counting out loud and working. Then, from nowhere, came a ripple along the small body. It ended in a cough of regurgitated sea water and a sharp intake of breath. After that, the thin chest rose and fell rhythmically.

But she did not wake up.

Maimouna was wrapped in a blanket and transported onto the stretcher, across the gangplank, aboard the ferry, across the water and into the ambulance. Sitting next to her as they hurtled through the afternoon traffic, Khadi turned unfocused eyes towards the small back window. It seemed to her that all had gone dark apart from a glimmer of light beyond the curtained square. The wail of the ambulance was remote, and in the darkness as they edged nearer to the hospital, she wondered how she would tell her father that she had killed her sister.

Suddenly the wailing stopped and she knew they had entered the precinct of the hospital. It was only then that Khadi dared to look at Maimouna. There was a small bruise on her head, but otherwise she appeared unmarked. The dress was not torn and seemed newly washed with its drops of scarlet on the clean white ground. The merest breath passed through her lips and on her face there was the impression of a smile.

9

SALIOU: TEARS OF THE WARRIOR

Saliou heard the ambulance approaching. He looked around at the functional exterior of the hospital with its struggling greenery and its steady tide of people. This was his world and, apart from the hands clenched behind his back, his body gave no indication of inner disturbance. From the sound of the siren, he knew that the ambulance was still a few minutes away. There was nothing to be done except wait. As a physician, he would keep his mind open, waiting for the evidence of his eyes before embarking down the path of tests, diagnosis, treatment, prognosis... It was vital that he didn't get ahead of himself, imagining catastrophes based on a sixty-second message left on his cell phone. He would see the patient before jumping to conclusions. As a father, he would lead by example, short-circuiting any hysteria that Ndeye and the others might veer towards. No. He was the head of the family and would conduct himself accordingly.

He lifted his eyes above the hospital gates and the surrounding neighbourhood until they settled on the stretch of sea beyond. He searched for the reef line. There it was, visibly white, its churning waters forming the gateway to the darker colours of deep ocean. Suddenly, nostalgia for his childhood on the Petite Côte pressed heavily on him. He remembered standing at the water's edge with the women and other children as the men pushed their pirogues through the morning tide and headed out, singing. Then, in the evening, oh the joy at their return with nets alive with shimmering fish! Sometimes they did not come back, leaving widows and orphans to mourn on the indifferent sands. But the fishing continued and, accepting both their duty and their destiny, the men went daily to cross the bar and hoped daily to return.

For a moment he felt unmanned by memories of those who

used to brave the wild white horses of the deep. Through the noise of the everyday, above the cry of the siren, he thought he could hear the lamentations of the orphans and the fishermen's songs as the white wall of death rose up before them. It took all his will to hold back the flood of emotion that threatened to swamp him but he remembered the counsel of his elders as they'd prepared him to cross the threshold into adulthood. *Gorgui do dioye*: a man does not cry. With his head bowed, he clamped his hands together and waited until composure returned.

When the ambulance swung into the driveway, Saliou stood ready to accept both his duty and his destiny, to make manifest the instruction that had taken him from child to youth to husband to father. The last stage – that of elder – lay ahead. As the ambulance came to a halt, he vowed he would be worthy.

He gave a scarcely perceptible nod to the support team that had gathered around him: a couple of orderlies, another doctor and a nurse. They leapt into action, throwing open the door, helping the driver to ease Maimouna out onto the gurney, pausing for a split second while Saliou's eyes raked over her, and then whisking her inside. It all happened so rapidly that under different circumstances, he would have been satisfied that the regular training he insisted on was having an effect. There was room only for the clearest thought, the surest action. And yet, as he readied himself, Saliou gave thought to his other daughter, the one whose silhouette emerging from the ambulance had been a blur. He turned back and found her standing on the spot where she'd stumbled out into the sunlight. The ambulance was gone but she remained, marooned on the driveway.

"Khadi." Saliou looked into her dazed face and when he put his arm around her, her weight collapsed against him.

He took her by the shoulders and held her at arm's length.

"Khadi. I must go now. Put some cold water on your face. You're in shock. Ask in the waiting room and they'll tell you where I am. Make sure they know who you are…" He turned and hurried off, feeling the pressure from Khadi's clutching fingers on his hand.

He didn't see her again for more than an hour during which time Ndeye arrived, self-controlled and dry-eyed. She stayed on the periphery while Maimouna was examined and put through a series of tests. Several medical and technical personnel were involved and things unfolded rapidly. But apart from the moment when the CAT scan technician was delayed, all procedures were carried out with promptness and efficiency. Saliou kept his distance, aware that his staff would be doubly anxious about making any mistakes, ensuring that he did not override anyone, allowing them to do the specific jobs they were trained to do – in short, practising what he had spent his working life preaching – that every life is precious; that every patient deserves to be given the best care available; that positive results are brought about by the teamwork of competent professionals. In his mind, though, he had to fight to keep calling the person in the bed "the patient", fearing the zone where she became Maimouna, the only one of his children ever to be critically ill. He also knew that if it had not been his, but the child of a fisherman on the Petite Côte, or some snot-nosed urchin from the Medina, the burial rites would have already begun.

It was hard, but he managed to stay on the sidelines, occasionally saying a few words to Ndeye who sat in silence, watching everything that was going on with dull, lifeless eyes.

There were a few minutes when he and Ndeye were alone in the room with Maimouna. Everything was sparkling and the equipment new; it was one of the two rooms for critical care made possible by a grant from the European Union. The irony did not escape him that this would be the first time it was being used.

Reluctantly, he looked at Ndeye and found her staring up at him. In a flat voice, she asked him when he thought Maimouna would wake up. Can't say for sure, he'd said, but probably not too much longer. Probably just a bad concussion… We'll know more when we get the results of the scan…

"Dr. Wade." The neurologist was at the door, beckoning him outside. Ndeye stood up, daring them to try to keep anything from her.

"It's all right, Charles. Just tell us."

The neurologist cleared his throat and launched into a highly technical discourse, which Ndeye immediately understood was another ruse. But she had been around doctors for a long time –

she'd first met Saliou when she worked at the hospital secretariat and up until her third child, she'd run the accounts section of Saliou's maternity clinic. So she knew enough medical jargon to be on the lookout for the giveaway phrase. She waited, searching through the thick camouflage and then, there they were, in rapid succession – "coma" and "deeply comatose". She sat down with a thud.

The neurologist had the sense to stop. With a stiff bow, he left the room.

Saliou went over to his wife but so palpable was the bright hard shell surrounding her that he was afraid to touch her.

The door opened and Khadi walked in.

"Papa... Ndeye..." Her swollen eyes sought out a response from them, but when there was none, moved on until they came to rest on the still figure in the bed with a partially shaven head, tubes stuck in her arm and her nostrils. She walked up to Maimouna's head, on the opposite side of the bed from the child's parents. As though in a trance, she stared down.

"Papa?"

"We've been able to stabilize her. Her breathing has improved. No fractures. We have to keep monitoring her vital signs though..."

"The head. Tell her about the head, Saliou." Ndeye's voice was quiet but accusing.

"I was coming to that," he said. "The trauma to the head is more severe than we'd at first imagined. There is significant swelling in the brain and..."

"Tell her about the coma, Saliou."

Khadi's breath became erratic. Her eyes pleaded with her father.

"I'm afraid it's true. Maimouna is in a coma..."

"A deep coma," Ndeye corrected him.

"All we can do is what we are doing now and hope that the swelling will subside and that her body will heal itself." Struggling to keep his tone businesslike, he ended with an abrupt, "That's it."

"Hope? We can hope? Nothing more than that?" Although she spoke them quietly, Khadi's questions seemed to fill the room.

She felt a return of the nausea that had kept her vomiting in the hospital toilets for the better part of an hour, the return of the swimming head and scrambled thoughts.

"Papa… Ndeye… we were getting onto the ferry… she was getting onto the ferry… rough, the water was rough… she seemed to have jumped across and then she just…" The threatened stream from her mouth suddenly diverted to her eyes, sending down a river of tears onto Maimouna's bed.

Ndeye rose. "You dare! You dare!" The absence of haste in her exclamations and the quietness of her voice, made the hardness of the words more wounding. "You dare to weep for this child? The child who's lying here because of you. Selfish! Thoughtless! Careless! You've wanted to kill her from the first time you saw her. This child you envied so much you could find no peace until she was dead. This child!" Ndeye rammed her hands onto the bed, making a strong triangle of her body as she leaned forward, her forehead nearly touching Khadi's, forming a bridge across Maimouna. Both Khadi and Saliou froze, mesmerized. Ndeye straightened up, threw out a hand and pointed.

"This child… this child is *mine!*" Her voice had the strength of a tolling bell, but when she reached the word "mine", she started to weaken. By the time Saliou had the courage to say, "Ndeye! Enough!" she had fallen back into her chair, impotent, quaking.

When Saliou knelt to console her, he found himself clinging to her, trying to hold on to the granite she had been only moments before. That's what he wanted to be – hard, clear, impervious. When she had leaned across the bed, her body a hard triangle, her words made of steel, she had been locked in a single vision, no matter how illogical. But that was over now. As he held her quivering shoulders, he saw that a lurch towards hysteria had begun and he was powerless to stop it. Not because it was invading his wife, but because it was inside him… His mind went blank for a moment. Then he roused himself and remembered Khadi. He had to talk to her. Make her understand the enormity of Ndeye's fear. He looked up and saw the swinging door. In a way he was glad.

Saliou didn't know how long he sat with Ndeye. Later, when he looked back at the events of that day, all he could remember of that time was the silence. The critical care rooms were some distance from the main hub of the hospital, but there seemed to be some powerful mechanism that filtered out all other sounds and made the room a sanctuary. Inside, all sighing, moaning and sobbing, all breathing, natural and artificial, were hushed the moment they escaped into the air.

"What can I do?"

He flinched at the unexpected sound and saw Hassim crouched in front of them, a look of anguish on his face.

"Stay with her." Saliou stood up while Hassim took his place beside Ndeye, who was weeping silently.

"I have some things to do. Some calls to make. Neurosurgeons. One in Marseilles. One in Abidjan." At the door, he stopped and turned. "I shouldn't be long." He paused. "And Hassim... well..."

Hassim shook his head and said, *"Mon frère,* the news is out. Everyone's here. And those who are not are on their way. Waiting for you to tell them something... I thought I should warn you."

Saliou left them, passed the empty room next to Maimouna's and made his way towards the main part of the building. This was something he did many times a day. He was usually in a hurry and rarely alone, always overwhelmed with greetings, often accosted for advice, sometimes pulled aside for revelations of the latest twists of hospital politics. Occasionally, he managed to walk alone and the corridor was long enough to allow him to formulate a plan, bring closure to some preoccupation – even evaluate some aspect of his life outside the hospital walls. He savoured those moments. Now, leaden feet slowed his progress and the air itself seemed heavy. Saliou was not given to flights of fancy but every person who passed seemed insubstantial, pressed against the walls, with eyes averted and lips tight. He remembered long ago someone saying that illness and death brought with them the aura of shame which attached itself like a stubborn smell to those involved. Nonsense, he'd said. Now he wasn't so sure. The news of his daughter's condition had made people afraid to look at him.

At the end of the corridor was the turn to the general wards. To the left was the waiting room. Saliou turned left and for a moment stood unobserved in the doorway. It was full. This was not unusual, but Saliou couldn't remember people sitting on the

132

floor when he'd rushed through earlier with Maimouna. He couldn't remember there being no space left at all. There hadn't been the intolerable noise of people all talking at once. He remembered Hassim's warning and started looking into the faces of the crowd. My God, he sighed, these are all mine.

"Look! It's Saliou!" someone called and every eye turned towards him. As repellent as misfortune was to some, to many it exerted a powerful fascination.

A group of children broke ranks and darted towards him.

"Papa! I want to see my mother! And Maimouna!"

"Amadou? What on earth... Omar? Malik?" Saliou's astonishment was absolute as the three boys surrounded him, grasping his legs. "Who brought you here? Who?" He looked around and his eyes lit upon Fatou bringing up the rear and holding little Lamine. "Fatou! Are you mad?" he hissed, the young girl shrinking away from his wrath in mute terror. "Who told you to bring these children here at a time like this?"

"I did."

Anyone else would have felt incinerated by Saliou's look, but not Hodia, who moved through the crowd like a vessel with noisily billowing sails.

Saliou groaned inwardly as Hodia steamed towards centre-stage. When she reached him, he stepped forward, placing himself between Hodia and everyone else.

"It was I who ordered the maid to bring the children here. I exercised my authority as the wife of your older brother."

Despite being unable to deliver these lines to a maximum audience, Hodia twisted her head, a smile playing around her thin lips. Saliou saw a forked tongue flicking. He tried to still the impulse towards violence. Bad enough that every last soul that he'd ever fed, watered, bandaged up or kept out of prison was here adding confusion to confusion... but to have the whole spectacle orchestrated by Hodia! His lip curled as he looked at her, dressed in full mourning white, presiding over this congregation of his kin. He turned away from her to address the assembly.

"*Asalaamu alaikum!*"

"*Alaikum salaam!*"

"I am very touched to see so many of you here to express your concern for the health of our daughter. I know that I speak for Ndeye when I say…" Saliou could hear his voice adopting the tone he used at meetings – calculated, persuasive. It was the voice of the successful politician and he knew that this was the time to use it. "…that your support brings us comfort at this time."

"*Yalla bahana!*"

Apart from the occasional call to the divine, there was total silence. The assembly had now grown and included medical staff, patients, their families, assorted others and, in a far corner, Magdalene and Khadi, who, until Saliou's address, had isolated themselves from the rest.

"I will not to attempt to deceive you. Despite the best efforts of this hospital, our daughter remains very ill."

"*Ndeye-san!*"

"The next forty-eight hours will be critical. But, and I say this with the utmost sincerity, it is a great consolation to know you hold us in your hearts. In your prayers."

"*Al-humdoulilahi!*"

"But, my dear brothers and sisters, it is Allah alone who will work the miracle, through the doctors who labour here. And it is in this knowledge that I urge you to return to your homes and pray for us there. Let this hospital continue its work in a manner that will be most favourable to our daughter's recovery." Saliou stopped and looked out at the people before him. Brothers, nieces, uncles, cousins, friends, colleagues, sisters, neighbours, nephews… These were his people, whose lives were, and always would be, his responsibility. That was just the way it was. He was educated. He was successful. He was their keeper, their daily bread. Even at this dark hour, he could not escape that stark truth. What had started as a deliberate appeal to reason had ended as a lump in the throat. "I want to thank you all. But please, please go home."

His voice trembled during the final sentence. There was a hush, someone stood up, then another and soon most of the occupants of the waiting room were on their feet. In the shuffling commotion that followed, Saliou did not lose focus.

"Fatou! Get the boys' things. Here's money for a taxi. Boys!" He squatted down. "You're going home now. We're busy here trying to make Mai better. When she is, you can come and see her."

"Is my mother going to be home for dinner?" Amadou wanted to know.

"She'll probably be late so you shouldn't wait."

"But she's always there…" he said, a big tear rolling down his cheek.

"Eh, Amadou! *Et le guerrier*? You know that the warrior is not supposed to cry." Saliou embraced his sons and watched them leave, his head aching, the lump rising in his throat again.

Most people honoured Saliou's request but a hard core remained, making themselves at home. A few spread out mats in preparation for the evening prayer. Hodia was, of course, among them and when Saliou passed, throwing her a cutting look, she simply said, "I will stay until my husband, your older brother, tells me otherwise. I at least will carry out my duty to my husband's family."

"Isn't Omar abroad?"

"Yes. Which means that I will be here until Allah's will for the child has been revealed." Then she settled herself comfortably and returned to regaling the group of older women stationed near her with juicy morsels of information about the calamity. Saliou walked away in disgust.

"Vultures!"

Saliou was perplexed. That was his exact thought but he was sure he hadn't spoken.

"Vultures," repeated Magdalene.

"Oh! I thought I saw you over there." After Hodia, it was a relief to see a human face.

"I want you to know that what you said just now, what you said to everyone… Well, it was just right. You see. It worked." She gestured to the waiting room, now practically empty except for Hodia's group and a few others not connected to the family. "At first I thought you were going to bullshit them. But you treated them with… respect."

"And what did you expect? That I scream at them to go?" Saliou hadn't meant to speak so sharply and prepared himself for her response. But it didn't come. She just stood there, waiting. He made some restless movements with his hands while he tried to work out what she wanted.

"Maimouna's condition is…"

"I'm not a doctor, Saliou. I don't need to know any more than what you just told us all. We have to wait and see. Wait and pray."

"Then what… What do you… I'm sorry, Madeleine, but I have to go. I have some calls to…"

"You have to talk to her, Saliou. She's in a bad way. She wouldn't even come up here with me to talk to you." Magdalene's head made a slight turn to the left, indicating with her chin a figure whose back was to them, seated near the entrance.

"Oh." Saliou raised and dropped his shoulders wearily. "She told you what happened inside? What Ndeye said?" He made a despairing flip of his hand. "She must realize that Ndeye is hysterical. She doesn't know what she's saying…"

"But you're not. She has to hear it from you. You need to tell her that you don't blame her. That it was an accident. You need to tell her right now. She is your daughter too!"

Magdalene levelled her unblinking golden eyes at him and for the second time that afternoon Saliou felt transfixed by a mother.

"Fine! Ask to be taken to the small conference room and wait for me there. I have to go to my office and make some calls. I won't be long." He set off, almost at a run, glad he had calls to make, glad he could seek some solace in a few minutes of doctorspeak, where science obliterates chaos, at least for a moment. He needed to be relieved of the weight of his family, the burden of these women… When he put the phone down, he stayed a while longer, pacing the floor, raking his hands across his head. He remembered how he'd felt standing waiting for the ambulance to arrive. Child to youth to husband to father to elder. Yes, he was on that path and he would continue. He would show that a man's strength was not in his muscles but in his heart and the white hairs earned by enduring and leading in hard times. As he set off to join Magdalene and Khadi, he felt fortified by this knowledge.

He opened the door.

"Saliou!" His wife rushed to him and hid in his arms.

Over her head, he saw Hassim, Magdalene and Khadi. His mind went blank again.

"Yes," he said at last, "here we all are!"

Hassim had thought that Ndeye needed a break from sitting

with Maimouna and had suggested that she wait in this room while he fetched her something to drink. They had come in and found Khadi and Magdalene, just before Saliou arrived.

Hassim was about to excuse himself but then thought better of it. He sat down and tried not to look at Khadi's ashen face.

Magdalene cleared her throat and approached Ndeye who clung more closely to her husband. Magdalene dropped back.

"Ndeye. You must believe me when I say how sorry I am, how sorry we both are, about what has happened. We are all praying that she will get better. Absolutely and completely better. We are praying in our different ways to God who is omnipotent. Your God and mine. There is only one."

"And His name is Allah and Mohamed is His prophet." Ndeye's voice was tremulous and her eyes bright behind her tears.

Magdalene was taken aback. One minute she had been talking to the back of a cowering head… She regrouped.

"Ndeye. We share in your sorrow. We don't wish for there to be any dissention between us at a time like this. Maimouna needs us to be unified." At the mention of Maimouna's name, a surge of electricity shot from one mother to the other but Magdalene persevered. "Khadi…" – another electric surge – "Khadi feels this tragedy very deeply. Look at her! I'm just asking you to remember her intention, which was to take her sister – the sister she adores and has longed for all her life – to take her out for the afternoon." Magdalene spoke calmly though Ndeye's threatening glare did not make it easy. She paused and said, "What happened was an accident. It was an accident, wasn't it, Saliou?"

Her eyes rose in challenge.

"Yes, it was an accident." His voice was a whisper.

Ndeye's wasn't. "How do you know? Were you there? You will take her side instead of mine? Hassim! Take me home. I need to be with people who respect me." She flung aside Saliou's arms and moved towards her one ally, chin raised and carriage erect.

With a look of consternation, Hassim ushered Ndeye out.

This was too much. Saliou felt on the edge and he didn't care who knew it.

"Now see what you've done!"

"Me? Me! What can you accuse me of doing this time?"

"Couldn't leave well enough alone! Couldn't see that Ndeye is practically out of her mind... Oh no! Not you! Just go barging in. As usual! My God! You never know when to stop! No, not you..." Striding back and forth, flinging words about, his anger welled up from the depths of his powerlessness, his fatigue, his frustration and his fear, dragging with it the debris of ancient trauma.

"Why did you come here?"

"You asked me to, Saliou." Magdalene struggled to resist being dragged into this whirlpool spinning around him. She spoke with great care. No one could afford for him to be like this, especially not Khadi.

"Why did you come?" he repeated. "Did you come to wreck this marriage too?" He did not hear Magdalene gasp or Khadi moan. He wanted the single vision Ndeye had shown, the impervious rock of righteousness no matter how unjust, the granite certainty that blocks pain. Yes, it was within his sights. He must grasp it.

"One wasn't enough, I guess. You needed to come to where I'd built a new life, a new family. To come and sow the catastrophe that follows you like a..."

"Saliou, you'd better stop before you say something you're going to regret..." Magdalene willed herself not to explode for Khadi's sake, who was twisting herself away from this encounter.

"Regret? Ha! What I regret is ever laying eyes on you!"

"Saliou! Remember your daughter!"

Magdalene grieved to see Khadi burying her head in her hands. But Saliou had not yet emptied the contents of his spleen; it was old and bitter on his tongue.

"What possessed me to think that I could bridge the gap between us? Gap? More like an ocean. A universe..." He stamped up and down the room. He seemed unhinged. "Different gods. Different worlds. No language either of us could understand. And you wouldn't change! How could there be a meeting between us?" He shot a glance at Magdalene. But she did not see. She was looking away, trying not to witness his humiliation. He rambled on, incoherent.

"...And you brought with you all your thieving ways."

"What did you say?" Magdalene asked, incredulous. Despite

her determination not to respond, these words couldn't pass. "What the hell did you say?"

"You heard. You, *ma chère* Madeleine, are a thief, pure and simple." He was slurring his words, although he had not touched alcohol since his student days. He looked at her with the red eyes of a drunk and did not recoil from the outrage of Magdalene's response.

"And what did I steal from you?"

"Where shall I start, *chère* Madeleine?" He was on the move again, up and down, up and down. "What about... my reputation? My name. It took me years to get it back."

"That's shit! My leaving you did your reputation nothing but good. Made you into a martyr. You should thank me." She paused, not wanting to go on. But Saliou was just getting started.

"My name! My name! Wrecked in a single night. But then you have no idea what it feels like to be respected, even admired by your community and then the next day to be scorned. Pitied. That was your handiwork, Madeleine. Yours."

Saliou's finger was inches from Magdalene's face. She said nothing. He was too far gone for any reasoning. Whatever her response, whether screams of abuse or silence, it was guaranteed to push him further in the direction of that white light towards which he had been moving since Ndeye had stalked away.

"Yes! But worse than that, worse than the shame you brought on me and the family that welcomed you like a sister, like a daughter, worse than all that..." Saliou's voice suddenly was lower, "...was the way you stole *her*!" His arm was a spear aimed at Khadi, impaling her against the wall where she sought refuge.

"You took away my child like a thief in the night. You took my innocent child when you ran to the arms of your lover – the man I thought was my friend, my brother. While I slept in our bed, you snatched my child away and took her to be part of your disgusting affair."

Magdalene wept now, shaking her head.

"And in that filthy air you made her breathe, you polluted her, contaminated her. Now you've brought her back to me as this... this..." He pointed at Khadi cringing like a threatened forest creature. "This... this stranger who looks like us but is not of us.

139

Whose smile is warm but whose blood is cold. Someone who brings trinkets but whose purpose is to steal the most precious jewel we possess. Yes, she saw in Maimouna the person that she could never be, so all she wanted was to take her away. To Gorée, to America. Anywhere, as long as it wasn't with us." He paused. "A thief, like her mother. You trained her well." Then the madness haemorrhaged from his body, leaving him empty, deflated, like a carcass by the roadside. He leaned back against the wall and closed his eyes.

But madness had not quit the room.

Magdalene strode towards him and landed a ringing slap on his cheek – loud, hard and shocking, putting an end to everything.

Through the bristling silence that followed came another sound, wailing, sacramental, familiar.

"*Allahu Akbar!*"

"*Allahu Akbar!*"

When he heard the muezzin's call, Saliou stared down at his trembling hands and covered his face with them. Magdalene stood uncertainly before him as shudders overtook him and felt him lean towards her. For a moment she held him.

He straightened, wiped his face with his hand, threw a sorrowful look at Khadi, who stood with her fists clenching and unclenching, and ran from the room.

Magdalene followed, not knowing why, but certain that it was the only thing to do. Saliou's white coat flew down the central corridor, his long legs keeping him well ahead, Magdalene barely keeping up without breaking into a run. When they came to the waiting room, there was no decrease in speed as they skirted the faithful who were turned towards Mecca and intoning praise to God.

So swift was their passage through the waiting room that it was only the ever-watchful Hodia who saw them rush through the main doors into the gathering dusk. Despite the urge to leap up and see what was going on, she felt trapped by the conspicuous piety of her devotions, so she was forced to continue her prostrations with the other supplicants.

In a little used corner of the hospital grounds, Saliou sought release from his grief. The loss of two daughters, the loss of two wives, the loss of the person he thought he was... It poured out in racking sobs, in strangled words and unstoppable weeping. Magdalene stood beside him, daring to touch him on the shoulder only once, transfixed by a Saliou she had never imagined. She scanned the darkness around, ready to put herself between him and any unwelcome visitor. But no-one came. At last he grew quiet.

She passed him a tissue and he blew his nose.

"I'm going to Khadi now," she said. "I have to hurry. I'll take the short cut."

He looked as though he wanted to speak but could not. She turned to go. He made a sound that she did not understand. She gave a faint smile.

"*Merci*," he murmured after she'd rounded the corner and entered the building through a side door.

He walked towards the main entrance and in the falling darkness caught sight of Khadi in a taxi just as it was moving off. She stared straight ahead, refusing to see her father.

10

MAGDALENE: SEARCHING IN THE RAIN

"*Dem-na.*"

"Gone? What do you mean gone? Gone where?"

Fatou shrugged. Another tiresome family member, forcing her out of her domestic routine and making her account for the actions of others. First Hodia, then Saliou, then Khadi. Now this one. Although she was well treated by Dakar standards, the past several hours at the house of Saliou Wade had reminded her of the endless complaints of other maids she knew. Fatou had howled when she'd heard the news of Maimouna's accident, but if things carried on like this, she might just find herself rolling up her bundle and taking the next *car rapide* back to her village.

"Khadi *dem-na.*" Somewhere in the yard, a child started crying and Fatou began to walk off. Over her shoulder, she added, "She took a suitcase."

Magdalene hurried to their bedroom. The closet was still full of the colourful outfits Khadi had received as gifts over the past two weeks. It was her western clothes that were missing, her toiletries, her underwear, her shoes, her wallet, her passport. Magdalene sat on the bed, her head in her hands.

It was the first time she'd been alone since she'd returned from her afternoon with Anne-Marie to find the house in uproar. When she'd found out what had happened, she'd raced to the hospital to find Khadi in a near catatonic state. She'd tried to coax her to talk and witnessed the gathering of the clan in the waiting room. She needed to clear her head. Where could her daughter have gone?

The years as a single woman raising a daughter, as a teacher in rundown North London schools, as a community activist, as a filmmaker, small-time admittedly, but still with shoots to organize and funds to generate: all that experience was there to call on. She sat at the small table by the window and start scribbling on the yellow pad that had been lying on Khadi's bed. She did what she always did when confronting a problem – she transferred the disorder in her mind onto paper and then, amidst arrows and interlocking spheres and spidery connections, tried to make sense of it all. She'd had to learn this technique early in her life. Her friends used to laugh when she did this. They'd say it went against her spontaneous nature. But she would just smile and carry on. Hard knocks had taught her that not having a plan was never a good idea.

The page quickly filled up with speculations about Khadi's state of mind, about places she might be drawn to, things she might do, people she might seek out. Using the telephone directory and her own address book, Magdalene produced a single neat column of telephone numbers and addresses.

Ignoring the people milling about the house, she appropriated the phone in the living room and looked down at her list. It started with the city's main hotels. She dialled the first number.

"Hello?"

Before she could get any further, there was a loud clap, a white flash, and a moment later the din of torrential rainfall. Lamps flickered, held, flickered again, then expired. Everywhere there were sighs of resignation followed by the noise of splashing footsteps as someone sprinted into the yard to switch on the generator. Life returned to the bulbs, but they gave only a dim facsimile of their usual brightness, increasing the atmosphere of gloom. The thunder continued to roll overhead, punctuated by the crackling staccato of shafts of lightning. Inside, a moist breeze made the curtains billow, informing everyone that after several weeks' flirtation with the rains, the season was here in earnest.

Magdalene dialled again, heard a disconcerting sound on the line and recognized it as the despairing cry of the Dakar telephone system in the rainy season. Until the storm spent itself, there would be no getting through to anyone. A cigarette or, better still, a good, stiff drink was what she needed. Neither was possible here. No, she would have to brave the elements without nicotine or alcohol to take the edge off her troubles. It was night-time and the city was flooding. She had no means of getting anywhere as taxis were out of the question and both of the family cars were at the hospital. But luck smiled on her when one of Saliou's many nephews appeared at the door, wanting news of Maimouna. Abdou was a frequent visitor, and he had a car, a battered old Peugeot. It took Magdalene only a few minutes to persuade him to help her find Khadi who, she explained, was distressed and alone in some hotel in the city.

They set off amid exclamations of *"Toubab!"* from those they left at home. Only a *toubab* would dream of going out on a night like this. Inside the car, she was relieved to find that exact details of Khadi's problem would not be required by this reserved young man with shadows under his eyes. His attention was on the road and the wavering beams of his headlights. Although the centre of the storm was now heading further down the coast, there were still residual pockets of the thunder's baleful grumbling. Magdalene noticed how hard the young man was gripping the steering wheel and was glad that she was not the only one feeling awed as the natural world roared and wept around them.

"Let's start at the Teranga," she said, trying to sound confident. Abdou nodded and swerved to avoid another deep puddle.

Magdalene's thoughts went back to how Khadi had been throughout her childhood – on the surface brave but in fact timorous and fragile when faced with the might of nature or situations beyond her control. There was Khadi, aged six, reciting her poem in total darkness when the assembly hall lights failed as she stepped on stage. She was there again with a couple of other teenagers spending an unexpected night on a Welsh hillside when a mist, white and sudden, came down and enveloped them. There was the summer at Maracas Bay in Trinidad when they went island-hopping, and huge green Atlantic swells curled over them. Each time Khadi had stood firm, but she had smelled her daughter's fear. And as rain washed over the city, Magdalene was sure this smell would be there again, a palpable thing. If only that smell could lead her to her daughter. But that would be too goddamn easy...

At the Teranga, she crossed the lobby swiftly, ignoring the trail of water which followed her across the elegant mosaic tiles.

"Good evening, *madame*," said a receptionist seated next to a large arrangement of flowers. "How can I help?"

"Do you have a guest by the name of Khadiatou Wade registered here?"

The young woman moved her chair over and paused, seeming to admire her impeccable red nails before making contact with the computer keyboard. She was no Anne-Marie. More like Mademoiselle Coly. God! The city girls really were all over the place. But Magdalene's anxiety deleted any compassion she might feel for their plight.

"I'm so sorry." The receptionist frowned charmingly at the screen, "Our system's down. With all the rain, you know." She looked up, folded her arms and gave an engaging smile.

"And?"

"*Pardon, madame?*"

"And what's next? How do I get my question answered?" Magdalene drew herself up to her full five foot two, her grey locks springing from her head, her amber eyes bellicose.

"But, *madame*, I told you that the computer is not working at the moment…"

Magdalene slammed her hand down on the polished counter, causing both the birds of paradise and the receptionist to tremble. "Look here, mademoiselle…" She peered at the hapless girl's badge. "Diarra, is it? Mademoiselle Diarra. Ten years ago, there were no computers at all in this country… None! But there were hotels and people stayed at them. And…" Magdalene threw her arms out in a big gesture. Conversations stopped and eyes swivelled round. "And amazingly, the hotels knew who those people were. How did they know? Mademoiselle Diarra, how did they know who was staying with them?'

"They… they…"

"They had lists. Yes! Lists! On paper! Do you think you can find such a list and tell me if Khadiatou Wade's name is on it?"

Five minutes later, Magdalene was striding out to the waiting car, her mind already on their next stop. One of the hotel's managers grimaced and returned to his office. The front desk receptionist tried to fit what had just happened into the training course she had recently passed with distinction.

Magdalene spent the next hour clambering in and out of Abdou's car, going from one hotel to another, having the register checked, often getting angry and offending or frightening someone behind the front desk, and then returning deflated to the car. When the fifth front desk proved fruitless, Magdalene slid in next to Abdou and sat there tapping her fingers.

"Shall I take you home now?"

"No! Not yet!" Softening the sharpness in her voice, she added, "If you wouldn't mind, I'd like to go to the airport. There's a flight to New York late tonight."

The young man turned the key in the ignition.

"But wait!" She looked at her watch. "It's only just gone nine. The flight leaves at two. Nobody will be there before eleven."

Abdou switched off the engine and waited. Magdalene gave a weary sigh.

"Madame Madeleine, I live near here," he said. "Come to my house and rest for a while. Then later I'll take you to the airport."

"But Abdou… I don't want to put you or your family out. It's a terrible night to be having unexpected guests."

"It would be an honour." He turned on the engine again.

Although his house was not far from the last hotel, it seemed to exist in a parallel universe. The road was narrow and unlit and Abdou had to guide her across the choked ditch into the flooded courtyard. What she could not see, she could smell. At the zinc door, Abdou said something in a low voice. A young boy in torn shorts let them in and disappeared. The room was small and hot. On one wall there was the framed photograph of an unsmiling patriarch, and on the other some embroidered Koranic verses. The other two sides of the room were curtained off and from behind the curtains there came the muffled sound of people preparing to sleep.

"Excuse me a minute," Abdou said.

A few moments later, he reappeared with a pretty young woman, small-boned and very pregnant.

"Madame Madeleine, this is my wife, Aminata."

After exchanging greetings, Magdalene settled back. She was given food and drink and for a little while she slept in the room's one upholstered chair. Before they left for the airport, Abdou told her – in a whisper so as not to disturb the others – that he was not Saliou's nephew at all but just called him "uncle" as a token of his gratitude and respect. He had left his village and come to work in the capital a year ago after his wife had nearly died giving birth to their first child. He had found work as a part-time driver at Saliou's Clinique Aurore.

"One day, I was driving him and we started to talk. I told him what had happened to Aminata. He gave me a full-time job as a handyman and said that if she became pregnant again, he would make sure she received good care. So now she gets checked at the hospital every week. In a few weeks, the child will come in safety." Abdou faltered a little. "With the money I make now, I've been able to bring most of my family to the city. I see all the rich women who come to have their babies at the Clinique. We are not like them." He summoned up the spirit of the house, with its ditch of raw sewage and its many sleepers behind the curtain. Magdalene remembered Anne-Marie's description of her accommodation. "Could be better". She probably lived somewhere like this.

"But we are doing all right," Abdou concluded. "And it's all thanks to Saliou."

They reached the airport at half past eleven. Here, Magdalene was unable to bully or cajole anyone into revealing whether or not Khadi's name was on their list. 9 / 11 and all that; by now she felt certain that she would not find Khadi that night. But absorbed as she was in her own drama, she had been humbled by her visit to Abdou's home. In the end, he was able to persuade her to just sit and wait to see who checked in. The flight was full, but there came a moment when the last of the travellers had gone through the barrier, their squadrons of family and friends had departed and Magdalene and Abdou found themselves alone except for a few listless workers pushing brooms across the floor. It was almost two in the morning.

After a few hours of broken sleep at Saliou's house, Magdalene spent most of the morning reordering her thoughts, drawing more diagrams and coming up with another plan. She needed to find Hassim. Her instinct told her that he loved her daughter, whatever the pain that Khadi had undoubtedly put him through. She would try to reach him by phone. But though the rain had relented and the phone system was working, she was unable to use the one phone in the house as much as she wanted. There were so many calls coming in and being made about Maimouna. The official bulletin was that her condition was "unchanged", but the rumour was that she was worse. In the vacuum of Saliou's, Ndeye's and Hodia's absence from the home, there was some jockeying for power among the remaining assorted relatives. Magdalene kept her head down. When at last she was able to use the phone, she learned that from Dakar to the Petite Côte, no-one – friend or relative – knew where Khadi was.

Like a faithful soldier, Abdou turned up for duty. "Madame Madeleine, I am here," he said in his soft voice. He saw how exhausted Magdalene looked and added, "It's raining again. Why don't you stay home this afternoon while I look around the hotels for you? I'm likely to be able to find out more…"

Magdalene knew this was probably true.

"How is your wife?"

"She is well. She sends her greetings."

Magdalene smiled. "Yes, I think you're right. You'll be able to do much more without me. And Abdou," she said, "Please see if you can find Hassim. Tell him I've been trying to reach him."

She lent him an umbrella, waved him off, went into her room, lay on the bed and closed her eyes. The sound of steady rain failed to soothe the tight muscles in her stomach and back. She had been in this place at other times of her life. She thought of Saliou, convulsed with grief, shocked by his own unfocused rage. Poor Saliou! To think that it was only now that he was facing up to the things that happened when they were young. Whilst she… she almost chuckled, that's all she'd been doing since then.

Back then, she'd felt trapped. Living in a world she didn't understand and that didn't understand her. Resenting the constraints of an ancient society, so unlike the fluid one that had made her. How many times had she asked why she couldn't do this or that? Always the same answer: "*Ça ne se fait pas.*" It is not done. How could she argue with that? Then there was the change in Saliou. After a few months back home, what had happened to the funny, passionate student who'd swept her off her feet in Paris? The one whose face had shone when he'd talked about their future in Africa? Where had this other person come from? The humourless one whose judging eyes always seemed to wonder why it was so hard for her to fit into his world.

There'd been the fateful night when the British Institute guy had driven her home from work......

"Hey, Maggie, aren't you staying?"

"What for?" Magdalene asked.

"Don't you remember? It's Karen's last day."

"Oh yes! I'd forgotten!" Magdalene put her bag down. "I'll just stay for a minute." She wasn't in a rush. Saliou was on night shift at the hospital and Khadi had her usual retinue of minders at home. It wasn't much of a job, this British Institute thing, just a few hours teaching a week, but Magdalene loved it and jumped at the opportunity to spend some time in this environment.

They had never intended it to be more than a few drinks as a send-off to a colleague going back home. But like the loaves and fishes, the single bottle of wine multiplied. Somebody produced a cassette player and a few tapes and before she knew it, it had become a full blown English expat party and Magdalene was the life and soul of it.

There'd been about a dozen of them, mostly in their twenties, with varying degrees of commitment to the developing world. It was the end of the working week, all of their English classes were over, their earnest Senegalese students had gone and with them the ever-present anxieties about making cultural faux-pas. No! They could let their hair down, have a few drinks, do a few Monty Python impressions and go wild on the dance floor. Magdalene laughed as usual at the spectacle of "white people dancing", but there was affection in her laughter. This was a night off. She was having a great time, without the burden of having to think about what was or was not done.

When one of her colleagues nearly knocked her over with his flailing arms, she had to get a grip of the situation.

"No, Roger, that's not how you do it. You don't dance with your arms and your head. You dance with this!" She put her hands on her hips and did a little jook.

"Ooooooo!" the others cried. "Show us how!"

Magdalene attempted to teach Roger to move to the rhythm while the others cheered her on.

"Better not let that gorgeous husband of yours see you!" someone chimed.

"Why not?" Magdalene replied, holding her dance student by the waist and trying to get him to desist from leaping about and listen instead to the beat. "One – two three four... Pay attention! Forget that music in your head. Concentrate! Two – two three four... No! My husband is happy when I'm happy... Come on, Rog, you can do it! Three – two three four... And, besides, he's working late tonight!"

"Oooooooo!"

In the end, Magdalene gave up on Roger but there were speeches to be made, a gift to be presented and a few tears to be shed. It was almost ten o'clock when they called it a night. A man called Bob offered to take Magdalene home. She hardly knew him.

During the ride home, she started to simmer down. She'd had a glass of wine but that wasn't what had made her high. It was the feeling of freedom, one that she hadn't felt for a long time. As the breeze blew in through the car window, she thought of her little daughter. There was no guilt, only delight at the prospect of seeing her in the next few minutes. She would be a better mother for having had an evening off. And a better wife too.

When they pulled up, there were a couple of cars in the driveway, including Saliou's, although he was still supposed to be at work. Magdalene was puzzled.

"Good night," she said. "And thanks."

"I'll wait till you go in," he called as she got out. She smiled and walked quickly towards the door. As she reached for the handle, the door was flung wide by Hodia, triumphant, her acute senses not missing the white man in the car and the faint smell of wine on Magdalene's breath. Behind Hodia stepped Saliou holding three-year-old Khadi, fretting in his arms.

"She's running a high fever," he said, glancing at the car as it pulled out. "It's a good thing Hodia happened to be passing. The maid would not have known what to do." He closed the door...

Lying on her bed, hearing the rain falling outside, Magdalene remembered that sound. During the twenty odd years that followed the British Institute party, whenever Magdalene felt she could no longer bear her loneliness or the feeling that she'd thrown away the pearl with the oyster shell, she reminded herself of the shutting of that door. She quit her job, of course. At home, apart from Hodia's sly crowing, nobody mistreated her. On the surface, Saliou put it behind him and things went on as before. But inside, she knew that when that door opened again, she would walk out through it. And it did when Antoine called saying he would be coming for a visit.

Eventually, she fell asleep. She slept for hours and when she awoke, the altered light told her that it would soon be evening.

There was a knock and a timid head appeared around the door.

"Madame Madeleine?"

"Oh, come in, Abdou. Please."

"Do you have a photograph of Khadi?"

Magdalene sprang to her feet.

"What's happened? Have you found her?"

"No. But there are people who match her description in one or two places. Although the name isn't right."

"Do you think she could be using an assumed name?" Magdalene was rummaging through her bag as she spoke. "Why would she…" She stopped. "She doesn't want to be found. Of course." She handed over the photograph, shaking her head. "Of course." She tried to hold back tears coming to her eyes.

"Madame?"

"I'm fine," she said, moving towards the door. "Let's go." As she walked through Ndeye's crowded *salon*, she felt flayed by the unspoken hostility of those who watched her. She, her daughter and their *toubab* ways were responsible for this tragedy. She straightened her back, passed through without a word, grateful for Abdou's presence.

The first stop was the Novotel and there at the front desk was Mademoiselle Ba, the one who had passed Magdalene on to Anne-Marie. That seemed so long ago. She recognized the person in the photograph as one of their guests, registered as Katy Joseph from the United Kingdom.

"Joseph. It's my maiden name." Magdalene tapped the counter

for a moment and then looked up at Abdou. "I'll be fine now. I'll go up and talk to her and then bring her home."

'Don't you want me to wait here?"

"No. No. It may take a while. The talking, I mean. I'll bring her home when it's all done."

"Please call me if you need me." He scribbled on a piece of paper. "Here's the number of my *mobile*," he added with shy pride.

Magdalene smiled. "What! Does everybody in this town have a cell phone?" She chuckled. "Ah! Progress!"

She embraced him and disappeared into the elevator.

She knocked at the door several times. Eventually, there was the sound of the dead bolt being released and there she was.

The first thing Magdalene felt like doing was giving Khadi a good hard shake; the next was to hold her in her arms and rock her. She did neither but simply followed her daughter into the room and watched as she pulled a crumpled T-shirt around her while resuming her place on the edge of the bed. The television was on, but on mute.

"I don't want to talk, Mum," Khadi said in a flat tone. "I want to be left alone. And I'm not leaving here."

"Hats off for the alias, kiddo," Magdalene said. "Katy Joseph. My maiden name and the name all your New York friends call you. It really pisses me off the way Americans can't be bothered to make the slightest effort. Never heard of Kha – di. Kha- di. "Kha," as in "car". How hard is that? But no, they turn it into some ridiculous approximation… Katy! How could anybody look at you and call you Katy! Katy's the name of that blue-eyed blonde in those books for blue-eyed blondes – "What Katy Did". "What Katy Did Next". Even when you were a kid, you refused to read that shit. And what do you do now? You become Katy!"

Khadi continued to stare at the silent pictures on the screen.

"Maimouna is no worse," Magdalene said. "Your father is trying to fly in a specialist to look at her." She decided that Khadi's absorption in the television was real and not the pantomime she had originally thought. Each line and sinew, each limb and feature strained to comprehend the images that unfolded before her.

"Your father is very sorry for everything he said to us at the hospital."

Khadi remained deaf and dumb.

"He was just overwrought." Magdalene was surprised at how sad she felt as she spoke these words and saw Saliou again in the empty corner of the hospital grounds. Then, almost to herself, she added, "I've been trying to find Hassim but he seems to have gone missing. So unlike him…"

No response.

Time passed. Magdalene walked over to the sealed window, opened the curtain and looked out. Rain falling from a dark sky, its music drowned by the clatter of air conditioning. She could not bear to look at Khadi, rigid, wishing her gone.

She stood in front of the television. Khadi's face twitched momentarily then became impassive again.

"I need to talk to you about your Tonton Antoine."

Khadi stared through Magdalene at the screen behind.

"Okay," Magdalene said, "if this is going to be a monologue, so be it." She switched the television off.

"What your father said yesterday – about me and Antoine – it wasn't true. Not exactly." Khadi turned her face away.

"Do you remember him? What am I saying? Of course you do. You were sixteen years old when he died. Over ten years ago… And before that, there were those times he came and visited us in London. But what I don't know is whether you remember when we left this city. And went to him in the middle of the night. You were four years old…" She paused, her eyes filling with tears. "Do you remember it, Khadi?"

Nothing.

"Do you remember the months we stayed in Paris with Antoine?"

Khadi remained stiff, turned away from her mother. Magdalene cleared her throat.

"I don't know how to begin. How to get you to understand what it was like back then… You see me now. I'm back in Africa after all these years. And I seem fine. I am fine! Now. But it's been a long and winding road, Khadi. Back then, when you were a baby, I wasn't up to it. I wasn't up to the challenge… And neither was Saliou. He thought he could rewrite the script of his life but when it came to it, he couldn't. But this is not about him. It's about me."

Magdalene took a deep breath. "I wasn't ready for this." Her hand encompassed the whole continent. "I was too young to be able to cope with the change… the transformation… that would have been necessary to make our marriage work. I was so… unformed, Khadi. When I was your age, I already had you. But for all intents and purposes, I was not much more than a child."

The air seemed static. Khadi was sitting on the edge of the bed looking down and Magdalene was standing as though rooted, growing out of the floor. When she spoke, it was as if to herself.

"I didn't grow up until I was back in England, trying to raise you on my own. That's when I started to understand the upside of Africa. It struck me every single day when I realized that I was completely alone with you. That I was responsible for everything. That there was no system of support, no automatic sense of belonging, no army of relatives to help mould you and keep you safe. It was down to me and me alone. I remember it as clear as day – the moment that I really understood this. It was your first day at infant school. You went in – brave, of course – but I stood at the school gates and I couldn't stop crying. I understood what I had lost. What you had lost. I also understood that whatever happened next was all down to me.

"I don't know why I'm talking about all these things. About me and your father. I didn't come here for that. You see what happens when I can't do my spider charts and make some sort of order." She gave a dispirited chuckle. "My thoughts just come any old way… I wanted to tell you about Antoine…"

"I don't want to hear this, Mum." Khadi stood up, walked around her mother and switched on the television.

Magdalene grabbed the remote and switched it off again.

"I want to watch CNN. There's a hurricane in the Atlantic." Khadi's manner was mild, resigned.

"What can be more important than for you to hear what I have to say?"

"My father said it all. You and Tonton Antoine had an affair. So? That sort of thing happens all the time." Khadi's shoulders were hunched and her steps sluggish as she moved back towards the bed. "If it wasn't true, you would have denied it by now and not given me some long preamble…"

154

"Khadi! Listen to me! Why won't you listen to what I have to say?"

"Because it doesn't matter. I didn't know you and Antoine had an affair; but now I do, I can see that it's just the way it would be. Just like everything else that has anything to do with me. It's business as usual."

"Don't talk like that! Don't try to make everything ugly!"

Magdalene sat on the bed next to Khadi. She did not have the courage to reach over for her hand.

"It's very difficult for parents to tell their children exactly what happened in the past. No matter what culture we come from, it's… taboo… crossing the territory between parent and child. But anyway… When you were four years old, Antoine came to visit us. I was desperately unhappy. Thought I would drown in the life that I was living with your father. On Antoine's last day, we all went to Gorée for the afternoon. When we were walking around the *Maison*, it was as though I was seeing it for the first time. I was seeing it with someone who had a history like mine, or at least someone who understand my history from the inside. I felt very moved… not just by what I saw but because Antoine understood what I was seeing. Sounds strange, I guess. But that's the way it was. And, just like that…" Magdalene snapped her fingers, "He became my saviour.

"He helped us to get out of the country and put us up in his apartment in Paris for four months. When we moved back to England, he stayed in touch and came to visit often. Well, you remember that. When there was literally no one else, he was our friend, someone we could count on."

The only sounds in the room were the rattling of the air conditioner and the labour of Magdalene's breathing.

"He was a big womanizer. Other than his work – which he loved, running around the world covering the news – he liked two things. Women and booze. But in all of that time, he never once tried it on with me. I wondered about that… Because I knew his other side. Was I so unattractive? But no. He saw his role as making sure that we were all right. That we had enough money, had a decent place to live and that kind of thing. Only once or twice did he admit how much he missed Saliou's friendship."

She stood up and looked towards the window.

"A few weeks before he died, he went on holiday to Guadeloupe, some R and R before his next assignment in Kuwait where the bomb killed him… You remember that. It was you who answered the phone when his friend from Agence France Presse called. Anyway, he wrote me a letter from a hotel in Point-à-Pitre. But it went missing. It arrived after I'd received the news of his death."

Magdalene glanced over and saw that although Khadi was still looking at the floor, she was listening.

"He told me that he loved me. That he loved both of us. But that he had stayed away because he knew that family life was not something he could manage." Magdalene struggled to control her voice. "He also said that I should take you back to St. Lucia to live. Because England was not doing either of us any good. And because there are 'riches' in the Caribbean too. That's how he put it. 'Go home', he said. 'Be reconciled'."

She gave a painful a sigh. "So you see, your dad was wrong about Antoine and me. It was never what he said it was. But he was right too. Because it was… something."

There were tears in Khadi's eyes as she stood up.

"All right, Mum. All right. I'm sorry."

"What for, love?"

"I'm sorry your life has been so hard. I'm sorry I've made it so hard."

"What are you talking about? You've made it… worthwhile. You've given me a reason to get up in the morning!"

Magdalene reached over to touch her.

"No, Mum, please!" Khadi backed away. "No! No!"

"You're scaring me. Why can't I even touch you?"

"Because…"

"Because what?" Despite Magdalene's misgivings, she caught Khadi's hand in hers. It was limp and clammy.

"Because… whatever I touch turns to ashes."

"Sweetheart, no…"

Khadi pulled her hand out of her mother's and fled to the other side of the room.

"Stay there, Mum. Please! Stay there."

Magdalene fought the desire to rush over and take Khadi in her arms. Khadi stayed pressed against the wall, her head down. She was so still it looked as though she was asleep.

"If it wasn't for me, you'd be over my father now. But as long as I'm around, you'll always be tied to him."

"Well, I *will* always be tied to him but not in the way you think. We made you together, Khadi. He'll always be part of my life. But I have a separate life now and so does he."

"If it wasn't for me," Khadi continued, "my father would be able to get on with his life with his new family. It's torture for him having me around!"

"That's not true! He loves you!"

"And if it wasn't for me, Maimouna, that lovely child, would be playing in her yard with her brothers, listening to stories, drawing her pictures, reading her books, dreaming her dreams. But instead, she's lying there… Nothing will ever be the same when she dies."

"But she's not dead…" Magdalene would have continued but Khadi quelled her with a look.

"I am a wrecker. I kill people." The tone was matter-of-fact.

"Didi! You need to stop talking like this!" She crossed the room and shook Khadi hard, just as she'd wanted to do at first. "Look at me!" Khadi, limp as a rag doll, acquiesced, then looked away. "Look at me! I think… for the past few days and certainly tonight, you're a little crazy." Khadi started to slump down onto the bed but her mother held her up, forcing her to look into her eyes. "More than a little! I don't know what your New York shrink would say about your analysis of yourself but here's what I think. Khadi! Are you listening?"

"All I know is I'm not leaving this room," Khadi murmured.

Magdalene gave her another shake, a rough one. "You're not some creature of myth that wrecks and kills people. You are just a human being. And human beings hurt others and are hurt by them. That's life. Look at me!"

"Never leaving…" Khadi's voice was a whisper.

Magdalene grabbed Khadi's drooping chin and held it firm.

"What you need to know is that you were not responsible for your parents' divorce. We did that to ourselves. Don't look away! You did not make me miss my chance with Antoine all those years ago. It was my choice. I didn't want to face the feelings between us. And when I did, it was too late... And last, and very much to the point – are you listening, Khadi? You did not cause Maimouna to fall. Life is full of unexplainable grief... That's all."

Khadi looked into her mother's face searching for the blame and recrimination that would justify the agony she felt. All she found was the face she knew best in the world, etched with a network of lines.

"And how can you ask me *if* I remember, Mum? I remember it all! I remember my *bonne* Yacine and how she used to carry me on her back! I remember the night we left and how scared I was. I remember waking up in Tonton Antoine's car with woollen clothes on. I was covered in a blanket with yellow roses on it. And it smelled so bad..."

Her long thin body collapsed against Magdalene's breast, limp and lifeless until finally the shuddering started, then the sobs and at last the tears that would set her free.

For the rest of the weekend, Magdalene looked after her daughter. She coaxed her to eat, saw that she bathed, combed her hair. Although she never mentioned Hassim by name, she said how terrible it was to refuse love. Sometimes, they opened the curtains and looked out at the city under rain. From time to time, they turned on the television and watched the CNN weathermen track the storm as it left its birthplace off West Africa, gained energy from the warm Caribbean, turned north and finally roared across Bermuda. Despite the wretchedness in the hurricane's wake, there was something strangely cathartic about watching this manifestation of the natural world, single-minded and wholly unrepentant. And when eating and grooming and viewing were done, Magdalene lay down with her daughter and sang her to sleep with songs from her childhood.

"Ma belle ka di maman li
Pourquoi le monde si joli..."

When the words of the lullaby that Khadi had loved so much as a child came back to her, she thought how true they were, how there was so much in life that couldn't be known or understood.

"Un jour et mille ans cest meme temps
Pour le bon Dieu, pour le bon Dieu..."

As Magdalene waited for her own sleep to come, she thought of Antoine, the lover that she never had, but the man who had set her on the path that could give her back her life. He would have been happy to know that she had gone back home and was trying to reconcile herself to it.

On the morning of Magdalene's second day at the Novotel, there was a knock at the door. It was Abdou.

"Khadi! You have to get up. We've got to go." There was a timbre in Magdalene's voice that Khadi recognized. She sat up.

"We've got to get to the hospital." Magdalene paused. "It's Maimouna," she added unnecessarily.

Khadi hesitated for the merest second and then reached for her clothes.

LIVING WATER

MAIMOUNA: THE DOORWAY

"Sea and *karite*. Water and earth," she said again.

"I'm sorry, Yaye Coumba." Saliou scratched his head and looked around the room at the others. "Our poor brains can't understand what you want us to do."

Yaye Coumba raised her eyes in exasperation. When she spoke this time, it seemed she was making allowances for his dull wits.

"If you want this child to be released from the torture of your toubab learning..." She threw a withering look at the tubes in Maimouna's nostrils and the other one piercing her arm. "If you want her to be cured, she will have to be taken to the sea, given a salt bath and her limbs oiled with *karite*. A double anointing of water and earth."

Saliou knew a declaration of war when he heard one. Yaye Coumba's frail body did not disguise the fact that from this moment on she would be his implacable foe.

He squared his shoulders and said, "That will not be possible, Yaye. Maimouna cannot be moved."

Nobody spoke. Yaye and Saliou looked about them. There was the specialist from France, his face flushed from the heat, his mind bewildered by this tower of Babel into which he had landed. He stuck close to Saliou, the only point of reference that made any sense to him. There was Ndeye, appearing not to hear what was going on, leaning listlessly against Hassim's shoulder. There were Magdalene and Khadi, both struggling to make sense of what Yaye was saying in her highly figurative use of Serrer. All were conscious of Maimouna's physical deterioration, as she lay motionless, her skin the colour of ash.

Yaye Coumba moved closer to the bed and reached out to touch the pouch containing the medicine brought by the specialist from

France. No one breathed as her gnarled hand traced the line from the plastic pouch, along the tube right to the spot where it entered Maimouna's arm. She placed her hands on the child's body and said in a clear voice, "Will someone help me to take the one who suffers to the sea? Or must I alone carry out the wishes of the ancestors? Must I bear the burden alone?" She looked around.

Ndeye and Hassim hung their heads in shame. Saliou was impervious to Yaye's blackmail, and ready to act if she made a false move.

Ten, twenty years ago, she would have been quick and strong enough to pick up the child and clutch her to her breast before anyone was able to do anything. Now, by the time she started to lean over Maimouna and take hold of one of her arms, Saliou was already across the room confronting her. For a long moment, they stared at each other. Saliou removed Yaye's hand, exerting more pressure than he cared to consider, removing each bony finger, one by one, releasing the child's arm from the iron grip.

"No, Yaye. Maimouna cannot be moved."

The old woman let out a sigh, picked up her huge basket and began to creak towards the door.

"Yaye!" Ndeye sprang to life, barring Yaye's path. "Where are you going?"

Without even a glance, the old woman said, "Do not weep, my child. When I am back sitting under my shade tree, hearing the waves on the shore, I will pray for our daughter sleeping here. I will intercede on her behalf with the ancestors."

"But what about now?" said Ndeye, wringing Yaye's hand. "What about the cure? You said you could cure her!"

"I can do nothing alone, my child." Her back was to Saliou but her words were addressed to him. "I am a poor helpless old woman…" Saliou ground his teeth together and threw a furious glance at Hassim. Traitor! He was the one who'd gone to the Petite Côte and brought Yaye Coumba to sow more confusion, false hopes and grief. Not for the first time, Saliou felt the impulse towards violence well up inside his chest. He took a breath, closed his eyes and let it pass through him.

"I do not have the learning of the toubab…" Yaye continued. "But this I know. For the ancestors to speak and show their

164

mercy, certain things must be done in certain ways by certain people..."

"Due process!" Saliou thought sourly. "She's saying the spirits require due process!" In another situation, he might have laughed inwardly, but try as he might to keep up the appearance of professional optimism, he knew that this was a day for tears.

"For example, we must immerse the one who suffers in the incoming tide..."

"But Yaye..." The tremor in Ndeye's voice did not obscure the fact that she had broken through the barrier that had always kept her in fear and trembling of the old woman. Today she would take her on for Maimouna's sake. "Yaye, Saliou has said that we cannot move her. It's too dangerous." With this brief nod to her husband's status, she forged ahead with the idea that had formed in her mind. "You say she needs to be bathed in the sea... Well, couldn't... couldn't the sea be brought to her?"

"My child, it is said that I am a wise woman," Yaye replied with a modest chuckle. "But that is a task that even Yaye Coumba of Nianing cannot perform."

Ndeye grasped both the old woman's hands. Her body, which had spent the past three days in a kind of swoon, now had an intense energy. She looked Yaye Coumba straight in the eye and spoke with heightened confidence.

"My mother, you are indeed wise. And your wisdom has been handed to you from those who have gone before." She drew a deep breath. "My spirit tells me – the spirit that has guided me all my life – the spirit that speaks to me in the dark night..." Saliou winced but Ndeye took no heed, oblivious of everyone except for the wrinkled matriarch in the dark blue gown. "My spirit tells me that we must sometimes take a different path to reach the same end. That even the laws set down by the ancients can be bent a little here, a little there, in the way of vines twisting and turning but always breaking through to the light."

The old woman clucked with surprise when she heard the new rhythms in Ndeye's speech, but she said nothing.

"When the wise woman places the one who suffers in the incoming tide, what does she do?" Ndeye asked.

"She lets the water flow over the whole body," Yaye answered.

165

"Then, with a man – yes, it must be a man for balance to be maintained... man and woman, earth and water – with a man holding the body out of the water, she makes a cup of one of her hands..." All eyes were fixed on Yaye's hands – dull black, desiccated, their palms still bearing a faded henna pattern – and as they mimed the action, everyone in the room could smell the sea air and feel the warm water escaping between the cupped fingers. "...and with the other, she dips from that cup and touches the body of the one who suffers. That is the blessing of the sea."

"What parts of the body does the wise woman touch, Yaye?" Ndeye pressed hard.

"The important ones." She paused, as though she had said enough. Then, remembering the ignorance of those around her, she went on. "The parts that give us sight, smell, sound, taste... and thought." Yaye's fingers made a tour of the head. "Then the one that gives us breath..." She gestured towards her chest. "The parts that give us touch..." She rubbed her hands together, making the sound of dry leaves fretting in the wind. "And the one that brings forth life..." Her hands pressed hard on the spot where her thighs met, causing all eyes except Ndeye's to drop and shift away. But their discomfort was of no concern to Yaye. All that mattered was to make the procedure clear to these simpletons. "But for one as young as our daughter lying here, one whose power to bring forth life still lies buried deep within her, it would be enough to place a drop of sacred water on her belly where the life-giving spirits slumber."

Only Ndeye, Saliou and Hassim could follow what the old woman was saying. The others could only guess at her meaning, but they felt the authority emanating from her shrunken form. Hassim stood very still, his eyes half closed, a hand unconsciously scraping at his hairline. Saliou shifted from foot to foot, trying to gauge the right moment to intervene.

"So Yaye..." Ndeye had a hold of Yaye's hands again. "Yaye! It seems as though the important thing is the touch of the anointing fingers. Perhaps it is not essential to place the one who suffers in the tide. Perhaps it is enough to bring the sea to her and place it on her body! Perhaps that will be enough to bring about the blessing!" Ndeye's face was transfigured, its glow lighting up the room.

"Ndeye… please…" Saliou's voice was soft as he stepped forward and put his hand on her shoulder.

Ndeye swatted it off as though it were a fly.

"Won't it be enough, Yaye?" Her tone was strong, insistent. "Won't it?"

"I'm not sure… We cannot change the law to suit our desires…"

"I will go myself! I will go to the sea and bring you the water… One bucket. Ten! Whatever you need!"

The specialist from France looked ever more ill at ease. He couldn't understand what was going on. Now he began to regret having allowed himself to be persuaded to make this mercy dash. The child was not yet responding to the experimental drug that had shown so many positive results in his hospital in Marseilles… And the women were becoming hysterical … It was too much…

Saliou tried to steer Ndeye away to a corner for a semblance of a private conversation, begging her not to upset herself, but she was not having any of it.

"Do I look upset to you?" she demanded, glaring.

She didn't. In fact, she had never looked less upset, less dependent on him. It was all so confusing. Among the many things that Maimouna's fall had unleashed, the most difficult for him to fathom was the emergence of this new person inhabiting his wife's body.

"But what you are proposing to do," he said, "is not… *raisonable*."

The luminous glow died in Ndeye's cheeks as she struggled to assemble words which would adequately describe the three days and nights that she had watched over her child as she was violated by tubes and syringes, as she was checked and rechecked by a constant stream of doctors and nurses, as she continued to sleep, as she refused to return to the land of the living. All that time Ndeye had been in absolute despair. Since Yaye Coumba had appeared in the hospital, hope had blossomed in her chest and nothing would rob her of it. She pointed an accusing finger at Saliou as he wavered at her side.

"*Raisonable! Raisonable!* That's all you know, isn't it?" Her eyes never left the face of the old woman as she aimed her words at her husband. "You've tried *raisonable* on our daughter, Saliou," Ndeye continued. "Look where it's got us!"

Saliou retreated to the wall he had been occupying with the man from France. Ndeye turned her back on him and was about to launch a fresh assault on Yaye Coumba when Hassim took her by the shoulders and said, "You stay here. I'll go."

"Hassim, what do you think you're doing? Have you lost your mind?" Saliou spoke in rapid French. At first he looked more perplexed than angry. "Why are you sabotaging me in this way? First you go behind my back and bring Yaye here. Now this! Yaye Coumba is a woman worthy of the greatest respect, but I will not permit her to practice any of her nonsense on this child!" His eyes flashed. "You're not a *marabout*! You're a doctor! Act like one!"

For a moment Hassim was held by the rebuke. Then he walked to the door. "That's what I'm doing, Saliou." Then he was gone.

Saliou threw out his arms in disbelief and flopped into a chair while the specialist from France began looking for something in his pocket, wondering when it would be appropriate to ask about the next flight out. Meanwhile the alliance between Ndeye and Yaye Coumba was sealed and they stood side by side at the foot of Maimouna's bed, murmuring the occasional word.

Khadi stood apart, watching, with her arms crossed around her body. Magdalene walked to the other side of the room and looked out of the window at the morning rain. It was at moments like these that she regretted having abandoned her faith so many years ago. It was what was giving Ndeye the strength to live through this cruel hour. Immersed in these thoughts, she didn't see that her daughter was trying to hide a smile as Hassim made his rebellious exit.

He sped through the hospital trying to formulate a plan which would bring some sort of order to the chaos. He couldn't afford to think of the implications of what he was doing, only that he had to do it. It might seem mad but it also seemed right. He snatched up one or two things that might be useful and, dragging along an orderly who seemed to be doing nothing in particular, jumped into his car for the short drive to the sea. The tide was only just coming in, so they had to leave the car and make a punishing run across the sand until they reached the surf. With a few crude receptacles and a bemused assistant to help him, Hassim set to work to capture the sea and bring it to Maimouna.

They were soon back, carrying an unwieldy cooler, the kind

that medicines were transported in. It was full of sea water which sloshed around and splashed out from its ineffective lid. Yaye's eyes were sceptical as she appraised this unprepossessing vessel.

"We're in luck, Yaye!" Hassim said, sweating and breathing hard. "The tide was coming in!"

The old woman threw back her head and laughed, showing her few remaining teeth. She laughed until it looked as though she might fall. The more she laughed, the less it sounded like laughter until, swaying from exertion, she let out a cry that hung in the air like the call of an unseen forest bird, melodious but tinged with danger, an eerie sound that seized the hearts of all who heard it. At last she was silent and her head fell to her chest. When she looked up again, the crotchety old matriarch was gone, and Yaye Coumba, wise woman of Nianing stood in her place. Saliou looked away, knowing defeat when he saw it.

First, she motioned Ndeye to bring a chair and place it next to her. She covered the seat with a wad of folded cloth. Next, she took a large conch shell from her basket, filled it with sea water and balanced it on the chair. Light shimmered on the water dancing in the shell's translucent heart. Slowly, she lowered her hands into the water, up to her wrists, and kept them there as her lips began to move. She lifted her hands from the water, held them steady as salt rivulets drained back into the shell, then brought them to her lips, as she mouthed her exhortations. Her hands returned to the shell – fingers to water, fingers to lips, fingers to water – and the prayers from Yaye's mouth fused with the salt sea water in a circle repeated many times until its sanctification was complete.

"Will a man who loves this child hold her body so that she can receive the blessing from the sea?" The air in the room shivered with a new sound. Yaye Coumba's voice was always strong, but now it had none of the hectoring quality that she was known for, none of the querulousness or the sheer irritation felt by the very old at still being alive.

Saliou felt tears threatening his eyes. He heard the compassion in Yaye's voice, but felt the breath of her world hot in his face. He wanted to leap up, press Maimouna to his chest and let the ancients guide her back into life. But he could not. His feet were soldered to the floor, his buttocks welded to the chair. For what had been all those years of scientific study? Would it be an admission of personal failure? He didn't know. All he was able to do was to turn towards his wife's cousin, the half-Lebanese outsider, a fellow doctor who, unlike him, seemed able to put down his stethoscope to listen to the pulse of the spirits.

Hassim nodded and went over to the other side of the bed, opposite to where Yaye continued to pray. As he passed Khadi and her mother, he felt a light hand on his shoulder. He knew instinctively that it was Magdalene wishing him well, not Khadi, whose arms were still locked around her body.

"What must I do, Yaye?" he asked.

"Lift her from the bed and hold her so that she may receive the blessing."

Hassim tried to ignore the sudden outburst of coughing coming from Saliou who, he knew, would be silently screaming warnings about tampering with the tubes or disturbing the fragile head. He drew back the sheet that was covering Maimouna. She looked so tiny lying there in her short hospital gown, her limbs so thin and black against the stark white sheet. With tender care, he undid the first two ties of her gown, exposing the sharp definition of her ribcage and its faint rise and fall. Then he squatted beside the bed and began to make his arms into a hammock on which Maimouna could safely lie. He arranged her legs so that her knees were the apex of a triangle and slipped his arm beneath it. Making sure that the I.V. remained unblocked, he braced himself against one of her shoulders and curled his other arm up and around her head, so that his finger tips touched her other shoulder, holding Maimouna beneath her knees and her shoulders, supporting but not putting pressure on her stricken head.

In this pose, Hassim waited. Could this be called "lifting the one who suffers from the bed"? Could it be interpreted as "immersing her in the incoming tide"? Had due process been observed? He waited for Yaye Coumba to make her ruling.

Yaye paused from her silent supplications, perhaps just long enough for her to blink once, twice at Hassim, crouched and awkward by the bed. And then she started up again, filling her lungs, her lips moving rapidly, mouthing words.

Then the prayers ceased. In the stillness, it seemed that Maimouna alone drew breath, and her breathing was so quiet it could scarcely be heard. Yaye became active again, bringing the chair closer, repositioning the shell so that it was within easy reach of her hand. She glanced at Hassim, his arms strong and protective around the sleeping child. From her corner of the room, Khadi dropped her eyes, hoping that no one noticed the unseemly flush she felt at seeing the strength of Hassim's arms around Maimouna.

He felt sweat soaking his shirt as one of Yaye Coumba's hands disappeared into the water and emerged like a weathered cup made of the hide of animals, shining with the water that seeped between her fingers. Into that cup she dipped her other hand and in swift smooth movements, her fingers touched the closed eyelids, the bridge of the nose, the lower lip, the upper lip, the temples, the ears. Her touch was so light that the water left only the barest shimmer on Maimouna's skin.

"Where are you, my daughter? What do you see? What do you hear?" As she turned to the shell again, her questions hung in the air. She was oblivious of anything else in the room: life began and ended with the words from her mouth and the actions of her hands. There was desire in every heart that Yaye Coumba perform a miracle, but the certainty in every mind that she could not.

Saliou went over to his wife. It was not about modernity versus the old ways any more. The time for that debate had passed. All he could do was to clasp Ndeye to him, bearing her up, being borne up by her. They both wanted the same thing: for Yaye Coumba to open up a channel, hidden from the I.V. drip and the brain scan, through which Maimouna could pass and return to their waiting arms. But as they waited, they called out to Allah in the prayer for the dying. Saliou took a string of beads out of his wife's hands and started to say them while Ndeye spoke the prayer out loud, over and over again.

"Oh Allah, I ask of thee a perfect faith, a sincere assurance, a reverent heart…" Her voice was part of the air, a background out of which Yaye's older voice emerged.

"What do you feel, my daughter?" Yaye Coumba spoke softly as she placed her wet fingers on the child's hands, then her breast bone and left them there for a moment while the wasted chest rose and fell.

"…a remembering tongue, a good conduct of commendation, and a true repentance…"

Magdalene began murmuring "Hail Mary, full of grace…" and fragments of phrases of the sacrament of extreme unction came to her from her Catholic childhood in a St. Lucian valley, beneath the benevolent gaze of the black saints painted on the church walls. She made the sign of the cross and caught her daughter's questioning eye.

"What will you do, my daughter?" Yaye asked, turning away again, busying herself with the water.

Hassim shifted slightly, to get some relief for his aching thigh muscles. But despite his physical discomfort, he felt at peace. This wasn't about faith. He had seen too many hypocrites around to give religion any place in his life. Whatever grief might be awaiting them, he had no regrets about fetching Yaye Coumba. She alone had been able to bring them all together in the dignity of this ceremony, to be in this room at this moment, either willing life back into Maimouna or preparing her and themselves for her journey out of it. Either way, he had "done no harm", the first principle of his profession.

"…repentance before death, and forgiveness and mercy after death, clemency at the reckoning, victory in paradise…" intoned Ndeye, rocking back and forth.

Yaye turned back to the child and said, "Will you continue the journey you began when the sea called you three days ago?"

As Yaye's whispered question floated on the back of the Arabic prayer, Khadi stood apart, feeling more alone than she had ever felt in her life. She was not one of God's people. There was nothing in her life to help her here. Everyone else – her mother, her father, Ndeye, Hassim – had found some way to bear witness as the outriders of death blew into the room. She and the specialist from France had to watch, futile and godless, as she who was most favoured slipped away.

Ndeye's words mirrored the inevitability of it all. "…May my closing acts be my best acts and the best of my days be the day when I shall meet thee…"

Something in Yaye Coumba was changing. Her body seemed stronger, her voice more resonant, her words and her actions challenging the acceptance of fate. "Or will you fulfil the journey that you began seven years ago on the day of your birth?" She allowed almost all of the water to drain from her fingers and in a powerful gesture, held her hand high over Maimouna's body.

"Will you grow and ripen…" – Yaye let a few drops of water drip onto her hospital gown, just below her navel – "…and nourish the many lives that yet lie sleeping inside you?"

"Will you return?" Her outstretched arm reached up, solid and strong, and her voice boomed with the sound of the shore.

Yaye, who had appeared to grow younger, stronger, seemed now to shrink back to her accustomed wizened proportions. Even her voice seemed diminished.

"The sea has given her blessing."

No one dared to speak.

The old woman stood panting and trembling. She looked as though she would faint. She held onto the chair and fought to keep herself upright. Furtive glances were exchanged among the others but no-one dared to budge.

Just as Saliou was about to offer assistance, Yaye straightened herself and was on the move again. Reaching into her battered basket, she took out a jar with a torn label declaring it to be "*confiture fraises*". It contained a thick beige-coloured paste which smelled of rotting vegetation. She applied a small knob to her palms. As she worked the paste into her skin, the sound of dry leaves scraping together died away as the butter warmed and liquified.

With her hennaed palms held up to reveal their gleaming surfaces, she said, "Will a woman who loves this child help to anoint her with *karite* so that she can receive the blessing from the earth?"

Before Ndeye had taken a full step forward, Yaye shook her head. "It cannot be the mother." Ndeye leaned back, speechless and shaken.

"I will, Yaye Coumba."

Magdalene extended her hands and flinched at the old wom-an's touch. Her hands were burning! Magdalene closed her eyes and bit her bottom lip as the ancient hands transferred the oil of healing onto hers. She walked to the other side of the bed, her head light, her hands tingling from the contact. She took her place at the bedside, looking straight at Yaye, with Maimouna, lying grey and faltering between them.

"With the touch of our hands, we will render the earth's blessing."

Magdalene watched as Yaye laid hands on Maimouna's arm and travelled its length, flexing the joints, stretching the arm and each of the fingers. Yaye's eyes were closed and she hummed as her hands explored the contours beneath them. Magdalene took a deep breath and placed her hands on the other arm, the one pierced by the tube through which a clear liquid flowed. It was smooth and cool and as Magdalene's hand moved towards the child's fingertips, the coldness deepened. So did Magdalene's sense of dread. She looked over at Yaye whose eyes were still closed, who continued to hum in rhythm with the movement of her hands. It seemed that Yaye never let go for an instant. Skin against skin; old skin against young, holding on with eloquent fingers.

And so Magdalene put aside her fear and tried to learn the language of touch. She didn't let go but kept on kneading the flesh, feeling the resistance of muscle and bone, seeing the skin drink in the oil, like desert sand under rain.

There was a change in Yaye's humming and Magdalene saw her dip her fingers into the jar decorated with faded pictures of French strawberries, saw her recharge her hands with *karite* and prepare to massage the legs. Magdalene leaned over to receive her share from Yaye's hands and found less of the earlier heat. The humming started up again and for a few minutes, the two women found a rhythm of touch and of pressure. Maimouna's skin gleamed and Magdalene was sure that the leg seemed warmer. But soon Yaye Coumba's strokes became irregular, her humming erratic until finally, she stopped, looked at Magdalene and tilted towards the floor. Ndeye caught her and led her to a chair. Magdalene saw this but did not stop.

Without losing her rhythm and without looking around, she said in English, "Come here, Khadi. Maimouna needs you."

Khadi was trembling violently as she walked to the side of the bed. Saliou's hands supported her from behind as her mother leaned across and held out her hands so that Khadi could get her share of the oil. Their eyes touched before their hands did and in that look Khadi found a calm centre from which to carry out the duty before her. So it was no surprise to her that her mother's touch seared her hands and that Maimouna's leg seemed made of marble and that the movement of her hands brought warmth to the coldness and the skin sang with the oil from the earth and the strength from her fingers could feel the living bone beneath and the water from her eyes and the oil from her hands mixed and merged in a double anointing.

Then Yaye raised her ancient eyes to Magdalene and Khadi, made a short humming sound, then stopped. She struggled to her feet and once more the power was upon her. Her feet sent roots into the ground and her arms were the stretching boughs of an ancient tree. When she spoke, it was thunder rolling over the ocean.

"Will you return, my daughter?"

Silence fell into the void as Yaye shut her eyes and willed her body to become stone.

"Maimouna! Answer!"

The anointing was over.

Where are you, my daughter?

The doorway! Pulling me… pulling me in…

Maimouna could not finish but once more felt a mighty pull down into the liquid darkness of her mind, tumbling down ever down into the timeless ocean. No day no night no sea no shore no yesterday no tomorrow only now. Only now.

Now came the visions of the dark world.

People in rows… Screaming…

Shadows slipped past her, their necks taut and bloody in iron collars, walking on wounded feet in sunlight while clanking chains cut into their ankles; then locked in darkness in the belly of a ship which heaved and wailed as a river of vomit and blood and pus and shit churned around them.

It's me screaming… My voice… Can you hear it, Yaye? Oh help me…

She squeezed her eyes shut and blocked her ears and let the current roll her away.

What do you feel?

Maman! … Don't leave me here… I promise to be quiet… to be good…

The power of the ocean surge abated and all was suddenly calm. Maimouna's trembling eased as she drifted through the cool darkness. She drifted down, with her arms outstretched and turning, drifted down like a slowly spinning top, drifting into peace, into darkness.

This… I want this… sleep…

What will you do? Will you continue the journey you began when the sea called you three days ago?

Sleep, Yaye… that's all…

A rest from her travails was all that she wanted. The sea where she was now dwelling kept soothing her with sweet lullabies, only to cast her into more rough journeys, more strange vistas. New terrors were presented to her.

No more!

Human flesh weighed and sold. Shamed. Scourged. Stamped with burning brands.

No more seeing or hearing…

Empty eyes that could not weep. Silent tongues too lost to speak.

No more talking, Yaye...

Or will you fulfil the journey that you began seven years ago on the day of your birth? Will you grow and ripen and nourish the many lives that yet lie sleeping inside you?

Grow? Ripen? Live? Why?

She yearned for an escape from the nightmare as she plunged further down towards the ocean floor, away from the swarming phantoms, all dancing in a fearful masquerade of children. Children of war, of disease, of hunger, of abandonment, of despair. She did not want to look upon the child soldiers, the child gangsters, the child whores, the child corpses and the rest of the monstrous cavalcade. She longed only to feel the weight of the mighty waters on her, pressing her down, spinning her soul into a complete and final oblivion.

Why come back?... It's so lovely here...

For the ocean had revealed its other face to her, its beauties, its luminous darkness, its great creatures and its small, its stars and its flowers. She would just lie there, cradled as though by a strong hammock, with gentle drops of water cooling her, and fall into a dreamless eternity of no sound or speech or image or thought.

Just sleep, Yaye, just rest...

Will you return?

Do I have to? I told you I just want to... But you won't let me, Yaye. I feel you... I feel your hands touching me... Pulling me up... Pulling and stretching... No! I don't want to... I like it down here... quiet and cool... Your hands are hot, Yaye! And the other ones, too... They won't let me go, won't let me go... I feel myself rising, Yaye... feel the bottom of the ocean dropping beneath me, yet still trying to hold on to me. And you, you keep pulling me up towards you. Out of the darkness... Yaye, where are you? Where have you gone! Oh, don't leave me!... My mind! It's spinning and falling back down again. But... someone else has taken your place... Who is she? I feel like I know her... Rising again... The water is warmer... clearer. Something bright is shining through it, coming closer and closer. I am sailing towards it... Oh! The light is so bright, Yaye, and it's shaped like an arch. No, not an arch. A hole... Something... A door to somewhere... And it's all on fire!

Will you return, my daughter?

No, Yaye! Can't! Afraid... afraid of it. It took me too far... But I'll try...

Maimouna!

My name! I'd forgotten, just like I've forgotten the people who are with you... And there it is just ahead. The doorway! I'll pass through it again, Yaye. I'll try to come back to you and the others. I'll be brave like the warriors Papa used to tell me about. Papa! He's there with you... I remember him now... I'll be the strongest warrior and I won't be vanquished... I won't be afraid. Or at least I'll try not to be... I'll try...

Answer!

1 2.

KHADI: ECHOES OF THE DEEP

"*Allahu Akbar!* Almighty God, the Most Gracious, Most Compassionate, grant thy everlasting mercy to this, thy daughter. Grant her thy perfect forgiveness; reward her for her good works and keep her with the righteous in the Hereafter. Admit her this day, Most Merciful God, to dwell with Thee forever in Paradise."

The imam said these words in a whisper, conscious that at his side the monseigneur of the district was addressing similar exhortations to the Father, Son and Holy Ghost. They were seated in a stifling room among the bereaved, and both were aware that in this place, at this time, their gods were outranked by more ancient deities. The burial had already taken place, all rites performed and in this brief hiatus before the great mass of mourners descended, both men of God had seized the opportunity to acknowledge, in their different ways, the passing of Yaye Coumba.

A few hours after the anointing of *karite* and sea water, Maimouna had opened her eyes, smiled and squeezed her mother's hand. Yaye Coumba had slept on a mat in the child's room that night and the next morning had almost come to blows with Saliou and Hassim when she'd refused to let either of them drive her home. No, she and Bintou, the unmarried great-niece who looked after her, would take a bush taxi, stop off along the way to have lunch with a relative and then complete the journey in the afternoon. It was useless to try and change her mind. By the time Saliou and Hassim had gathered everyone together to say goodbye, Yaye had gone.

She and Bintou had arrived in Nianing in the heat of the afternoon, siesta time, and were able to slip in unnoticed, with Yaye making straight for her spot beneath the shade tree, easing her bones down onto the carved stool which, over time, had worn comfortably to her contours.

"Do you hear it?" Her old head turned slowly.

"Yes, Yaye. It's calm today." There was the quiet whisper of waves breaking on the sand just beyond the yard's palm frond boundary.

"Yes." Yaye's hands fidgeted with a part of her boubou.

"You are not content, Yaye? The child woke up. The child is well."

"No, not yet content... She does not speak."

Tests showed the effective functioning of all her vital organs, but why was the bright-eyed child mute?

"But Yaye," said the great-niece, "she will. She is just tired now. Tired from too much dreaming."

There was a soft light in Yaye's milky eyes as she lifted them to this plain, self-effacing woman, now nearing sixty, so often taken for granted. "You are right, Bintou. Too much dreaming. I will sit for a while now... Bring me some water." She let go of the cloth that she had been twisting and pointed towards the corner of the yard with a steady hand. As the great-niece turned to go, Yaye added, "The others will do the rest."

Accustomed as she was to Yaye's riddles, Bintou went without comment to the clay *canari*.

"No. From the bottle."

Bintou shrugged her shoulders, entered the dark house and, squinting, located the two bottles of mineral water that were brought for Yaye every day – and which Yaye never used. But the years had taught Bintou to expect the unexpected. She smiled as she wiped and filled the cup then stepped back outside. The sunlight blinded her at first. Then she saw the empty stool.

The cup fell from her hands as she grasped what had happened. There was never any question as to where she should look. She found Yaye lying on her back, just where the smallest waves broke. When the sea drew back, she lay on a bed of shining sand. And when the sea returned, it washed right over her, making her blue gown smooth and iridescent with refracted light.

The ululations announcing the death tore the air, sounding like a congregation of cormorant, ibis and tern, as the family, the clan, the village and almost, it seemed, the entire region made ready to say farewell to the matriarch whose life had become legend long before she had closed her eyes for the last time. By sunset, Yaye was in the hands of women – the closest by blood, the oldest, the wisest, as well as the young ones in the full flood of fertility – all there to keep watch over her, to sing to her, to whisper messages in her ear in what the men – banished and for the moment irrelevant – knew was a secret language. During their long night vigil they prepared her for her transition, bathing her in scented water, as they did a young girl on the eve of her wedding, then winding her in her final garment, the white cloth that women had woven. In a place of honour sat the great-niece, Bintou, acknowledged at last for her years of uncomplaining service. When the sun had fully risen the next day, the men came and claimed her, coming in silence through the crowded yard and bearing her away to the place of burial. They committed her body to the earth, amidst prayers to the ancestors, in a shady corner near to the sound of the shore.

Saliou was among the men who laid Yaye Coumba to rest and when it was time for them to place the tiny shrouded body in the grave, he felt a prickling behind the eyes. He was thinking about the hasty conversation he'd had with his colleague from Marseilles, jubilant that his experimental drug had at last pulled the child out of deep unconsciousness. The specialist from France was now in a state of excitement at the new challenge posed by Maimouna's inability to speak. Yes, he was sure there were things that could be done, strategies that could be tried. In the gleam of those blue eyes, Saliou could see the text of his colleague's article in a prestigious medical journal.

But as he walked among the press of people, as he heard the expressions of condolence, some elaborate, some simple, some genuine, some self-serving, as he passed the bowed heads of the imam and the priest, as he glimpsed the mobilization of resources needed to feed and accommodate the multitude that was gathering, his deepest feelings were of gratitude to the old woman. Some mystery had dictated that there should be a death and Yaye Coumba had seen to it that it was hers. He had been in that hospital room. In his heart he knew that whatever the congress of learned physicians said, it was Yaye who had returned Maimouna to them.

Back in Dakar, Ndeye was steadfast at Maimouna's bedside. At her request, Saliou had arranged for a cot to be set up in the room so she could be there as much as she wanted to. She would be going nowhere. The birth cord that had almost been severed was once more intact as she talked softly to the child and watched as Maimouna drank in the comfort of her mother's presence like an infant at the breast.

All other witnesses to Yaye Coumba's double anointing of Maimouna were either preparing to go to pay their respects, were en route or already there. Saliou, *le responsable*, looked detached as he took his place at the heart of his people; Hassim said nothing as he sat with the men, solemn after the burial; Magdalene, in a hot, packed car, fixed her eyes on the pale quivering leaves of the neem trees at the side of the highway; Khadi still in the city, fussed over what to wear, finding it hard to get into a car that would take her away from Maimouna.

When all were there, each felt alone in the presence of the community around them, as it lived the ferment of the hour – the healing and succumbing, the living and dying. Each of them felt as though they were in a cocoon of silence, no matter what was going on around them. When night fell and the village bulged and burst with its flood of people, when the vast assembly was fed to fullness, when drums sounded and dust whirls danced among the stamping feet, when veteran storytellers grew hoarse trying to outdo each other with tales of Yaye Coumba, when the celebrations of her life reached their climax, for them there was only stillness and separation.

Later that day, from the corners of the village, they drifted towards one another.

"Hello! Hello!" Magdalene called in English, seeing Saliou ahead. He turned and with a slight smile, guided her towards the periphery of a courtyard where a griot from a distant village was eulogizing the departed. When they found some space, they stopped to listen, only to hear a familiar voice.

"Mummy! Papa!" Their sudden appearance together took Khadi by surprise and she rushed forward. Pressing herself between them, she felt like a little girl again, no more than four years old. Embarrassed, she dropped back and gestured to her parents to listen to the singer's strong voice floating high above the cascading kora. The three of them stood still with the music swirling around them. Saliou was the first to become aware of Hassim's approach. He was almost in front of Khadi before she realized who it was.

"Oh, Hassim, I'm so glad you're here!" Magdalene exclaimed. "Is there anywhere we can go and sit down?" she asked Saliou. "My feet are killing me."

He took them away from the music and dancing to a small darkened house on its own in the middle of a spacious yard. In a village where more and more dwellings were constructed of cement and galvanize, this was of painted mud brick. No one was around as they crossed the yard and went into a room where a paraffin lamp was burning. Each found a chair or a stool. In one corner there was a small table with a few upturned glasses and some bottles of mineral water; in another a stack of towels in a plastic box and a neat bed enrobed with fine mosquito netting. On the shelf next to the bed were several framed photographs and a battery-powered fan.

Magdalene broke the silence. "Whose house is this? It's not your average…"

"It belongs to Ndeye." Saliou tried to speak in a matter-of-fact way, but failed to conceal the sudden yearning in his voice. Hassim came to his rescue.

"When each of old Malik Diop's daughters got married, he built a house for her like this…"

"In case the husband turned out to be no good… His daughters would know they had somewhere to come back to…" Saliou's laugh was not altogether convincing.

"All of Ndeye's sisters," Hassim went on, "knocked down the houses built for them and rebuilt them in concrete, but Ndeye refused to. She kept the house her father built for her. Whenever she comes home, it's here she stays."

Magdalene was peering at the faces in the photographs; some she recognized, some she did not. The half light softened them, smudging the barriers between young and old, living and dead.

"It always looks like this," added Hassim. "Ready. As though she's just about to walk through the door."

When Magdalene had finished examining the photos, she resumed her seat and silence fell, broken only by the scampering of rats along the rafters.

"Ah, Ndeye…" Saliou's voice faltered.

"It's as though she's here," Magdalene said softly.

"*Comment?*"

"Your wife. It's like she's here. It feels as though we're all here – with Ndeye – in this room, Maimouna in all our hearts. And Yaye. Well, Yaye… everywhere." She paused. "Yes, we're all here."

There was a nodding of heads, acknowledging the bond the anointing had created. But still no one else spoke. The intensity of the silence increased as the sea breeze suddenly dropped. Saliou was mopping his face with a handkerchief while Magdalene fanned herself with the scarf draped around her shoulders. Even Khadi, who could normally appear cool in blistering heat, found herself wiping her brow. Hassim sat like a marble carving, seemingly impervious to heat or silence.

Then, as suddenly as it had disappeared, the breeze started up again, blowing straight off the dark waves breaking on the shore. Its cool breath unlocked their tongues.

"You would never know by looking at her…"

"Trauma. It's the trauma…"

"But the specialist says there's some drug therapy that can…"

"A short term loss… that's what we can hope for…'

"Just sitting up as bright and breezy, like nothing happened…"

"She might have to learn how to talk again… as though she'd had a stroke…"

"People who've had a stroke don't look like they're just about to go out to play…"

"Always writing things down on that notepad they gave her…"

"Yes, writing, when gestures aren't enough…"

"She'll have her own sign language soon…"

"Have you seen the pictures?"

"Pictures? What pictures?"

"Of who?"

"Of everybody. All of us. Her brothers. The nurses. You should have seen the one she did of Hodia, after she'd come to visit. A classic! Then she always did like to draw…"

Conversation paused as they looked outside at the dance of the fireflies.

"Well, Saliou, what do you think? Honestly." Magdalene paused. "It is, after all, the season of miracles."

"The miracle is that she is alive." His voice was firm. "As for not being able to speak, she'll have to go a more conventional route to get over this one, I fear." Even in the dimness, the hunching of Saliou's shoulders was visible, as was the straightening that followed. "What do you think, Hassim?"

Hassim didn't answer right away. At last, he said, "It's hard to say with brain injuries. There's so much we don't know. The scans don't indicate anything that looks like permanent damage. Etienne has all sorts of ideas about therapies that we can try... I think we must try them. And soon. The longer Maimouna continues without speech, the better she'll be able to manage without it, the harder it will be for her to get it back."

"Is it possible that she doesn't want to speak?" Magdalene was brave enough to ask.

Saliou stretched his legs and arms before getting up and slowly going over to get water for everyone. They knew him well enough to know that this activity was a means of deflecting his desire to issue a reprimand. By the time he handed Magdalene her glass, he was able to say in a calm voice, "No, Madeleine, it is not possible."

"It was just a question. An obvious one. I didn't mean to upset you."

"No," he continued, "everything she's done since she woke up shows that, more than anything, she wants to communicate. We don't know why she can't talk. But we know she wants to. We'll find a way. But it might take time."

Now Magdalene stood up, but unlike Saliou she did not pretend she had something to do, but took a few aimless steps forward and then back. She looked over at Khadi who had closed her eyes, fearing a scene between her parents. Magdalene circled the room until she stood behind Khadi, and began lightly massaging her shoulders.

"Saliou, so much has happened in the past few days, few weeks... It's been so good to be here... to be with everyone. Everything was going so well and then... Disaster..." Magdalene's gaze was fixed on Saliou, his face dark and attentive in the flickering light. She could not see that the water in Khadi's glass was trembling. "You know… We can't foresee disasters… We just wake up in the morning and there they are! Undeserved. Inexplicable. We talked about that, didn't we, Didi?" She sighed, her fingers still pressing into Khadi's flesh. "But we've been lucky. Maimouna's life has been spared. And I believe you when you say she'll talk again. If love brought her back from the brink, then love will make her talk again." Magdalene placed her hands flat on Khadi's shoulders. "I'd hoped to leave with Maimouna completely better, but I see that probably isn't going to happen. But at least, we'll be able to go, pretty confident that she's on the road to recovery."

"Leave?"

"When?"

Saliou and Hassim spoke almost at the same moment.

"Why… soon… In the next few days. On the Sunday flight. I thought you knew. We've already had to put back our booking once. I thought you knew. I'm sure I told you."

"Probably. But with all the confusion…"

Everyone was aware of the steady darkening in the room. Just outside there was the rustling music of the night and, more distantly, the pounding drumbeat of Yaye Coumba's fête. Inside the room, the oil lamp hissed its way to extinction.

Soon they sat in the dark.

"Yes," Magdalene said. "Sunday night to New York. Then back home for me the next day."

"*Sainte Lucie?*" Saliou asked.

"Where else?"

"Oh, I don't know. I got the feeling that you were less than enamoured of the place. That the return was not all that you'd hoped it would be."

"If not St. Lucia, where would you suggest I go?"

"Well, you lived all those years in London. You must have liked it. At least it didn't have all those – what do you call them – 'island irritations'…"

"But hasn't Europe – England – become unliveable for black people?"

"It has. And it hasn't. Well, it's true I did some good things there. But maybe I just overstayed my welcome... What do you think?"

Saliou hesitated. Magdalene had thrown him off balance. Here she was drawing him into this quasi-frivolous discussion about her future. He remembered it well – this knack she had of annoying and engaging him simultaneously, as well as her ability to land the occasional incapacitating blow to the solar plexus. There was a tiny corner of his heart where he missed it. Against his better judgment, he would let this conversation go wherever it wanted to.

"So why not here? You could stay in Senegal and make films. It's a great place for making films. Before Maimouna's fall, you'd started working on..."

"Wait a minute! Stay here? As what? Your second wife?"

"My what?"

"But how exactly would that work? I was your first wife. First in sequence. If I were to marry you again, that would stay the same. I would still be the first woman you'd married. But if you married me again, I would be co-wife with Ndeye... Now, let's see. I would need a house of my own, not just a handful of rooms in the villa. A car, of course. But then, even with a big house – equivalent to the villa – I would be second in hierarchy, in seniority, even though I'm a good ten years older. She would be first and I would be second in ranking order. No. No, I don't think so. As nice as Ndeye is and as handsome as you still are, I'm going to have to turn you down. Thanks for asking, though."

Although she could not see him, Magdalene knew he would be shaking his head at her brazenness. Then a deep bass note, started down in his belly, travelling through his chest into his throat in a series of guffaws and opening into the air as the great laugh he was known for. Magdalene added her riotous higher registers, and was joined by Hassim, glad to be swept up out of his brooding into this sudden music. Khadi hovered on the edge, unsure but envious, until she heard her mother topple from her stool onto the floor. Heaving her up and stabilizing the stool while the ample backside found its place once more, Khadi felt the laughter locked inside her burst out. It started as a groaned "Mum!", as she felt her hand sandwiched between stool and backside, but then it was transformed into helpless peals of laughter, making her part of the melody that rocked the house that old Malik Diop had built for his favourite daughter.

When decorum had been restored and they were walking out into the yard, Magdalene stopped and looked at Saliou.

"It really is time for me to go home. I can't be relied upon to behave myself for much longer." They both chuckled. "And, anyway, it's not only the islands that have 'irritations'! I'm sure you remember the French ones… And what about African irritations? I think we can agree that there are some!"

Saliou dropped his head and smiled.

"Yes. I've got to get back," she continued. "There are so many things I want to do." She looked straight ahead into the night. "I'm ready."

"You've always been looking for home, Madeleine. I don't know what that feels like."

"Well, of course, for you, home just *is*. A family, a system, a country, a continent… You're lucky. So lucky…" Magdalene paused. "But for me, it's not a place; it's a *feeling*. And strange as it might seem, ever since I got here, I've started to *feel* that other place, that island, in a way that I never have before. That it might suit me and I might suit it, no matter how much we get on each other's nerves. I love it here, Saliou, always have. So big. So… sure, despite all the chaos… But I've never felt it from the inside, the way you should about home."

He looked steadily at her.

"*Oui. C'est ça.*"

"And anyway, as Antoine used to say, wherever I go, I take Africa with me." She said this without looking at him. "And besides, I have some ideas for when I get back home. There's that lot of land my father left me. Wild and overgrown. On the Atlantic coast. A great place for a house. A very extraordinary house, of course. You know we have a pair of hills called Les Mamelles there too. Maybe on a clear day, I'll be able to look out and see…"

Saliou and Magdalene continued to walk towards the centre of the village, chatting companionably, their banter ranging from future plans to old times, to issues of the day. But for Khadi and

Hassim, there was still the abyss that had opened up the day their jeep had fallen into the ditch. Since that night, they had not exchanged a single word, or even looked at each other until just an hour or so ago when Khadi had looked up and found Hassim staring at her as the kora player sang to the memory of Yaye Coumba. Their talk was tense and stilted. Both knew there was unfinished business between them.

It had begun well in the restaurant.

"Delicious!" Khadi exclaimed as she finished the last morsel of her dish of mutton couscous.

"I hope it's not too down-market for you," said Hassim, glancing at the modest decor. "I know you're used to a higher degree of... sophistication." There was an exaggerated leaning on the final word.

"You're the only person who thinks I'm 'sophisticated'. When anyone else sees me, they see a *fille du pays.*"

They laughed, nervous, brittle laughter. However, inside, each of them had been in good spirits. Hassim had congratulated himself on the choice of *La Marocaine* – absence of chic, but good location and good food – and Khadi for choosing from the simpler end of her wardrobe. Yes, this had been promising. So when they were leaving and Hassim asked if she minded if they stopped by his house, she'd replied "Of course not!" with the minimum of clumsiness.

His house was in darkness when they entered. As soon as he'd flicked the switch and light had spilled into the tousled space that looked and smelled and felt so like him, she had felt the freezing begin and knew that another fiasco was at hand. But instead of turning away from his first caress, she had locked herself down and gone into full performance mode, faking every look, every moan, every touch as they made their way to his rumpled bed. But he had seen through her.

"Put your things back on," he said in a tone that made her want to crawl away into a hole and never emerge. "I'll wait for you in the car."

It had been a quieter, much sadder disaster than the first time, but Khadi carried the feeling around with her like a stone lodged in her gut. As her departure drew nearer, she longed to be rid of the weight of it, to try to mend fences and lift relations with Hassim to a more civilized plane. To maybe say she was sorry...

So she'd jumped at the opportunity when it presented itself in the form of an overheard conversation. Lunch was over, and Saliou was trying to persuade Ndeye to stay at home with the family that night. She'd agreed to do so but only if he stayed at the hospital instead.

"But she's getting so much stronger," he said. "She's only there under observation."

Ndeye shook her head.

"Can't she stay without either one of us for just one night?"

"Suppose something happens?"

"Nothing's going to happen, Ndeye. She's in good hands. She's getting the best care."

She looked at him, steely-eyed. "Either you sleep next to Maimouna or I sleep next to her. That's all there is to it."

Saliou sat in silence for a while. "What about Hassim? We could ask him!" He saw her knitted eyebrows become smooth at the mention of Hassim's name, so he pressed his advantage. "You would feel as confident about Hassim watching over her as me! That way, you could be home... and I could be home... at the same time."

Hassim readily accepted. From her half-hidden spot in the corner, Khadi decided to go to see Hassim at the hospital that night. Yes, she would go and see him and make things better.

And he wouldn't be able to act up with Maimouna right there.

In two days, Khadi said to herself, in two days, I'll be back in New York. She tried to concentrate on that thought but her mind failed to deliver a single image that connected her to her apartment or office in the metropolis. Instead, she'd kept rehearsing what she would say to Hassim. Now, through the door's narrow pane of glass, she could see him reading and sitting on the low cot where Ndeye usually slept. *Yes, I was on my way home from dinner at Tanti Naba's and I felt I just had to see Mai. So I told the taxi driver to...*

Hassim looked up from his book and saw her face. He beckoned her to come in. Her explanatory monologue evaporated. She stood for a moment while he looked pointedly at the clock. It was after midnight.

"Yes. *Bon soir*. I was on my way home from…"

"Well, now you're here, I'll be on my way." Hassim was almost at the door when Maimouna tossed off her cover, flung her arms out and made some gurgling sounds in her throat. Khadi quickly replaced the sheet, smoothing it across Mai's shoulders and stood looking down, a little anxious but glad that her body was itself again, free of tubes, with a shadow of hair growing where sections of her head had been shaved. Maimouna threw the sheet off again and continued searching for a comfortable spot.

"Is she always this restless?"

"Not at all. She was fine until you came."

Khadi glanced over to see if there were even the tiniest bit of humour in his eyes. No. She had known concrete blocks more expressive.

"I'm just down the hall, if she wakes up." His hand was on the door handle when Khadi said, "Aren't you forgetting something?" She held out the book he'd left lying on the floor. "*New Paradigms in Sub-Saharan Health Care* – Wow! This looks like a laugh a minute!" He did not react. She knew she sounded as arch as she had on the day they'd first met, and she tried to think of something more adult to say. She cast around for a lifeline.

There it was, stuck to the walls.

"So these are the pictures."

Maimouna turned over, once, twice, three times and then lay quiet.

"So these are the famous pictures," Khadi repeated, this time in a stage whisper, and started a tour of the drawings Maimouna had made in the seven days since her awakening.

"Hey! These are good! No, really! Some of them are really good, Hassim."

He stayed there, his hand on the handle, not moving.

"Look! There's storytelling in the yard! And this one – the boys, Amadou, Malik and Omar. She's even got Fatou holding Lamine, and looking her usual sour self." Khadi continued her commentary, not daring to look in Hassim's direction. "The bump on the head has evidently improved her technique… I'm

191

looking for the one of Hodia… You know, the one my father was talking about. It's got to be here somewhere…" Khadi heard the words tumbling from her mouth, pointless, empty, filling time. "Oh it's in this folder… with some of the others that aren't too flattering… That's Ndeye's censorship… Look how well she's managed Hodia's snarl… it's really…" She was replacing the folder on the table when she heard a noise. Maimouna was squirming again, making rasping sounds under her breath.

"You're disturbing her." Hassim's voice was quiet and cold. "If you want to talk to me, it'll have to be outside."

"Who said I wanted to…" Khadi stopped. "O.K. O.K." She followed him out to the hall.

"Why are you here?"

She opened and shut her mouth then managed to say, "Maimouna."

"I don't believe you."

"Believe what you like… Believe what you like." She blew air out of her mouth. This is not going well. She was suddenly aware that Hassim was riveted to the oblong pane of glass in the door, not paying her the slightest attention.

"What's wrong?"

He didn't answer but went back into the room. Khadi followed.

Maimouna was sitting upright on her bed, swaying a little, with her legs dangling over the edge. She showed no trace of the agitation that had made her turn and twist only a few minutes before. Khadi bolted forward, fearing Maimouna would fall. But when she stood directly in front of the child, the dull open eyes showed no flicker of recognition and her lips seemed to speak in a silent, unknown language.

Khadi drew back.

Maimouna sighed deeply and then raised her two thin arms from her sides until they were two straight black lines, perfectly straight, perfectly parallel, lifted to the ceiling.

"What's she…" Khadi began. She stepped forward, but found her path blocked by what seemed like the iron bar of Hassim's arm.

Maimouna sighed again. Then the circling began.

It was a strange movement, somewhere between music and dance. Her small hands described slow circles away from her body, thin arms following the lead of the hands; her small head, crowned with an uneven scattering of braids, rolled front, side, back, side, front, in a smooth imitation of the hands. The top half of her body had become a sweetly turning wheel. She edged her feet onto the floor, her arms still circling, her head rotating. She stood for a moment, then sank to her knees, her eyes now shut and a look of serenity on her face. Finally, she lay on the floor with one arm under her head and the other relaxed beside her.

Hassim's iron arm continued to press Khadi back, though she had abandoned all thought of touching Maimouna. From a remote part of her mind, Khadi heard the injunction, "Never touch a sleepwalker."

Moments passed. Khadi both saw and heard the hand of the clock jerk to the next minute. Hassim dropped his arm and started scraping his fingers through his hair. Maimouna slept the sleep of angels on the cold hospital tiles.

"What should we do?" Khadi whispered.

Hassim shook his head in reply.

"It looks like it's over…"

"Shhhhh…"

"Why are you shushing me? She's dead to the world. She can't hear us. Even when her eyes were open, she couldn't see us. I'm sure she couldn't…"

But something was happening. Gone was the repose. The loose limbs were tightening and Maimouna was curled up into a fierce foetus, her short hospital gown accentuating the hard line of her back, as she lay on her side. She took a long breath and, with that breath, seemed to open the gates to marauders, to violators, to assassins. She fought them, her flailing arms and legs making powerful movements of defence.

Hassim lunged towards her but Khadi grabbed him, trying to pull him back, holding on to his shirt as he tried to throw her off.

"What's wrong with you? Can't you see she's going to hurt herself?" Hassim's eyes were wild.

"Don't touch her! Don't ask me why… But we shouldn't touch her!" He tried to take a step forward and she pulled him back by his shirt. He retreated to the wall as Maimouna writhed and battled on the floor.

Then it was over and her body resumed the position of the peaceful sleeper.

Hassim and Khadi hovered around her, their faces tight with the effort of trying to figure out what was going on. The clock on the wall grew loud as five times its hand clicked from one minute to the next.

"Think we should put her back to bed?"

Khadi nodded.

As they bent down, they could hear the grinding of teeth and her uneven breathing. They stumbled back as Maimouna stood and tried to cross the room. But there seemed agony in every step as she reached down to clutch her ankles and then reached up to soothe her neck. She couldn't continue and fell to her knees with her back exposed and cringing. Then the rolling began.

"Oh my God…"

"What's happening…"

Khadi and Hassim rushed to push the bed out of the way, then the table – anything that might hurt her. As Maimouna rolled around at their feet, her body flexed, in a posture between lying and sitting, her spine arched, her muscles bristling.

They did what they could to protect her but did not restrain her.

"Make her stop!" Hassim groaned, covering his eyes with his hand.

"She has to do it." Tears streamed down Khadi's face as she watched this cruel travesty of innocence.

Maimouna struggled to her knees with her arms loose at her sides and her head and shoulders slumped forward. Slowly, her hands grasped the sides of the drooping head and when she straightened up, her mouth was broken open in a scream, silent, malevolent, engulfing.

Some time later – they could not say how long – they put Maimouna back to bed. Hassim examined her thoroughly; her heart and lungs were working normally. They prodded her; she did not wake. For all the world, she looked like a seven year old in the midst of a good night's sleep.

Hassim collapsed in the chair, his head in his hands.

Khadi, though, was all nervous energy, walking around the room, picking up things, putting them down, studying the drawings, rearranging the bedside table. Anything was preferable to doing what Hassim was doing, sitting there, trying to find explanations for what they had seen.

Hassim got up.

"I'm going to call your father."

"What, now? In the middle of the night?"

"Yes. Right now. He needs to know." Hassim looked absent for a moment, then became focused. "Yes. He needs to know."

"Of course he does. But not right now. Not at almost two in the morning."

He moved towards the door.

"And what are you going to tell him?"

"That Maimouna has to be taken home. Immediately."

She looked puzzled.

"Because… because…" He came closer to her and spoke in a whisper. "Because if anyone else sees what we've just seen, it will make Maimouna… it will make her…"

"Make her what?"

He drew a long breath. "Vulnerable… to all the cranks in the country. To every would-be *marabout* in this city. To everyone wanting to make a franc, claiming to be able to cast out demons. Or there'll be barren women and beggars who will want her to bless them and bring them boy-children and wealth. To everyone who will want to take this… this…" Hassim waved towards where Maimouna had lain. He looked up and Khadi could see his eyes were full. "They will want to take it and use it and hurt her with it."

"No! That can't happen. We can't let that happen." Her thoughts were confused. "But aren't you the one who went and got Yaye Coumba? You weren't a man of science then! You went and got the sea water for her. And now… Now you're calling them all cranks! So, was Yaye a… crank? A con artist?"

"Of course not! She was the real thing." He moved closer.

"No!" Khadi shouted, holding up her hand. "Keep away! Just keep away."

"*De grâce!* Keep your voice down!" he urged in a loud whisper. "You're going to wake her!"

"She can't hear us!" Khadie snapped. "She won't wake up! You! You! I can't believe a word you say! First you make me

195

believe that Yaye Coumba reached down and pulled Mai back…"
She was breathing heavily.

"I never said that…"

"Not in words. But you meant it! You did!"

Hassim shook his head and said nothing.

"Now you say that this thing… whatever it is… that's now in Maimouna… that Yaye put it there when she was pulling her up… that…" Khadi was sobbing incoherently. "Now you say that other people like Yaye…"

"They're not like Yaye!" he cried.

"Other people like Yaye…"

"No!" Again he tried to come closer, desperate to be understood. A blistering look stopped him in his tracks. "There are so many *petits voyous* out there… So few healers…"

"They'll try to hurt her and make her into a…" She was sobbing so hard she could hardly catch her breath, "into a… a… freak show! Is this your precious Africa? Is that what you're telling me, Hassim?"

She clamped her arms around her body as if trying to keep herself from crumbling altogether. She had her back to him but heard him take a step towards her and then stop.

He cleared his throat.

"You are very … distressed. I know why you are in this state," he said softly. "It's not about the crooks and the false prophets. You've lived in America. You know all about those!" He paused. "It's about what happened in this room. Right here. What we experienced with Yaye Coumba. Then what we just saw."

Her back was still hard against him.

"I am a man of science, despite what Saliou may think. But I think science is broader and deeper than we imagine. Yaye helped to bring Mai back, of that I have no doubt. But what we saw tonight… I… I would have to say… that it was really just… the physical trauma she experienced manifesting itself… physically."

"Physical trauma manifesting itself physically? Hmph! I ask you… Did you see her face? Did you see the movements she was making? They didn't remind you of something? Huh?" She was right up in his face, goading. "Go on! Give me some more of your psycho-babble! Look me in the eye and tell me they were just 'physical manifestations'!"

Hassim looked her in the eye without flinching. "I don't know what we saw."

"I do!" The anger was leaving her, leaving emptiness, making room for the return of tears. "I was with her... in the last hours, minutes and seconds before she went in the water. I was there! I saw her face when she went into the *Maison*. She never had a clue about slavery before and I was there when she understood, when her mind took hold of it." Khadi remembered the heaviness that had draped the child as they'd waited for the ferry and the look of sorrow as she'd turned to take a last look at Gorée, how her head had fallen forward, as though she were incapable of keeping it upright.

"That may be it." Hassim's voice was calm, after a long silence. "Maybe... what she saw in Gorée was somehow... imprinted on her mind... on her body... Does that make any sense?"

"Maybe... You might be right... Who knows?" She looked drained.

"Come. Sit down." Hassim led her to the cot.

"Why are you so good to me?"

He tried not to hear her. "Sit."

"Why?"

"You need to rest." She did as she was told, grateful for this kindness. Grateful for him. She sat on the cot looking up at him and reached up and touched his cheek.

He was caught off guard and when he felt the warmth of her hand, his first instinct was towards flight. But the atmosphere in the room was still so charged that he found it hard to fling the hand off, as his mind directed him to. No, he would catch it by the wrist and gently put it from him. But he was too late. Khadi's other hand was on his other cheek and slowly drawing him to her.

She found his mouth and the kisses felt to him like being brushed by the wings of a hundred fluttering butterflies. Even so, he was afraid. He closed his eyes and tried not to respond as her fingers travelled the territory of his face, as if mapping him for the first time. She sought out the unvisited places, behind the ears, on the sides of the nostrils, the tender darkness beneath the eyes, the uneven coastline where his hair sprang from his scalp, the naked space between his lower lip and the growth on his chin. When he opened his eyes, he found her watching him, studying what had come to life beneath her hands, the image deeper than skin and flesh. Behind her tears was a bright and certain flame.

The utilitarian cot was not made for lovemaking, but Hassim and Khadi were thankful for it – it kept them off the cold, tile floor. She took him in her arms and their bodies made fresh discoveries. Their memories had played them false. He found her skin more luminous than before, her breasts richer, her limbs more welcoming. She had not remembered the hiding places afforded by the fine hair on his chest, or the glory in the sculpted muscles of his back and buttocks. They took their time as they paid homage to each other, to their bodies, to the souls that lived within. They were in no hurry and did not hear the cot creaking and groaning beneath them. They would not have heard if someone, some nurse, some night porter, some nocturnal wanderer, had walked in on them. But when Hassim lowered himself between Khadi's thighs, Maimouna, in her bed less than a foot away, made a noise and turned over. Khadi's eyes flew open in agitation.

He took her head between his hands and gently turned it towards him.

"She won't wake up," he said.

"How do you know?"

"Because you said so."

"Did I…" With one powerful movement, Hassim entered her body. "Yes…" Their eyes remained locked open as they began. "Yes…" The room became very hot. They gasped for air and the sweat poured from them. He was the blind man feeling the path forward and she was the guide, showing him the way. Their rhythm gained pace as desire consumed them. And there it was, the light in the distance, and how to get there was in giving and receiving and holding and releasing until the light in the distance became the light right before them: the light that blinded them and the light that made them see; the light that destroyed them and the light that made them whole. On their unlikely altar, they celebrated the communion of their lives.

It was very late.

Khadi yawned, her eyelids heavy, her limbs intoxicated with

love and sleep. Out of the corner of her eye, she saw Hassim walking to the door.

"Where are you going?"

"To get a chair. I promised Ndeye that I'd stay with Maimouna the whole night, remember. And I don't think we'll both be able to get much sleep on this thing." He patted the cot.

She smiled.

"Hassim?" Khadi turned to look at the steady rise and fall of Maimouna's chest.

"Yes?"

"Do you think she's done this before? Do you think anybody else knows about it?"

"This isn't the kind of thing you can keep secret. No. Nobody else knows. I'm sure of that."

When he returned with the chair, he found Khadi sleeping. He placed his chair alongside and tried to get comfortable. It was impossible so he squeezed himself next to her on the cot and they slept, like two spoons in a drawer.

Hassim woke just as the mourning doves had started their dawn lament outside the window. He shook Khadi lightly.

"We'd better get dressed. The nurses will be coming around soon."

They had only just dressed and positioned themselves, with Khadi sitting primly in the chair and Hassim standing looking like a doctor on his rounds, when they heard approaching voices. It was Ndeye and Saliou.

Trying to shake off any evidence of their night together, Khadi and Hassim braced themselves for this brusque return to the real world. Khadi plunged in first, anticipating a stern interrogation from Ndeye about her presence at the hospital during the night. "I came here from Tanti Naba's…"

"It's all right, Khadi." Saliou held up his hand. "Your mother told us." His manner was strained and there was a puzzling look on Ndeye's face. Despite this, Hassim decided that the moment had come for him to speak.

"Saliou. Ndeye. We have something to tell you." Khadi dropped her eyes and Ndeye's hand fluttered up to her mouth. "Something happened last night…"

His voice faltered and there was a brief silence, while he and Khadi struggled not to exchange a glance.

"Don't say any more, Hassim." Saliou looked at his wife, touched her shoulder and nodded by way of encouragement.

"Ndeye?"

Ndeye had said nothing until then, not even a greeting. She seemed to be in shadow, with no light coming from her. With a trembling hand, she reached into her bag, brought out a folded sheet and gave it to Hassim. He looked at it and passed it to Khadi.

Less than an hour later, Maimouna was awake and they were all making jokes with her as she ate the breakfast of *sombi* her mother had brought. She was excited, "talking" to them with signs and words written on a pad, delighted with the news that she was going home. Saliou left to make arrangements for Maimouna's release, while Hassim offered to drop Khadi home. Ndeye stayed to comb her daughter's hair and prepare her for her homecoming.

Later that morning, in the quiet of his office, Saliou shut his door and unfolded the sheet of paper his wife had shown him in the sanctuary of their bedroom. Never had he felt so much tenderness towards her as when she had woken him up in the night in tears and told her story of what she'd seen one night when she'd been alone with their daughter. Of how she had tried to keep it to herself until she'd found this drawing among all the others. *Xale-bi, dof-na!* Was their daughter really mad? Or was she something even worse... even more frightening... He had tried to comfort her as best he could.

Saliou looked at it as though trying to break the code on some ancient obelisk. The drawing was clear enough with parts of it done in great detail. But it was unfinished. It showed the hold of a ship whose timbers curved like the ribcage of some great sea creature. The hold seemed to breathe with some demonic life, and in it there were figures packed together closely, row upon row of them, neither sitting nor lying, their trunks and limbs interlocked, positioned for maximum storage. Neat, like sardines. Locked together in this hell chamber. The figures were only in outline but there was one, in the foreground, which was nearly finished. Its hands covered its ears and provided a frame for the face. It could hardly be called a face. Rather it was a mouth, magnified into a single, monumental scream.

The drawing was framed by what looked like an arch, the entrance of a tunnel, a doorway. The doorway was on fire.

13.

EBB TIDE

The farewell party was in full swing with a large crowd of well-wishers congregated at the Wades. It was intended as a goodbye to Magdalene and Khadi who were leaving that night, but it had merged into a welcome home celebration for Maimouna.

Magdalene was in her element, trying to organize a large troop of children into a game of "Pass the Parcel". The children had been restless and unwilling to sit in a quiet circle on the ground until Magdalene appeared holding an enormous, brightly wrapped parcel and told them that buried deep inside the many layers of paper, there was a prize. On the edge of the circle was Abdou, smiling, with a proprietary arm around Aminata.

"Was she really this much fun when I was seven?" Khadi asked with a sulk in her voice as Magdalene cranked up the music – Akon, singing about the ghetto – while the parcel began its journey around the circle of eager hands.

"Of course she was," Hassim laughed. "But you just couldn't see it. She's your mother."

"All I can remember her doing was telling me to do my homework."

"What do you want me to say? That she shouldn't have given you what you needed to become Miss Big Shot lawyer?"

"But when did she play 'Pass the Parcel' with me?"

Hassim raised his eyebrows.

"O.K. Every year, she gave some kind of party for me but…"

"But what?"

"Well…" She stopped. "Why aren't you on my side?" She made a face.

"Is this a pout I see?"

"And why are you so cheerful? I'm leaving tonight! How can you be so happy?"

"Because I know you're coming back."

"Oh!" This time she gave him a real smile. "But getting back to my mother… It's true. She was always on at me to work, work, work. And she's still doing it. I spent almost the whole morning working on that damn parcel with her. By the way, every layer has a prize. That's our Magdalene! Ever the egalitarian…"

Just then, a young woman tapped Magdalene on her shoulder and was instantly put in charge of the game.

"Who's that?" Hassim whispered.

"My mother's latest protégée. Her name is Anne-Marie Secka and Mum is determined that she should go back to school."

They walked away from the "Pass the Parcel" circle to an area across the yard where *tieb ou dien* was being prepared on a grand scale. It had been going on since early morning. A large cooler full of freshly caught snapper had been brought down by car from the Petite Côte and a contingent of girls and women had been pressed into service to gut, scale, slice and marinade it. A mixture of garlic and hot pepper was inserted into each slice, which was fried and dropped into a tomato sauce in which root vegetables were simmering. After the fish and vegetables were cooked and put to one side, the exquisitely flavoured broth was used to cook the rice, all fifty kilos of it in a cauldron the height of a school child. The rice had been picked through and washed and was waiting in a series of bowls to be added to the bubbling sauce. This was the critical moment. Any failure of nerve would mean either crunchy red rice guaranteed to produce indigestion or a red porridge guaranteed to produce nausea. Several veterans of rice wars barked orders but it was Ndeye who was the undisputed head of operations. She stirred the sauce with a large wooden paddle and gestured to Fatou to start adding the rice. Fatou poured in the shining grains, bowl after bowl, while Ndeye stirred, looking with a practised eye from the pot to the rice that remained. Even from where Khadi stood, she could see the muscles in Ndeye's arms as she stirred. Then she held up her hand to Fatou and placed the paddle on the ground. The rice was in; the charm was set. All they could do now was wait.

After this effort, Ndeye was relaxing with her team. The words of a now departed African leader came to Khadi's mind: I move among my people *comme un poisson dans l'eau*. Yes, that was Ndeye.

Ndeye suddenly looked up, feeling Khadi's eyes on her. The smile froze and died on her face, but then she nodded, as though in slow motion. Then she turned back to the other women.

"She's different," Khadi said as she and Hassim continued to make their way through the yard. "Tougher…"

"Hard times will do that."

"I don't mean it in a bad way," she added quickly. "I mean she seems to have more…"

"Authority?"

"Yes. That's it."

They were on the fringe of various activities. In one corner, near the *fromager*, feverish fingers tore at the diminishing bulk of the parcel. In another, the cooks took the weight off their feet, fanning themselves between rounds, as the great pot sent up clouds of steam into the air. Inside the house, groups of people sat, fleeing the late afternoon heat, drinking glasses of sorrel and exchanging stories of the latest political intrigues.

"Look at her!" The music had stopped and the parcel was in Maimouna's hands. The megawatt smile that had been on her face all day grew brighter as she wavered between ripping through the paper and going with care so as not to miss the mini-prize.

"She's got it!" Hassim said, as Maimouna found her stick of chewing gum and started waving it around. For an instant, she seemed on the point of saying something, with her chest appearing to contract and expand with the effort of trying to expel something. But then she passed the parcel to the next child and the music started again.

"Let's get some fresh air," Hassim said. "It'll be a while before the rice is ready."

They slipped away from the festivities to the nearby beach and found it deserted apart from three or four young men making noise and setting up for a session of tea drinking.

"It used to be just the *apprentis-chauffeurs*, lying around smoking yamba all day!" Hassim snorted. "Now it's everybody."

"Why, Hassim," she chided. "I'm surprised at you, judging people by appearances. You don't know who these boys are. I'm sure they're just on the beach for an afternoon drinking tea and liming. Although I have to say that your so-called "tea" is as much a narcotic as any innocent little spliff."

Hassim just managed to prevent himself from being drawn into an exchange about idle youth and mumbled something about "waste". As they passed, they saw that the young men had all the proper tea-making equipment – a small coal pot, an ornate pewter teapot, slabs of rock sugar, four tiny Moroccan glasses and a packet marked *Thé La Force, produit en Chine*. When they walked past, breathing in the pungent smoke surrounding the boys, Khadi smiled and Hassim emitted a grunt. She laughed when she heard him and set off at a run, calling to him to catch her. She was surprisingly fast and it took him longer than expected to reach her as she streaked along the beach. The tide was going out, and as there was hardly any wind, the waves were moderate, with none of the crashing and boiling they were known for. Over the sea and the curling coastline, there hung a haze, lit up in the west by the sun. When he was nearly upon her, she began a dodging manoeuvre which turned into a dance with her arms out wide, spinning and twirling on the tips of her toes, until dizziness overcame her and she fell laughing onto the sand. They sat catching their breath, brushed off their clothes and started to walk. It was some time before either of them spoke.

"My father and I had a long talk last night about looking after Mai." She paused and gave a small, almost secret smile. "That was when he asked me to come back and help."

"Yes, he told me."

"We agreed about everything. That we have to see how she adjusts to being at home... Well, look at how she was with the other children just now!"

"But we have to really wait and see."

"Yes. That's what he said. We have to see what happens over the next days and weeks. We have to monitor her closely. As few people as possible will be told... about the sleepwalking and the drawing. We must try for... What did he call it? Some kind of absorption..."

"A natural absorption."

"That's it. A natural absorption back into the family. He thinks that when that happens, the nightmares, sleepwalking, whatever you want to call them, will start to go away. And then, he hopes, she will start to talk again. That's when I can be helpful, he said. What with me being Mai's special friend and all…" Khadi bent down and picked up a piece of driftwood. She remained on her haunches, looking up. "Ndeye was there. She didn't say much, but she was there from start to finish." She trailed the stick in the sand. "Do you think she still blames me?"

"No." Hassim made his fingers into a temple and touched his forehead with it. "Yes."

Khadi shook her head. "When will that stop?"

Hassim squatted down beside her. "When Maimouna gets better. And maybe not even then… It'll take a long time for her to forget that she nearly lost her child."

"And now she has something else to hate me for." She reached over and squeezed his hand. He smiled.

"She's always wanted me to do the decent thing."

Khadi stood up. "Yes, but with a decent woman. Not some crazy black-skinned toubab." Khadi's face was sombre. "Suppose I hurt you?"

"Well that will be my problem, not Ndeye's." He seemed to want to continue walking but she did not move.

"I could hurt you, you know."

He said nothing.

"I'm coming back, but I'm coming back because I promised Maimouna. And my father. And Ndeye. Even she thinks I can help make Mai speak again."

Still he said nothing.

"I can't promise you anything, Hassim. I'm what is called an unreliable witness. I could come back next month and we could live happily ever after or I could come back next month and spit in your eye. Both equally possible."

Hassim found a stone and hurled it into the waves, watching it disappear without a trace.

"And then there's the problem of work. If… when… I come back, what will I do? I'm my mother's child. I have to work! I won't miss my life in New York. It was pretty empty. All right. Very empty. Except for… my one friend." Khadi's face broke into a smile. "One of these days, I'm going to bring my friend Tim with me. I think you'd really like him!"

Hassim shrugged while the lights continued to twinkle in Khadi's eyes.

"Anyway, back to serious things... What would I do here? What would I do?"

He stretched out his arms. "There's everything to do." He started to walk and over his shoulder he said, "And as for us, we'll just have to see. Just like with Maimouna."

"Do you really have to be so damn... solid?"

He put his arm around her and they continued to walk along to the sound of the surf as the sun slid towards the western horizon. Over and over they rehashed the topics of the hour: Maimouna and themselves; themselves and Maimouna until the two topics became so intertwined that they didn't know where one ended and the other began. They sat down on the warm sand.

"I told your father about my theory."

There was no response.

"The one about the imprinting of images on the mind."

"Yes, I remember." Khadi's voice was quiet.

"Like you, he was sceptical at first. Then like you, he started to consider it. Bearing in mind that Maimouna is the most intelligent, most precocious and most sensitive child any of us is likely to meet, it follows that when she went to Gorée, it traumatized her. When she went into the water, she was already deeply traumatized. The blow to the head when she fell in, the near death... they just acted as a seal to the primary trauma."

"I don't like your theory, Hassim. It's just... just sounds too rational."

"But aren't you the rational one? The lawyer prosecuting facts?"

"Even at my highest, or should I say, my lowest point in the law business, I never fully believed that it was only facts that mattered. I tried to force myself to believe that but I never really did." She picked up some sand and sifted it through her fingers. "I remember what she looked like when she was leaving the slave house... the intensity of it all. It doesn't seem like anything that can be explained by a single theory... Why can't you accept that something inexplicable happened when she was in the coma?"

"But I do!" Hassim exclaimed. "When she was in the *Maison*, she saw and heard terrible things – the doorway of no return, the ankle chains, the neck chains, the drawings of the hold of the slave ships. And they were literally stamped into her consciousness. How that happened, what that mechanism was – that's the mystery, Khadi. How we encourage her to let go of it – that's our challenge."

Still she didn't respond. He looked at her face and saw that she was struggling with something.

"What's wrong?"

"We didn't go upstairs."

"*Pardon?*"

"Upstairs! We didn't go upstairs!"

"Where?"

Khadi was moving her hands about as though trying to capture the thought and fix it in place.

"You mean in Gorée?"

"Yes! At the *Maison*! Listen. Your theory says that what Maimouna saw and heard during the tour of the slave house imprinted itself on her. Which is why she is doing the things she's doing now. Yes?"

"Yes. Yes!"

"But, we didn't go upstairs in the *Maison*, Hassim. We were supposed to, but when I saw that Mai was already so upset, I decided not to take her upstairs. Where the drawings of the slave ships are. Where all those drawings are. She never saw them. Not a single one!"

"Did the tour guide say anything about the conditions in the slave ships? Maybe it was something she heard?"

Khadi raced through the commentary in her mind. She played it back, remembering the guide's voice, his intonation, his pointing fingers, his words.

"No." She stared at Hassim with eyes wide open. "There was nothing in the tour that could have given her the idea of the close packing and how they had to sit. Nothing in the tour mentioned that! So where did the incredible detail she needed for her picture come from?"

Hassim looked away from the burning amber eyes and shook

his head. "I... I think that the tour guide probably did say something about it, Khadi. You may have forgotten..."

He looked out to sea and did not turn to her until he was sure that his racing heart had returned to normal. "And the rest of it was filled in by Maimouna's imagination."

"You're probably right," she said at last. "I'm sure you're right. You. My father. Your theory. Yes. It makes a kind of sense." She paused. "And it helps us to handle it all."

Khadi sighed and stretched out her legs. Between where they were sitting and the first fingerprints of the outgoing tide, a gull had landed.

The gull twisted its head around and stalked a few steps across the wet sand, leaving sharp prints on it. "Look! The Sankofa bird."

"You mean that gull?"

"It reminds me of the Sankofa bird.'

Hassim's face was blank.

"You know, the Sankofa bird, the one that flies forward while looking back. Ask Magdalene about it. She used to hurt my head with it when I was a kid. It never really meant much to me until... Oh!" With one swift motion, the gull lifted off and hovered over the water. They followed it with their eyes as it flew inland.

They had talked themselves to a standstill and were surprised when they saw what time it was.

"Better turn back," he said.

When they were in sight of the tea-drinking youths, they stopped for a moment. The sea was golden with the sunset.

"Where is it?"

"What?"

"Gorée."

"Somewhere in that direction," Hassim pointed. "Too misty to see it though."

Their moment of contemplation was interrupted by the raucous shouts of the young men, no doubt recounting one scandalous tale after another. In turn, they held the teapot high off the ground, watched as the tea fell in a thin tawny arc into the waiting glasses and laughed appreciation of their skill.

Hassim took Khadi by the hand and they turned away from the shore towards the city, towards the house, towards the child.

They trudged across the softness of the sand, leaving tentative footprints. It was the same sand that was carried on the wind and distributed on both sides of the ocean; the same sand that Maimouna had first learned to draw in; the same that Hassim had run across to capture the incoming tide for Yaye Coumba. Overhead a family of gulls screamed and whirled as they headed home to roost. And always there was the sea, rhythmic, persistent, enigmatic.

One of the tea drinkers detached himself from his companions and stepped into the water. He was clad only in loose faded trousers drawn by a string at his waist; a mane of dreadlocks fell on his naked shoulders. A strap around his neck held a drum in place and when he was up to his knees in the surf, he began to play. A ray from the setting sun touched his hair with brightness as he drummed to the sea, drummed to the sky. Over his head a bird on the wing flew straight and strong, vanishing in the haze, making for the far horizon.

ABOUT THE AUTHOR

Born and raised in Bermuda, Angela Barry lived for over twenty years in Britain, first as a student then as an English teacher. She started writing fiction in the 1980s, with her first short story, "Anansi in Babylon", forming part of a Master's degree at Sussex University. On her return to Bermuda, her interest in Caribbean literature deepened when she participated in a series of writing workshops taught by Barbadian novelist, George Lamming. A recipient of the James Michener Writing Fellowship, she has had essays and stories published in journals and magazines and was on the editorial board of the Bermuda Writers' Collective which published two anthologies of short stories. Her own first collection of stories, *Endangered Species*, was published by Peepal Tree in 2002.

ALSO BY ANGELA BARRY

Endangered Species
ISBN: 9781900715713; pp. 232; pub. 2002; Price: £8.99

Eve has to watch her husband bring his paler mistress to the party she has so carefully prepared; Esther to deal with her rebellious daughter, and the guilt which attaches to the consequences of her own youthful revolt against racial oppression; Joelle and Maryse must find ways of dealing with the incomprehension between village Africa and chic Frenchness in their Ivoirean lives; Gambian Doudou wants a traditional wife to end his loneliness in London; and Julia, in the title story, must fight to find herself again when her oldest friend dies of cancer.

Whether living in Bermuda, America, London, the Gambia or the Cote d'Ivoire, the characters in these stories not only confront their individual traumas, but the ways in which, as people of the African diaspora, differences of colour, class and colonial heritage divide them both from each other and themselves.

We are given revealing insights into Bermudian society, its tensions of race and culture and the geography that pulls some of its people closer to the USA, while others look to links with the Caribbean or the even more submerged links with Africa. But if we see the pain and alienation of uprooted people, what also moves through the stories is a sense of identity not as something fixed, but as an Atlantic flow, a circuit of peoples and cultures which has Africa as one of its starting points. And in that lies a unity that is real, if submarine.

When Doudou listens to the Gambian music of his homeland in London, it is a music of multiple Atlantic crossings, powerfully influenced by Cuban rumba, itself born from African and European roots. And as Mame Koumba, pointing to Doudou's Black British grandchildren, tells him, grieving for the loss of ancestral wholeness, "They're not what you would have had in the Gambia. But they're what you have. And there's Africa in them all." Angela Barry's stories demand an alertness to that kind of connection.

Visit www.peepaltreepress.com for safe on-line ordering and a wealth of information about Caribbean writing.